"[*Hammer's Slammers*] is a book by a man who has been there, and who has studied enough military history to understand, incompletely, as all of us understand only incompletely, why men fight; a book about a man who has that intangible but very real quality, the ability to lead men into Hell. . . .

"For all great captains there is the great temptation; for those who can lead men to Hell, there is the vision that they might lead them to Paradise. Hammer is no exception, but history records few instances of success.

"Of course Hammer knows that. All the great warrior captains have. But humility has never been a military virtue . . ."

—**Jerry Pournelle**
From his *Introduction*

Hammer's Slammers

DAVID DRAKE

ACE SCIENCE FICTION BOOKS
NEW YORK

Dedication
To my wife, Jo

HAMMER'S SLAMMERS

An Ace Science Fiction Book / published by arrangement with
the author

PRINTING HISTORY
Ace Original / April 1979
Ninth printing / March 1986

"But Loyal to his Own" was first published in the October 1975 issue of
Galaxy, copyright © 1975 by UPD Publishing Corporation.

"The Butcher's Bill" was first published in the November 1974 issue of
Galaxy, copyright © 1974 by UPD Publishing Corporation.

"Under the Hammer" was first published in the October 1974 issue of
Galaxy, copyright © 1974 by UPD Publishing Corporation.

"Cultural Conflict" was first published in the January 1979 issue of
Destinies, copyright © 1979 by Charter Communications Inc.

"Caught in the Crossfire" copyright © 1978 by David A. Drake; was
first published in *Chrysalis II,* copyright © 1978 by Zebra Books.

ISBN: 0-441-31602-6

Ace Science Fiction Books are published by The Berkley Publishing Group,
200 Madison Avenue, New York, New York 10016.
PRINTED IN THE UNITED STATES OF AMERICA

INTRODUCTION

MERCENARIES AND MILITARY VIRTUE

by
Jerry Pournelle

IN EUROPE and especially in England, military history is a respected intellectual discipline. Not so here. I doubt there are a dozen academic posts devoted to the study of the military arts.

The public esteem of the profession of arms is at a rather low ebb just now—at least in the United States. The Soviet Union retains the pomp and ceremony of military glory, and the officer class is highly regarded, if not by the public (who can know the true feelings of Soviet citizens?) then at least by the rulers of the Kremlin. Nor did the intellectuals always despise soldiers in the United States. Many of the very universities which delight in making mock of uniforms were endowed by land grants and were founded in the expectation that they would train officers for the state militia. It has not been all that many years since US combat troops were routinely expected to take part in parades; when soldiers were proud to wear uniform off post, and when my uniform was sufficient for free entry into movie houses, the New York Museum of Modern Art, the New York Ballet, and as I recall the Met (as well as to other establishments catering to less cultural needs of the soldier).

But now both the military and anyone who studies war are held in a good deal of contempt.

I do not expect this state of affairs to last—in fact, I am certain that it cannot. A nation which despises its soldiers will all too soon have a despicable army.

The depressing fact is that history is remarkably clear on one point: wealthy republics do not last long. Time after time they have risen to wealth and freedom; the citizens become wealthy and sophisticated; unwilling to volunteer to protect themselves, they go to conscription; this too becomes intolerable; and soon enough they turn to mercenaries.

Machiavelli understood that, and things have not changed much since his time—except that Americans know far less history than did the rulers of Florence and Milan and Venice.

For mercenaries are a dangerous necessity. If they are incompetent, they will ruin you. If they are competent there is always the temptation to rob the paymaster.

Why should they not? They know their employers will not fight. They may, if called a national army, retain loyalty to the country—but if the nation despises them, and takes every possible opportunity to let them know it, then that incentive falls as well—and they have a monopoly on the means of violence.

After all, it should be fairly clear that no one

fights purely for money; that anyone who does is probably not worth hiring. As Montesquieu put it, "a rational army *would* run away." To stand on the firing parapet and expose yourself to danger; to stand and fight a thousand miles from home when you're all alone and outnumbered and probably beaten; to spit on your hands and lower the pike; to stand fast over the body of Leonidas the King; to be rear guard at Kunu-ri; to stand and be still to the Birkenhead drill; these are not rational acts.

They are often merely necessary.

Through history, through painful experience, military professionals have built up a specialized knowledge: how to induce men (including most especially themselves) to fight, aye, and to die. To charge the guns at Breed's Hill and New Orleans, at Chippewa and at Cold Harbor; to climb the wall of the Embassy Compound at Peking; to go ashore at Betio and Saipan; to load and fire with precision and accuracy while the *Bon Homme Richard* is sinking; to fly in that thin air five miles above a hostile land and bring the ship straight and level for thirty seconds over Regensberg and Ploesti; to endure at Heartbreak Ridge and Porkchop Hill and the Iron Triangle and Dien Bien Phu and Hue and Firebase 34 and a thousand nameless hills and villages.

It's a rather remarkable achievement, when you think about it. It's even more remarkable when you look closer and see just how many mercenary units have performed creditably, honorably, even gallantly; how many of those who have changed history on the battlefield have been professional soldiers. For despite the silly sayings about violence never settling anything, history is changed on the battlefield: ask the National Socialist German Workers' Party, or the Carthaginians, or the Confederate States of America, Pompey and Richard III and Harold of Wessex, Don Juan of Austria and Aetius the last Roman. Yet you could search through the armies of history and you would find few competent troopers who fought for money and money alone.

This is the mistake so often made by those who despise the military, and because they despise it refuse to understand it: they fail to see that few are so foolish as to give their lives for money; yet an army whose soldiers are not willing to die is an army that wins few victories.

Yet certainly there have always existed mercenary soldiers.

We can piously hope that there will be no armies in the future. It is an unlikely hope; at least history is against it. On the evidence, peace is a purely theoretical state of affairs whose existence we deduce because there have been intervals between wars. But I did not speak contemptuously when I spoke of pious hopes; nor do I find it an irony that the Strategic Air Command, whose commanders hold leashed more firepower than has been expended by all the armies of all time, has as its motto "Peace is our profession." Most of those young men who guard us as we sleep believe in that, believe it wholeheartedly and give up a very great deal for it. I too can piously hope for peace; that we shall heed the advice of the carol we sing annually and "hush the noise, ye men of strife, and hear the angels sing."

But to hope is nothing. When Appius Claudius told the Senate of Rome that "If you would have peace, be thou then prepared for war" he said nothing that history has not repeatedly affirmed. It may be wrong advice. Certainly there is an argument against it. But I think there is no argument at all against a similar aphorism: "If you would have peace, then understand war."

Which is to say, understand armies; understand why men fight; understand the organization of violence.

And that, at last, brings us to this book.

Military science fiction is a highly specialized art form. It is attempted often, but there are few writers who know science, society, and the military well enough to write a good story of war in the future.

This is unfortunate: although science fiction, like all literature, must entertain and divert if it is to have readers, it often has a serious purpose as well: to look at future societies, and the impact of technology on history. Any attempt to look into the future while ignoring war and the military is probably doomed to failure: if five thousand years of recorded history have given us no formula for controlling violence and greed, we would be fortunate indeed if this generation has indeed fought the war to end all wars; if the armies that exist today were the last this planet will ever see.

Hammer's Slammers is a serious book. This is

not to say it is not a whacking good story, with real people fighting real conflicts, for it is all of that; nor is it a tract, preachifying for or against war. It is a serious book because while it tells a good story it depicts much of the reality of conflict. It is a book by a man who has been there, and who has studied enough military history to understand, incompletely, as all of us understand only incompletely, why men fight; a book about a man who has that intangible but very real quality, the ability to lead men into Hell.

But like many of the great conquerors, Hammer is despised by those who employ him; his country has no use for his talents. He is not often admirable, except to his own men, and not always to them. Like all the great warriors, real and imaginary, he may be seen, as you wish, as a saint or a fiend. That is true of my own John Christian Falkenberg, of Dickson's Donal Graeme and Drake's Alois Hammer, of Patton and MacArthur and Guderian and Robert E. Lee and Ulysses Simpson Grant, Caesar and Alexander of Macedon and all the others: for the essence of war is violence, and those who make it their profession must be stained by it; yet for all that they have, they *must* have, that peculiar and elusive quality known as military virtue. And make no mistake, the military virtues are real, and they are indeed virtues—although one might make the case that they are perversions of the truly human virtues, and thus worse than vices. But perversions or no, the great commanders whose company Alois Hammer now joins truly hold and revere the military virtues. They must have them, for without them they would not be great captains; without them their men would not follow them to Hell.

For all great captains there is the great temptation; for those who can lead men to Hell, there is the vision that they might lead them to Paradise. Hammer is no exception: but history records few instances of success.

Of course Hammer knows that. All the great warrior captains have. But humility has never been a military virtue...

CONTENTS

BUT LOYAL TO HIS OWN

"IT JUST BLEW UP. Hammer and his men knew but they didn't say a thing," blurted the young captain as he looked past Secretary Tromp, his gaze compelled toward the milky noonday sky. It was not the sky of Friesland and that bothered Captain Stilchey almost as much as his near-death in the ambush an hour before. "He's insane! They all are."

"Others have said so," the councillor stated with the heavy ambiguity of an oracle replying to an ill-phrased question. Tromp's height was short of two meters by less than a hand's breadth, and he was broad in proportion. That size and the generally dull look on his face caused some visitors looking for Friesland's highest civil servant to believe they had surprised a retired policeman of some sort sitting at the desk of the Secretary to the Council of State.

Tromp did not always disabuse them.

Now his great left hand expanded over the grizzled fringe of hair remaining at the base of his skull. "Tell me about the ambush," he directed.

"He didn't make any trouble about coming to you here at the port," Stilchey said, for a moment watching his fingers writhe together rather than look at his superior. He glanced up. "Have you met Hammer?"

"No, I kept in the background when plans for the Auxilliary Regiment were drafted. I've seen his picture, of course."

"Not the same," the captain replied, beginning to talk very quickly. "He's not big but he, he moves, he's alive and it's like every time he speaks he's training a gun on you, waiting for you to slip. But he came along, no trouble—only he said we'd go with a platoon of combat cars instead of flying back, he wanted to check road security between Southport and the firebase where we were. I said sure, a couple hours wasn't crucial. . . ."

Tromp nodded. "Well done," he said. "Hammer's cooperation is very important if this . . . business is to be concluded smoothly. And," —here the councillor's face hardened without any noticeable shift of muscles—"the last thing we wanted was for the good colonel to become concerned while he was still with his troops. He is not a stupid man."

Gratification played about the edges of Stilchey's mouth, but the conversation had cycled the captain's mind back closer to the blast of cyan fire. His stomach began to spin. "There were six vehicles in the patrol, all but the second one open combat cars. That was a command car, same chassis and ground-effect curtain, but enclosed, you see? Better commo gear and an air-conditioned passenger compartment. I started toward it but Hammer said, no, I was to get in the next one with him and Joachim."

Stilchey coughed, halted. "That Joachim's here with him now; he calls him his aide. The bastard's queer, he tried to make me when I flew out. . . ."

Puzzlement. "Colonel Hammer is homosexual, Captain? Or his aide, or. . . ?"

"No, Via! Him, not the—I don't know. Via, maybe him too. The bastard scares me, he really does."

To statesmen patience is a tool; it is a palpable thing that can grind necessary information out of a young man whose aristocratic lineage and sparkling uniform have suddenly ceased to armor him against the universe. "The ambush, Captain." Tromp pressed stolidly.

With a visible effort, Stilchey regained the thread of his narrative.

"Joachim drove. Hammer and I were in the back along with a non-com from Curwin—Worzer, his name was. He and Joachim threw dice for who had to drive. The road was supposed to be clear but Hammer made me put on body armor. I thought it was cop, you know—make the staffer get hot and dusty.

"Via," he swore again, but softly this time. "I was at the leftside powergun but I wasn't paying much attention; nothing really to pay attention to. Hammer was on the radio a lot, but my helmet only had intercom so I didn't know what he was saying. The road was stabilized earth, just a gray line through hectares of those funny blue plants you see all over here, the ones with the fat leaves."

"Bluebrights," the older man said dryly. "Melpomone's only export; as you would know from the briefing cubes you were issued in transit, I should think."

"Would the Lord I'd never *heard* of this damned place!" Stilchey blazed back. His family controlled Karob Trading; no civil servant—not even Tromp, the Gray Eminence behind the Congress of the Republic—could cow him. But he was a soldier, too, and after a moment he continued, "Bluebrights in rows, waist high and ugly, and beyond that nothing but the soil blowing away as we passed.

"We were half an hour out from the firebase, maybe half the way to here. The ground was dimpled with frost heaves. A little copse was in sight ahead of us, trees ten, fifteen meters high. Hammer had the forward gun, and on the intercom he said, 'Want to double the bet, Blackie?' Then they armed their guns—I didn't know why—and Worzer said, 'I still think they'll be in the draw two kays south, but I won't take any more of your money.' They were laughing and I thought they were going to just . . . clear the guns, you know?"

The captain closed his eyes. He remembered how they had stared at him, two bulging circles and the hollow of his screaming mouth below them, reflected on the polished floorplate of the combat car. "The command car blew up just as we entered the trees. There was a flash like the sun and it *ate* the back half of the car, armor and all. The front flipped over and over into the trees, and the air *stank* with metal. Joachim laid us sideways to follow the part the mine had left, cutting in right behind when it hit a tree and stopped. The driver raised his head out of the hatch and maybe he could have got clear himself . . . but Hammer jumped off our deck to his and jerked him out, yanked him up in his armor as small as he is. Then they were back in our car. They were firing, everybody was firing, and we turned right, into the trees, into the guns."

"There were Mel troops in the grove, then?" Tromp asked.

"Must have been," Stilchey replied. He looked straight at the older man and said, very simply, "I was behind the bulkhead. Maybe if I'd known what to expect. . . . The other driver was at my gun, they didn't need me." Stilchey swallowed once, continued, "Some shots hit on my side. They didn't come through, but they made the whole car ring. The empties kept spattering me and the car was bouncing, jumping downed trees. Everything seemed to be on fire. We cleared the grove into another field of bluebrights. Shells from the firebase were already landing in the trees; the place was targeted. And Worzer pulled off his helmet and he spat and said, 'Cold meat, Colonel, you couldn't a called it better.' Via!"

"Well, it does sound like they reacted well to the ambush," Tromp admitted, puzzled because nothing Stilchey had told him explained the captain's fear and hatred of Hammer and his men.

"Nice extempore response, hey?" the aide suggested with bitter irony. "Only Hammer, seeing I didn't know what Worzer meant, turned to me, and said, 'We let the Mels get word that me and Secretary Tromp would take a convoy to Southport this morning. They still had fifty or so regulars here in Region 4 claiming to be an infantry battalion, and it looked like a good time to flush them for good and all.'"

Tromp said nothing. He spread his hands carefully on the citron-yellow of his desk top and seemed to be fixedly studying the contrast. Stilchey waited for a response. At last he said, "I don't like being used for bait, Secretary. And what if you'd decided to go out to the firebase yourself? I was all right for a stand-in, but do you think Hammer would have cared if you were there in person? He won't let anything stand in his way."

"Colonel Hammer does seem to have some unconventional attitudes," Tromp agreed. A bleak smile edged his voice as he continued, "But at that, it's rather fortunate that he brought a platoon in with him. We can begin the demobilization of his vaunted Slammers with them."

The dome of the Starport Lounge capped Southport's hundred-meter hotel tower. Its vitril panels were seamless and of the same refractive index as the atmosphere. As a tactician, Hammer was fascinated with the view: it swept beyond the equipment-thronged spaceport and over the shimmering billows of bluebright, to the mountains of the Crescent almost twenty kilometers away. But tankers' blood has in it a turtle component that is more comfortable on the ground than above it, and the little officer felt claws on his intestines as he looked out.

No similar discomfort seemed to be disturbing the other men in the room, all in the black and silver of the Guards of the Republic, though in name they were armor officers. "Had a bit of action today, Colonel?" said a cheerful, fit-looking major. Hammer did not remember him even though a year ago he had been Second in Command of the Guards.

"Umm, a skirmish," Hammer said as he turned. The Guardsman held out to him one of the two thimble-sized crystals he carried. In the heart of each flickered an azure fire. "Why, thank you—" the major's name was patterned in the silver highlights below his left lapel— "Mestern."

"No doubt you have seen much worse with your mercenaries, eh Colonel?" a voice called mockingly from across the room.

Karl August Raeder lounged in imperial state in the midst of a dozen admiring junior officers. He had been the executive officer of the Guards for the past year—ever since Hammer took command of the foreign regiment raised to smash the scattered units of the Army of Melpomone.

"Mercenaries, Karl?" Hammer repeated. A threat rasped through the surface mildness of his tone. "Yes, they cash their paychecks. There may be a few others in this room who do, hey?"

"Oh. . . ," someone murmured in the sudden quiet, but there was no way to tell what he meant by it. Raeder did not move. The blood had drawn back to yellow his smooth tan, and where the cushions had borne his languid hands they now were dimpled cruelly. Two men in the lounge had reached officer status in the Guards without enormous family wealth behind them. Hammer was one, Raeder was the other.

He strained at a breath. In build, he and Hammer were not dissimilar: the latter brown-haired and somewhat shorter, a trifle more of the hourglass in his shoulders and waist; Raeder blond and trim, slender in a rapier sort of way and quite as deadly. His uniform of natural silk and leather was in odd contrast to Hammer's khaki battledress, but there was nothing of fop or sloven in either man.

"Pardon," the Guardsman said, "I would not have thought this a company in which one need explain patriotism; there are men who fight for their homelands, and then there are the dregs, the gutter-sweepings of a galaxy, who fight for the same reason they pimped and sold themselves before our government—let me finish, please!" (though only Hammer's smile had moved) "—misguidedly, I submit, offered them more money to do what Friesland citizens could have done better!"

"My boys are better citizens than some born on Friesland who stayed there wiping their butts—"

"A soldier goes where he is ordered!" Raeder was standing.

"A *soldier*—"

Dead silence. Hammer's sentence broke like an axed cord. He looked about the lounge at the twenty-odd men, most of them his ex-comrades and all, like Raeder, men who had thought him mad to post out of the Guards for the sake of a combat command. Hammer laughed. He inverted the stim cone on the inside of his wrist and said approvingly, "Quite a view from up here. If it weren't such a good target, you could make it your operations center." As if in the midst of a normal conversation, he faced back toward the exterior and added, "By the way, what sort of operations are you expecting? I would have said the fighting here was pretty well over, and I'd be surprised at the government sending the Guards in for garrison duty."

The whispering that had begun when Hammer turned was stilled again. It was Raeder who cleared his throat and said in a tone between triumph and embarrassment, "Col Rijsdal may know. He . . . he has remained in his quarters since we landed." Rijsdal had not had a sober day in the past three years since he had acceded to an enormous estate on Friesland. "No doubt we are to provide proper, ah, background for such official pronouncements as the Secretary will make to the populace."

Hammer nodded absently as if he believed the black and silver of a parade regiment would over-awe the Mels more effectively than could his own scarred killers, the men who had rammed Frisian suzerainty down Mel throats after twelve regiments of regulars had tried and failed. But the Guards were impressively equipped . . . and all their gear had been landed.

Five hundred worlds had imported bluebright leaves, with most of the tonnage moving through Southport. The handful of Frisian vessels scattered on the field looked lost, but traffic would pick up now that danger was over. For the moment, hundreds of Guard vehicles gave it a specious life. In the broad wedge of his vision Hammer could see two rocket batteries positioned as neatly as chess pieces on the huge playing surface. The center of each cluster was an ammunition hauler, low and broad-chassied. Within their thin armor sheetings were the racks of 150 mm shells; everything from armor-piercing rounds with a second stage to accelerate them before impact, to antipersonnel cases loaded with hundreds of separate bomblets. The haulers rested on the field; no attempt had been made to dig them in.

The six howitzers of each battery were sited about their munitions in a regular hexagon, each joined to its hauler by the narrow strip of a conveyor. In action the hogs could kick out shells at five-second intervals, so the basic load of twenty rounds carried by the howitzer itself needed instant replenishment from the hauler's store. Their stubby gun-tubes gave them guidance and an initial boost, but most of the acceleration came beyond the muzzle. They looked grim and effective; still, it nagged Hammer to see that nobody had bothered to defilade them.

"A pretty sight," said Mestern. Conversation in the lounge was back to a normal level.

Hammer squeezed the last of his stim cone into the veins of his wrist and let the cool shudder pass through him before saying, "The Republic buys the best, and that's the only way to go when a battle's hanging on it. Not that you don't need good crews to man the gear."

Mestern pointed beyond the howitzers toward a wide-spaced ring of gun trucks. "Latest thing in arty defense," he said. "Each of those cars mounts an eight-barrel powergun, only 30 mm but they're high-intensity. They've got curst near the range of a tank's 200—thirty, forty kilometers if you've that long a sight line. With our radar hook-up and the satellite, we can just about detonate a shell as soon as it comes over the horizon."

"Nice theory," Hammer agreed. "I doubt you can swing the rig fast enough to catch the first salvo, but maybe placing them every ten degrees like that . . . where you've got the terrain to allow it. The Mels never had arty worth cop anyway, of course."

He paused, not sure he wanted to comment further. The grounded tanks and combat cars of the regiment were in an even perimeter at the edge of the circular field. Their dull iridium armor was in evident contrast to the ocher soil on which they rested. "You really ought to have dug in," Hammer said at last.

"Oh, the field's been stabilized to two meters down," the major protested innocently, "and I don't think the Mels are much of a threat now."

Hammer shook his head in irritation. "Lord!" he snorted, "The Mels aren't any threat at all after this morning. But just on general principles, when you set up in a war zone—*any* war zone—you set up as if you were going to be hit. Via, you may as well park your cars on Friesland for all the good they'd do if it dropped in the pot."

"The good colonel has been away from soldiers too long," whipped Raeder savagely. "Major Mestern, would you care to enlighten him as to how operations can be conducted by a real regiment—even though a gutter militia would be incapable of doing so?"

"I don't . . . think. . . ," Mestern stuttered in embarrassment. His fingers twiddled an empty stim cone.

"Very well, then I will," the blond XO snapped. Hammer was facing him again. This time the two men were within arm's length. "The Regiment of Guards is using satellite reconnaissance, Colonel," Raeder announced sneeringly. "The same system in operation when you were in charge here, but we are *using* it, you see."

"We used it. We—"

"Pardon, Colonel, permit me to explain and there will be fewer needless questions."

Hammer relaxed with a smile. There was a tiger's certainty behind its humor. "No, your pardon. Continue."

Hammer had killed two men in semi-legal duels fought on Friesland's moon. Raeder chuckled, unconcerned with his rival's sudden mildness. "So," he continued, "no Mel force could approach without being instantly sighted."

He stared at Hammer, who said nothing. If the Guardsman wanted to believe no produce truck could drop a Mel platoon into bunkers dug by a harvesting crew—spotting the activity was no problem, interpreting it though—well, it didn't matter now. But it proved again what Hammer had known since before he was landed, that a lack of common sense was what had so hamstrung the regular army that his Slammers had to be formed.

Of course, "common sense" meant to Hammer doing what was necessary to complete a task. And that sometimes created problems of its own.

"Our howitzers can shatter them ninety kilometers distant," Raeder lectured on, "and our tanks can pierce all but the heaviest armor at line of sight, Colonel." He gestured arrogantly toward the skyline behind Hammer. "Anything that can be seen can be destroyed."

"Yeah, it's always a mistake to underrate technology," agreed the man in khaki.

"So," Raeder said with a crisp nod. "It is possible to be quite efficient without being—" his eyes raked Hammer's stained, worn coveralls— "shoddy. When we hold the review tomorrow, it will be interesting to consider your . . . force . . . beside the Guard."

"Via, only two of my boys are in," Hammer said, "though for slickness I'd bet Joachim against anybody you've got." He looked disinterestedly at the drink dispenser. "We'll all be back in the field, as soon as I see what Tromp wants. We've got a clean-up operation mounted in the Crescent."

"There is a platoon present now," the Guardsman snapped. "It will remain, as you will remain, until you receive other orders."

Hammer walked away without answering. Bigger men silently moved aside, clearing a path to the dispenser. Raeder locked his lips, murder-tense; but a bustle at the central dropshaft caused him to spin around. His own aide, a 15-year old scion of his wife's house, had emerged when the column dilated. Rather than use the PA system built into the lounge before it was commandeered as an officer's club, messages were relayed through aides waiting on the floor below. Raeder's boy carried a small flag bearing the hollow rectangle of Raeder's rank, his ticket to enter the lounge and to set him apart from the officers. The boy might well be noble, but as yet he did not have a commission. He was to be made to remember it.

He whispered with animation into Raeder's ear, his own eyes open and fixed on the mercenary officer. Hammer ignored them both, talking idly as he blended another stim cone into his blood. The blond man's face slowly took on an expression of ruddy, mottled fury.

"Hammer!"

"The next time you determine where my boys will be, Colonel Raeder, I recommend that you ask me about it."

"You traitorous scum!" Raeder blazed, utter-

ly beyond curbing his anger. "I closed the perimeter to everyone, *everyone!* And you bull your
way through my guards, get them to pass—"

"Pass *my* men, Lieutenant-Colonel!" Hammer blasted as if he were shouting orders
through the howling fans of a tank. All the tension of the former confrontation shuddered in
the air again. Hammer was as set and grim as
one of his war cars.

Raeder raised a clenched fist.

"Touch me and I'll shoot you where you
stand," the mercenary said, and he had no need
to raise his voice for emphasis. As if only Raeder
and not the roomful of officers as well was listening, he said, "You give what orders you please,
but I've still got an independent command. As of
this moment. That platoon is blocking a pass in
the Crescent, because that's what I want it to do,
not sit around trying to polish away bullet scars
because some cop-head thinks that's a better
idea than fighting."

His body still as a gravestone, Raeder spoke;
"Now you've got a command," he said thickly.

The wing of violence lifted from the lounge.
Given time to consider, every man there knew
that the battle was in other hands than Raeder's
now—and that it would be fought very soon.

The dropshaft hissed again.

Joachim Steuben's dress was identical in design to his colonel's, but was in every other particular far superior. The khaki was unstained,
the waist-belt genuine leather, polished to a rich
chestnut sheen, and the coveralls themselves
tapered to follow the lines of his boyish-slim fig-

ure. Perhaps it was the very beauty of the face smoothly framing Joachim's liquid eyes that made the aide look not foppish, but softly feminine.

There was a rich urbanity as well in his careful elegance. Newland, his homeworld, was an old colony with an emphasis on civilized trappings worthy of Earth herself. Just as Joachim's uniform was of a synthetic sleeker and less rugged than Hammer's, his sidearm was hunched high on his right hip in a holster cut away to display the artistry of what it gripped. No weapon in the lounge, even that of Captain Ryssler—the Rysslers on whose land Friesland's second starport had been built—matched that of the Newlander for gorgeous detail. The receiver of the standard service pistol, a 1 cm powergun whose magazine held ten charged-plastic disks, had been gilded and carven by someone with a penchant for fleshy orchids. The stems and leaves had been filled with niello while the veins remained in a golden tracery. The petals themselves were formed from a breathtakingly-purple alloy of copper and gold. It was hard for anyone who glanced at it to realize that such a work of art was still, beneath its chasing, a lethal weapon.

"Colonel," he reported, his clear tenor a jewel in the velvet silence, "Secretary Tromp will see you now." Neither he nor Hammer showed the slightest concern as to whether the others in the lounge were listening. Hammer nodded, wiping his palms on his thighs.

Behind his back, Joachim winked at Col

Raeder before turning. The Guardsman's jaw
dropped and something mewled from deep in his
chest.

It may have been imagination that made
Joachim's hips seem to rotate a final purple
highlight from his pistol as the dropshaft
sphinctered shut.

When the Guards landed, all but the fifteenth
story of the Southport Tower was taken over for
officers' billets. That central floor was empty
save for Tromp, his staff, and the pair of scowl-
ing Guardsmen confronting the dropshaft as it
opened.

"I'll stay with you, sir," Joachim said. The
guards were in dress blacks but they carried full-
sized shoulder weapons, 2 cm powerguns in-
ferior only in rate of fire to the tribarrels
mounted on armored vehicles.

"Go on back to our quarters," Hammer replied. He stepped off the platform. His aide
showed no signs of closing the shaft in obe-
dience. "Martyrs' *blood*!" Hammer cursed, "Do
as I say!" He wiped his palms again and added,
more mildly, "That's where I'll need you, I
think."

"If you say so, sir." The door sighed closed
behind Hammer, leaving him with the guards.

"Follow the left corridor to the end—sir," one
of the big men directed grudgingly. The colonel
nodded and walked off without comment. The
two men were convinced their greatest worth lay
in the fact that they were Guardsmen. To them
it was an insult that another man would de-

liberately leave the Regiment, especially to take service with a band of foreign scum. Hammer could have used his glass-edged tongue on the pair as he had at the perimeter when he sent his platoon through, but there was no need. He was not the man to use any weapon for entertainment's sake.

The unmarked wood-veneer door opened before he could knock. "Why, good afternoon, Captain," the mercenary said, smiling into Stilchey's haggardness. "Recovering all right from this morning?"

"Go on through," the captain said. "He's expecting you."

Hammer closed the inner door behind him, making a soft echo to the thump of the hall panel. Tromp rose from behind his desk, a great gray bear confronting a panther.

"Colonel, be seated," he rumbled. Hammer nodded cautiously and obeyed.

"We have a few problems which must be cleared up soon," the big man said. He looked the soldier full in the face. "I'll be frank. You already know why I'm here."

"Our job's done," Hammer said without inflection. "It costs money to keep the Sl—the auxiliary regiment mobilized when it isn't needed, so it's time to bring my boys home according to contract, hey?"

The sky behind Tromp was a turgid mass, gray with harbingers of the first storm of autumn. It provided the only light in the room, but neither man moved to turn on the wall illuminators. "You were going to say 'Slammers,'" weren't you?" Tromp mused. "Interesting. I had wondered if the newscasters coined the nickname themselves or if they really picked up a usage here. . . ."

"The boys started it. . . . It seemed to catch on."

"But I'm less interested in that than another word," Tromp continued with the sudden weight of an anvil falling. " 'Home.' And that's the problem, Colonel. As you know."

"The only thing I could tell you is what I tell recruits when they sign on," Hammer said, his voice quiet but his forehead sweat-gemmed in the cool air. "By their contract, they became citizens of Friesland with all rights and privileges thereof. . . .Great Dying *Lord,* sir, that's what brought most of my boys here! Look, I don't have to tell you what's been happening everywhere the past ten years, twenty—there are thousands and thousands of soldiers, good soldiers, who wound up on one losing side or another. If everybody that fought alongside them had been as good, and maybe if they'd had the equipment Friesland could buy for them . . . I tell you, sir, there's no one in the galaxy to match them. And what they fight for isn't me, I don't care what cop you've heard, it's that chance at peace, at stability that their fathers had and their father's fathers, but they lost somewhere when everything started to go wrong. They'd *die* for that chance!"

"But instead," Tromp stated, "they killed for it."

"Don't give *me* any cop about morals!" the

soldier snarled. "Whose idea was it that we needed control of bluebright shipments to be sure of getting metals from Taunus?"

"Morals?" replied Tromp with a snort. "Morals be hanged, Colonel. This isn't a galaxy for men with morals, you don't have to tell me that. Oh, they can moan about what went on here and they have—but nobody, not even the reporters, has been looking very hard. And they wouldn't find many to listen if they had been. You and I are paid to get things done, Hammer, and there won't be any blame except for failure."

The soldier hunched his shoulders back against the chair. "Then it's all right?" he asked in wonder. "After all I worried, all I planned, my boys can go back to Friesland with me?"

Tromp smiled. "Over my dead body," he said pleasantly. The two men stared at each other without expression on either side.

"I'm missing something," said Hammer flatly. "Fill me in."

The civilian rotated a flat datavisor toward Hammer and touched the indexing tab with his thumb. A montage of horror flickered across the screen—smoke drifting sullenly from a dozen low-lying buildings; a mass grave, reopened and being inspected by a trio of Frisian generals; another village without evident damage but utterly empty of human life—

"Chakma," Hammer said in sudden recognition. "Via, you ought to thank me for the way we handled that one. I'd half thought of using a nuke."

"Gassing the village was better?" the councillor asked with mild amusement.

"It was quiet. No way you could have kept reporters from learning about a nuke," Hammer explained.

"And the convoy runs you made with hostages on each car?" Tromp asked smilingly.

"The only hostages we used were people we knew—and they knew we knew—" Hammer's finger slashed emphasis—"were related to Mel soldiers who hadn't turned themselves in. We cut ambushes by a factor of ten, and we even had some busted when a Mel saw his wife or a kid riding the lead car. Look, I won't pretend it didn't happen, but I didn't make any bones about what I planned when I put in for transfer. This is bloody late in the day to bring it up."

"Right, you did your duty," the big civilian agreed. "And I'm going to do mine by refusing to open Friesland to 5,000 men with the training you gave them. Lord and Martyrs, Colonel, you tell me we're going through a period when more governments are breaking up than aren't—what would happen to *our* planet if we set your animals loose in the middle of it?"

"There's twelve regiments of regulars here," Hammer argued.

"And if they were worth the cop in their trousers, we wouldn't have needed your auxiliaries," retorted Tromp inflexibly. "Face facts."

The colonel sagged. "OK," he muttered, turning his face toward the sidewall, "I won't pretend I didn't expect it, what you just said. I owed it to the boys, they . . . they believe when they ought to have better sense, and I owed them to try. . . ." The soldier's fingers beat a silent tattoo on the yielding material of his chair. He stood before speaking further. "There's a way out of it, Secretary," he said.

"I know there is."

"No!" Hammer shouted, his voice denying the flat finality of Tromp's as he spun to face the bigger man again. "No, there's a better way, a way that'll work. You didn't want to hire one of the freelance regiments you could have had because they didn't have the equipment to do the job fast. But it takes a government and a curst solvent one to equip an armored regiment—none of the privateers had that sort of capital."

He paused for breath. "Partly true," Tromp agreed. "Of course, we preferred to have a commander—" he smiled—"whose first loyalty was to Friesland."

Hammer spoke on, choking with his effort to convince the patient, gray iceberg of a man across from him. "Friesland's always made her money by trade. Let's go into another business—let's hire out the best equipped, best trained—by the Lord, *best*—regiment in the galaxy!"

"And the reason that won't work, Colonel," Tromp rumbled coolly, "is not that it would fail, but that it would succeed. It takes a very solvent government, as you noted, to afford the capital expense of maintaining a first-rate armored regiment. The Melpomonese, for instance, could never have fielded a regiment of their own. But if . . . the sort of unit you suggest was available, they could have hired it for a time, could they not?"

"A few months, sure," Hammer admitted with an angry flick of his hands, "But—"

"Nine months, perhaps a year, Colonel," the civilian went on inexorably. "It would have bankrupted them, but I think they would have paid for the same reason they resisted what was clearly overwhelming force. And not even Friesland could have economically taken Melpomone if the locals were stiffened by—by your Slammers, let us say."

"Lord!" Hammer shouted snapping erect, "Of course we wouldn't take contracts against Friesland."

"Men change, Colonel," Tromp replied, rising to his own feet. "Men die. And even if they don't, the very existence of a successful enterprise will free the capital for others to duplicate it. It won't be a wild gamble any more. And Friesland will *not* be the cause of that state of affairs while I am at her helm. If you're the patriot we assumed you were when we gave you this command, you will order your men to come in by platoons and be disarmed."

The smaller man's face was sallow and his hands shook until he hooked them in his pistol belt. "But you can't even let them go then, can you?" he whispered. "It might be all right on Friesland where there wouldn't be any recruiting by outsiders. But if you just turn my boys loose, somebody else will snap them up, somebody else who reads balance sheets. Maybe trained personnel would be enough of an edge to

pry loose equipment on the cuff. Life's rough,
sure, and there are plenty of people willing to
gamble a lot to make a lot more. Then we're
where you didn't want us, aren't we? Except
that the boys are going to have some notions of
their own about Friesland. . . .What do you
plan, Secretary? Blowing up the freighter with
everybody aboard? Or will you just have the
Guards shoot them down when they've been disarmed?"

Tromp turned away for the first time. Lightning was flashing from cloud peak to cloud peak,
and the mass that lowered over the Crescent was
already linked to the ground by a haze of rain.
"They put us in charge of things because we see
them as they are, Colonel," Tromp said. The
vitril sheet in front of him trembled to the distant
thunder. "Friesland got very good value from
you, because you didn't avoid unpleasant decisions; you saw the best way and took it—be
damned to appearances.

"I would not be where I am today if I were not
the same sort of man. I don't ask you to like this
course of action—I don't like it myself—but
you're a pragmatist too, Hammer, you see that
it's the only way clear for our own people."

"Secretary, anything short of having my boys
killed, but—"

"Curse it, man!" Tromp shouted, "haven't
you taken a look around you recently? Lives are
cheap, Colonel, lives are very cheap! You've got
to have loyalty to something more than just
men."

"No," said the man in khaki with quiet certainty. Then, "May I be excused, sir?"

"Get out of here."

Tromp was seated again, his own face a mirror of the storm, when Capt.Stilchey slipped in the door through which Hammer had just exited. "Your lapel mike picked it all up," the young officer said. He gloated conspiratorially. "The traitor."

Tromp's face forced itself into normal lines. "You did as I explained might be necessary?"

"Right. As soon as I heard the word 'disarmed' I ordered men to wait for Hammer in his quarters." Stilchey's gleeful expression expanded to a smile of real delight. "I added a . . . refinement, sir. There was the possibility that Hammer would—you know how he is, hard not to obey—tell the guards be cursed and leave them standing. So I took the liberty of suggesting to Colonel Raeder that he lead four men himself for the duty. I used your name,.sir, but I rather think the colonel would have gone along with the idea anyway."

The captain's laughter hacked loudly through the suite before he realized that Tromp still sat in iron gloom, cradling his chin in his hands.

The room was a shifting bowl of reds and hot orange in which the khaki uniforms of Worzer and Steuben seemed misplaced. The only sound was a faint buzzing, the leakage of the bone-conduction speakers implanted in either man's right mastoid. Hammer, like Tromp, had left his lapel mike keyed to his aides.

"Get us a drink, Joe," Worzer asked. With the

Slammers, you either did your job or you left, and nobody could fault Joachim's effectiveness. Still, there was a good deal of ambivalence about the Newlander in a unit made up in large measure of ex-farmers whose religious training had been fundamental if not scholarly. Tense, black-bearded Worzer got along with him better than most, perhaps because it had been a Newland ship which many years before had lifted him from Curwin and the Security Police with their questions about a bombed tax office.

Joachim stood and stretched, his eyes vacant. The walls and floor gave him a satanic cruelty that would have struck as incongruous those who knew him slightly. Yawning, he touched the lighting control, a slight concavity in the wall. The flames dulled, faded to a muted pattern of grays. The room was appreciably darker.

"Wanted you to do that all the time," Worzer grumbled. He seated himself on a bulging chair that faced the doorway.

"I liked it," Joachim said neutrally. He started for the kitchen alcove, then paused. "You'd best take your pistol off, you know. They'll be jumpy."

"You're the boss," Worzer grunts. Alone now in the room, he unlatches his holstered weapon and tosses the rig to the floor in front of him. It is a fixed blackness against the grays that shift beneath it. Glass tinkles in the kitchen. Men on every world have set up stills, generally as their first constructions. Even in a luxury hotel, Worzer's habits are those of a lifetime. Hammer's microphone no longer broadcasts voices.

The door valves open.

"Freeze!" orders the first man through. He is small and blond, his eyes as cold as the silver frosting his uniform. The glowing tab of a master door key is in his left hand, a pistol in his right. The Guardsmen fanning to each side of him swing heavy powerguns at waist level, the muzzles black screams in a glitter of iridium. Two more men stand beyond the door, facing either end of the hallway with their weapons ready.

"Move and you're dead," the officer hisses to Worzer. Then, to his tight-lipped subordinates, "Watch for the other one—the deviate."

The kitchen door rotates to pass Joachim. His left hand holds a silver tray with a fruit-garnished drink on it. Reflections shimmer from the metal and the condensate on the glass. He smiles.

"You foul *beast*!" says the officer and his pistol turns toward the aide of its own seeming will. The enlisted men wait, uncertain.

"Me, Colonel Raeder?" Joachim's voice lilts. He is raising the tray and it arcs away from his body in a gentle movement that catches Raeder's eyes for the instant that the Newlander's right hand dips and—a cyan flash from Joachim's pistol links the two men. Raeder's mouth is open but silent. His eyeballs are bulging outward against the pressure of exploding nerve tissue. There is a hole between them and it winks twice more in the flash of Joachim's shots. Two spent cases hang in the air to the Newlander's right; a third is jammed, smeared across his pistol's ejection port. None of the Guardsmen have begun to fall, though a gout of blood pours from the neck of the right-hand man.

It is two-fifths of a second from the moment Joachim reached for his pistol.

Worzer had been ready. He leaped as Steuben's shots flickered across the room, twisting the shoulder weapon from a Guardsman who did not realize he was already dead. The stocky Curwinite hit the floor on his right side, searching the doorway with the powergun. In the hall, a guard shouted as he spun himself to face the shooting. Joachim's jammed pistol had thudded on the floor but Worzer wasted no interest on what the aide might do—you did not worry about Joachim in a firefight, he took care of himself. The non-com had been squeezing even as he fell, and only a feather of trigger pressure was left to take up when the Guardsman's glittering uniform sprouted above the sights.

Heated air thumped the walls of the room. The body ballooned under the cyan impact. The big-bore packed enough joules to vaporize much of a man's abdomen at that range, and the Frisian hurtled back against the far wall. His tunic was afire and spilling coils of intestine.

The boots of the remaining Guardsman clattered on the tile as he bolted for the dropshaft. Joachim snaked his head and the pistol he had snatched from Raeder through the doorway. Worzer and the big gun plunged into the corridor low to cover the other end. The shaft entrance opened even before the Frisian's outflung arm touched the summoning plate. Hammer, standing on the platform, shot him twice in the chest. The Guardsman pitched into the wall. As he did so, Joachim shot him again at the base of the skull. Joachim generally doubted other men's kills, a practice that had saved his life in the past.

Hammer glanced down at the jellied skull of the last Guardsman and grimaced. "Didn't anybody tell you about aiming at the body instead of getting fancy?" he asked Joachim. Neither man commented that the final shot had been aimed within a meter of Hammer.

The Newlander shrugged. "They should've been wearing body armor," he said offhandedly. "Coppy fools."

The colonel scooped up both the powerguns from the corridor and gestured his men back into the room. The air within stank of blood and hot plastic. Death had been too sudden to be prefaced with pain, but the faces of the Guardsmen all held slack amazement. Hammer shook his head. "With five thousand of you to choose from," he said to Joachim, "didn't they think I could find a decent bodyguard?"

The Newlander smiled. After his third quick shot, the expended disk had been too hot to spin out whole and had instead flowed across the mechanism when struck by the jet of ejection gas. Joachim was carefully chipping away at the cooled plastic with a stylus while the pistol he had taken from his first victim lay on the table beside him. Its muzzle had charred the veneer surface. "There isn't enough gas in a handgun ejector to cool the chamber properly," he said, pretending to ignore his colonel's indirect praise.

"Via, you hurried 'cause you wanted all of them," Worzer laughed. He thumbed a loaded round into the magazine of the shoulder gun he had appropriated. "What's the matter—don't you want the Colonel to bother bringing me along the next time 'cause I scare away all your pretty friends?"

Hammer forced a smile at the interchange, but it was only a shimmer across lines of fear and anger. On one wall was a communicator, a flat, meter-broad screen whose surface was an optical pickup as well as a display. Hammer stepped in front of it and drew the curtain to blank the remainder of the room. His fingers flicked the controls, bringing Capt Stilchey into startled focus. Tromp's aide blinked, but before he could speak the colonel said, "We've got three minutes, Stilchey, and there's no time to cop around. Put me through."

Stilchey's mouth closed. Without comment he reached out and pressed his own control panel. With liquid abruptness his figure was replaced by the hulking power of Secretary Tromp, seated against the closing sky.

"Tell the Guard to ground arms, Secretary," Hammer ordered in a voice trembling with adrenalin. "Tell them now and I'll get on the horn to my boys—it'll be close."

"I'm sorry for the necessity of your arrest, Colonel," the big man began, "but—"

"Idiot!" Hammer shouted at the pickup, and his arm slashed aside the drapes to bare the room. "I heard your terms—now listen to mine. I've arranged for a freighter to land tomorrow at 0700 and the whole regiment's leaving on it. I'll leave you an indenture for the fair value of the gear, and it'll be paid off as soon as contracts start coming in. But the Lord help you, Tromp, if anybody tries to stop my boys."

"Capt Stilchey," Tromp ordered coolly, "sound general quarters. As for you, Colonel," he continued without taking verbal notice of the carnage behind the small officer, "I assure you that the possibility you planned something like this was in my mind when I ordered the Guards landed with me."

"Secretary, we planned what we'd do if we had to a month and a half ago. Don't be so curst a fool to doubt my boys can execute orders without me to hold their hands. If I don't radio in the next few seconds, you won't have the Guards to send back. Lord and *Martyrs,* man, don't you understand what you see back of me? This isn't some coppy parade!"

"Sir," came Stilchey's thin voice from off-screen, "Fire Central reports all satellite signals are being jammed. The armored units in the Crescent began assembling thirty—Lord! Lord! *Sir!*"

A huge scarlet dome swelled upward across the vitril behind Tromp. The window powdered harmlessly an instant later as the shock wave threw man and desk toward Hammer's image. The entire hotel shuddered to the blast.

"They're blowing up the artillery," the captain bleated. "The ammunition—" His words

were drowned in the twin detonations of the remaining batteries.

Hammer switched the communicator off.
"Early," he muttered. "Not that it mattered."
His face was set like that of a man who had told
his disbelieving mechanic that something was
wrong with the brakes, and who now feels the
pedal sink to the firewall to prove him fatally
correct. "Don't go to sleep," he grunted to his
companions. "Tromp knows he's lost, and I'm
not sure how he'll react."

But only Worzer was in the room with him.

Though Tromp was uninjured, he rose only to
his knees. He had seen Capt Stilchey when the
jagged sheet of iridium buzz-sawed into the suite
and through him. Scuttling like a stiff-legged
bear, the civilian made his way to the private
dropshaft built into the room. He pretended to
ignore the warm greasiness of the floor, but by
the time the platform began to sink his whole
body was trembling.

Ground floor was a chaos of half-dressed officers who had been on the way to their units
when fire raked the encampment. Tromp
pushed through a trio of chattering captains in
the branch corridor; the main lobby of bronze
and off-planet stonework was packed and static,
filled with men afraid to go out and uncertain
where to hide. The councillor cursed. The door
nearest him was ajar and he kicked it fully open.
The furniture within was in sleep-mode, the self-
cleaning sheets rumpled on the bed, but there
was no one present. The vitril outer wall had

pulverized; gouges in the interior suggested more than a shock wave had been responsible for the damage.

Seen through it, the starport had become a raving hell.

Four hundred meters from the hotel, one of the anti-artillery weapons was rippling sequential flame skyward from its eight barrels. High in a boiling thunderhead at its radar-chosen point of aim, man-made lightning flared magenta: high explosive caught in flight. Almost simultaneously a dart of cyan more intense than the sun lanced into the Guard vehicle. Metal heated too swiftly to melt and sublimed in a glowing ball that silhouetted the gun crew as it devoured them. Hammer's tanks, bunkered in the Crescent, were using satellite-computed deflections to rake the open Guard positions. Twenty kilometers and the thin armor of the lighter vehicles were no defense against the 200 mm powerguns.

Tromp stepped over the low sill and began to run. The field was wet and a new slash of rain pocked its gleam. Three shells popped high in the air. He ignored them, pounding across the field in a half-crouch. For a moment the whistling beginning to fill the sky as if from a thousand tiny mouths meant nothing to him either—then realization rammed a scream from his throat and he threw himself prone. The bomblets showering down from the shells went off on impact all across the field, orange flashes that each clipped the air with scores of fragments. Panic and Hammer's tanks had silenced the Guard's defensive weaponry. Now the rocket howitzers were free to rain in wilful death.

But the tanks, Tromp thought as he stumbled to his feet, they can't knock out the tanks from twenty kilometers and they can't capture the port while the Guard still has that punch. The surprise was over now. Lift fans keened from the perimeter as the great silvery forms of armored vehicles shifted from their targeted positions. The combatants were equal, and a stand-off meant disaster for the mercenaries.

Much of the blood staining Tromp's clothing was his own, licked from his veins by shrapnel. Incoming shells were bursting at ten-second intervals. Munitions shortages would force a slowdown soon, but for the moment anyone who stood to run would be scythed down before his third step. Even flat on his belly Tromp was being stung by hot metal. His goal, the ten-place courier vessel that had brought him to Melpomone, was still hopelessly far off. The remains, however, of one of the Guard's self-propelled howitzers lay like a cleat-kicked drink-can thirty meters distant. Painfully the councillor crawled into its shelter. Hammer's punishing fire had not been directed at the guns themselves but at the haulers in the midst of each battery. After three shots the secondary explosions had stripped the Guard of all its ill-sited artillery.

A line of rain rippled across the field, streaking dried blood from Tromp's face and whipping the pooled water. He was not running away. There was one service yet that he could perform for Friesland, and he had to be home to accomplish it. After that—and he thought of it not as revenge but as a final duty—he would not care that reaction would assuredly make him the scapegoat for the catastrophe now exploding all around him. It was obvious that Hammer had ordered his men to disturb the spaceport as little as possible so that the mercenaries would not hinder their own embarkation. The lightly-rattling shrapnel crumpled gun crews and the bewildered Guard infantry, but it would not harm the port facilities themselves nor the ships docked there.

For the past several minutes no powerguns had lighted the field. The bunkered mercenaries had either completed their programs or ceased fire when a lack of secondary explosions informed them that the remaining Guard vehicles had left their targeted positions. The defenders had at first fired wild volleys at no better target than the mountain range itself, but a few minutes' experience had taught them that the return blasts aimed at their muzzles were far more effective than their own could possibly be. Now there was a lull in the shelling as well.

Tromp eased a careful glance beyond the rim of his shelter, the buckled plenum chamber of the gun carriage. His ship was a horizontal needle three hundred meters distant. The vessel was unlighted, limned as a gray shadow by cloud-hopping lighting. The same flashes gleamed momentarily on the wet turtle-backs of a dozen tanks and combat cars in a nearby cluster, their fans idling. All the surviving Guard units must be clumped in similar hedgehogs across the port.

The big man tensed himself to run; then the

night popped and crackled as a Guard tank
began firing out into the storm. Tromp counted
three shots before a cyan dazzle struck the en-
gaged vehicle amidships and its own ammunition went off with an electric crash. The
clustered vehicles were lit by a blue-green fire
that expanded for three seconds, dissolving
everything within twenty meters of its center.
One of the remaining combat cars spun on howling fans, but it collapsed around another bolt
before it could pull clear. There were
Guardsmen on the ground now, running from
their vehicles. Tromp's eyes danced with afterimages of the exploding tank, and for the first
time he understood why Stilchey had been so
terrified by the destruction of the car he might
have ridden in.

Half a dozen shots ripped from beyond the perimeter and several struck home together. All the
Guard blowers were burning now, throwing
capering shadows beyond the councillor's
shelter. Then, threading their way around the
pools of slag, the steam and the dying fires, came
a trio of tanks. Even without the scarlet wand
wavering from each turret for identification,
Tromp would have realized these were not the
polished beauties of the Guard. The steel skirts
of their plenum chambers were rusty and
brushworn. One's gouged turret still glowed
where a heavy powergun had hit it glancingly;
the muzzle of its own weapon glowed too, and
the bubbling remains of the perimeter defense
left no doubt whose bolts had been more accurately directed. The fighting had been brief,

Hammer's platoons meeting the disorganized Guardsmen with pointblank volleys. The victors' hatches were open and as they swept in toward the central tower, Tromp could hear their radios crackling triumphant instructions. Other wands floated across the immense field, red foxfire in the rain.

The shooting had stopped. Now, before the combat cars and infantry followed up the penetrations their tanks had made, Tromp stood and ran to his ship. His career was ruined, of that he had no doubt. No amount of deceit would cover his role in the creation of the Slammers or his leadership in the attempted suppression. All that was left to Nicholas Tromp was the sapphire determination that the national power which he had worked four decades to build should not fall with him. They could still smash Hammer before he got started, using Friesland's own fleet and the fleets of a dozen other worlds. The cost would leave even Friesland groaning, but they could blast the Slammers inexorably from space wherever they were landed. For the sake of his planet's future, the excision had to be made, damn the cost.

And after Tromp fell in disgrace in the next week or two weeks at most, there would be no man left with the power to force the action or the foresight to see its necessity. Panting, he staggered through his vessel's open lock. The interior, too, was unlighted. That was not surprising in view of the combat outside, but one of the three crewmen should have been waiting at the lock. "Where are you?" Tromp called angrily.

The lights went on. There was a body at the big Frisian's feet. From the cockpit forward stretched another hairline of blood still fresh enough to ooze. "I'm here," said a cultured voice from behind.

Tromp froze. Very slowly, he began to turn his head.

"People like you," the voice continued, "with dreams too big for men to fit into, don't see the same sort of world that the rest of us do. And sometimes a fellow who does one job well can see where his job has to be done, even though a better man has overlooked it. Anyhow, Secretary, there always was one thing you and I could agree on—lives *are* cheap."

Surely Joachim's wrists were too slim, Tromp thought, to raise his heavy pistol so swiftly.

INTERLUDE: SUPERTANKS

TANKS WERE BORN in the muck and wire of World War One. Less than 60 years later, there were many who believed that technology had made the behemoths as obsolete as horse cavalry. Individual infantrymen of 1970 carried missiles whose warheads burned through the armor of any tank. Slightly larger missiles ranged kilometers to blast with pin-point accuracy vehicles costing a thousand times as much. Similar weaponry was mounted on helicopters which skimmed battlefields in the nape of the earth, protected by terrain irregularities. At the last instant the birds could pop up to rip tanks with their missiles. The future of armored vehicles looked bleak and brief.

Technology had dragged the tank to the brink of abandonment. Not surprisingly, it was technology again which brought the panzers back. The primary breakthrough was the development of portable fusion power plants. Just as the gasoline engine with its high horsepower-to-weight ratio had been necessary before the first tanks could take the field, so the fusion unit's almost limitless output was required to move the mass which made the new supertanks viable.

Fusion units were bulky and moderately heavy themselves, but loads could be increased on a fusion-powered chassis with almost no degradation of performance. Armor became thick—and thicker. With the whole galaxy available as a source of ores, iridium replaced the less effective steels and ceramics without regard for weight.

Armor alone is not adequate protection. Stationary fortresses can always be battered down —as the French learned in 1940, having forgotten the lesson Caesar taught their ancestors at Alesia two millenia before. Caterpillar treads had given the first tanks cross-country ability; but at the cost of slow speed, frequent breakage, and great vulnerability to attack. Now that power was no longer a factor, even the armored bulk of a tank could be mounted on an air cushion.

The air cushion principle is a very simple one. Fans fill the plenum chamber, a solid-skirted box under a vehicle, with air under pressure. To escape, the air must lift the edges of the skirts off the ground—and with the skirts, the whole vehicle rises. Fan tilt with the velocity and angle of attack of the blades determine the amount and direction of thrust. The vehicle skims over surfaces it does not touch.

On tanks and combat cars, the lift was provided by batteries of fans mounted on the roof of the plenum chamber. Each fan had its own armored nacelle. Mines could still do considerable damage; but while a single broken track block would deadline a tracked vehicle, a wrecked fan only made a blower a little more sluggish.

Successful protection for the supertanks went beyond armor and speed. Wire-guided missiles are still faster, and their shaped-charge warheads can burn holes in any practical thickness of any conceivable material—if they are allowed to hit. Reconnaissance satellites, computer fire control, and powerguns combined to claw missiles out of the air before they were dangerous. The satellites spotted missile launchers, usually before they fired and never later than the moment of ignition. Fire control computers, using data from the satellites, locked defensive weaponry on the missiles in microseconds. And a single light-swift tribarrel could hose any missile with enough fire in its seconds of flight to disintegrate it.

Hand-launched, unguided rockets—buzzbombs—were another problem, and in some ways a more dangerous one despite their short range and small bursting charges. Individual infantrymen fired them from such short ranges that not even a computer had time enough to lay a gun on the little rockets. But even here there was an answer—beyond the impossible one of killing every enemy before he came within 200 meters.

Many armored vehicles were already fitted with a band of anti-personnel directional mines just above the skirts. Radar detonated the mines when an object came within a set distance. Their blast of shrapnel was designed to stop infantry at close quarters. With only slight modification, the system could be adapted against buzzbombs. It was not perfect, since the pellets were far less destructive than powergun bolts, and the mines could not be used in close terrain which would itself set them off. Still, buzzbombs were apt to be ill-aimed in the chaos of battle, and a tank's armor could shrug off all but a direct hit by the small warheads.

So tanks roamed again as lords of battle, gray-gleaming phoenixes on air cushions. Their guns could defeat the thickest armor, their armor could blunt all but the most powerful attacks. They were fast enough to range continents in days, big enough to carry a battery of sensors and weaponry which made them impossible to escape when they hunted. The only real draw-back to the supertanks was their price.

A tank's fire control, its precisely-metered lift fans, the huge iridium casting that formed its turret—all were constructs of the highest sophis-tication. In all the human galaxy there were probably no more than a dozen worlds capable of manufacturing war tools as perfect as the panzers of Hammer's tank companies.

But Hammer paid for the best, man and tank alike; and out of them he forged the cutting edge of a weapon no enemy seemed able to stop.

THE BUTCHER'S BILL

"YOU CAN go a thousand kays any direction there and there's nothing to see but the wheat," said the brown man to the other tankers and the woman. His hair was deep chestnut, his face and hands burnt umber from the sun of Emporion the month before and the suns of seven other worlds in past years. He was twenty-five but looked several years older. The sleeves of his khaki coveralls were slipped down over his wrists against the chill of the breeze that had begun at twilight to feather the hillcrest. "We fed four planets from Dunstan—Hagener, Weststar, Mirage, and Jackson's Glade. And out of it we made enough to replace the tractors when they wore out, maybe something left over for a bit of pretty. A necklace of fireballs to set off a Lord's Day dress, till the charge drained six, eight months later. A static cleaner from Hagener, it was one year, never quite worked off our powerplant however much we tinkered with it . . .

"My mother, she wore out too. Dad just kept grinding on, guess he still does."

The girl asked a question from the shelter of the tank's scarred curtain. Her voice was too mild for the wind's tumbling, her accent that of

Thrush and strange to the tanker's ears. But Danny answered, "Hate them? Oh, I know about the Combine, now, that the four of them kept other merchants off Dunstan to freeze the price at what they thought to pay. But Via, wheat's a high bulk cargo, there's no way at all we'd have gotten rich on what it could bring over ninety minutes' transit. And why shouldn't I thank Weststar? If ever a world did me well, it was that one."

He spat, turning his head with the wind and lofting the gobbet invisibly into the darkness. The lamp trembled on its base, an overturned ration box. The glare skippered across the rusted steel skirts of the tank, the iridium armor of hull and turret; the faces of the men and the woman listening to the blower chief. The main gun, half shadowed by the curve of the hull, poked out into the night like a ghost of itself. Even with no human in the tank, at the whisper of a relay in Command Central the fat weapon would light the world cyan and smash to lava anything within line of sight of its muzzle.

"We sold our wheat to a Weststar agent, a Hindi named Sarim who'd lived, Via, twenty years at least on Dunstan but he still smelled funny. Sweetish, sort of; you know? But his people were all back in Ongole on Weststar. When the fighting started between the Scots and the Hindi settlers, he raised a battalion of farm boys like me and shipped us over in the hold of a freighter. Hoo Lordy, that was a transit!

"And I never looked back. Colonel Hammer docked in on the same day with the Regiment, and he took us all on spec. Six years, now, that's seven standard . . . and not all of us could stand the gaff, and not all who could wanted to. But I never looked back, and I never will."

From the mast of Command Central, a flag popped unseen in the wind. It bore a red lion rampant on a field of gold, the emblem of Hammer's Slammers; the banner of the toughest regiment that ever killed for a dollar.

"Hotel, Kitchen, Lariat, Michael, move to the front in company columns and advance."

The tiny adamantine glitter winking on the hilltop ten kays distant was the first break in the landscape since the Regiment had entered the hypothetical war zone, the Star Plain of Thrush. It warmed Pritchard in the bubble at the same time it tightened his muscles. "Goose it, Kowie," he ordered his driver in turn, "they want us panzers up front. Bet it's about to drop in the pot?"

Kowie said nothing, but the big blower responded with a howl and a billow of friable soil that seethed from under the ground effect curtain. Two Star in the lead, H Company threaded its way in line ahead through the grounded combat cars and a battalion from Infantry Section. The pongoes crouched on their one-man skimmers, watching the tanks. One blew an ironic kiss to Danny in Two Star's bubble. Moving parallel to Hotel, the other companies of Tank Section, K, L, and M, advanced through the center and right of the skirmish line.

The four man crew of a combat car nodded

unsmilingly from their open-topped vehicle as
Two Star boomed past. A trio of swivelmounted
powerguns, 2 cm hoses like the one on Danny's
bubble, gave them respectable firepower; and
their armor, a sandwich of ceramics and iridium,
was in fact adequate against most hand weapons. Buzzbombs aside, and tankers didn't like to
think about those either. But Danny would have
fought reassignment to combat cars if anybody
had suggested it—Lord, you may as well dance
in your skin for all the good that hull does you in
a firefight! And few car crewmen would be
caught dead on a panzer—or rather, were sure
that was how they would be caught if they
crewed one of those sluggish, clumsy, blind-
sided behemoths. Infantry Section scorned both,
knowing how the blowers drew fire but couldn't
flatten in the dirt when it dropped in on them.

One thing wouldn't get you an argument,
though: when it was ready to drop in the pot,
you sent in the heavies. And nothing on the Way
would stop the Tank Section of Hammer's Slammers when it got cranked up to move.

Even its 170 tonnes could not fully dampen
the vibration of Two Star's fans at max load.
The oval hull, all silvery-smooth above but of
gouged and rusty steel below where the skirts fell
sheer almost to the ground, slid its way through
the grass like a boat through yellow seas. They
were dropping into a swale before they reached
the upgrade. From the increasing rankness of the
vegetation that flattened before and beside the
tank, Pritchard suspected they would find a
meandering stream at the bottom. The brow of

the hill cut off sight of the unnatural glitter visible from a distance. In silhouette against the pale bronze sky writhed instead a grove of gnarled trees.

"Incoming, fourteen seconds to impact," Command Central blatted. A siren in the near distance underscored the words. "Three rounds only."

The watercourse was there. Two Star's fans blasted its surface into a fine mist as the tank bellowed over it. Danny cocked his powergun, throwing a cylinder of glossy black plastic into the lowest of the three rotating barrels. There was shrieking overhead.

WHAM

A poplar shape of dirt and black vapor spouted a kay to the rear, among the grounded infantry.

WHAM WHAM

They were detonating underground. Thrush didn't have much of an industrial base, the rebel portions least of all. Either they hadn't the plant to build proximity fuses at all, or they were substituting interference coils for miniature radar sets, and there was too little metal in the infantry's gear to set off the charges. With the main director out, Central wasn't even bothering to explode the shells in flight.

"Tank Section, hose down the ridge as you advance, they got an OP there somewhere."

"Incoming, three more in fourteen." The satellite net could pick up a golf ball in flight, much less a two hundred kilo shell.

Pritchard grinned like a death's head, laying

his 2 cm automatic on the rim of the hill and squeezing off. The motor whirred, spinning the barrels as rock and vegetation burst in the blue-green sleet. Spent cases, gray and porous, spun out of the mechanism in a jet of coolant gas. They bounced on the turret slope, some clinging to the iridium to cool there, ugly dark excrescences on the metal.

"Outgoing."

Simultaneously with Central's laconic warning, giants tore a strip off the sky. The rebel shells dropped but their bursts were smothered in the roar of the Regiment's own rocket howitzers boosting charges to titanic velocity for the several seconds before their motors burned out. Ten meters from the muzzles the rockets went supersonic, punctuating the ripping sound with thunderous slaps. Danny swung his hose toward the grove of trees, the only landmark visible on the hilltop. His burst laced it cyan. Water, flash-heated within the boles by the gunfire, blew the dense wood apart in blasts of steam and splinters. A dozen other guns joined Pritchard's, clawing at rock, air, and the remaining scraps of vegetation.

"Dead on," Central snapped to the artillery. "Now give it battery five and we'll show those freaks how they should've done it."

Kowie hadn't buttoned up. His head stuck up from the driver's hatch, trusting his eyes rather than the vision blocks built into his compartment. The tanks themselves were creations of the highest technical competence, built on Terra itself; but the crews were generally from frontier worlds, claustrophobic in an armored coffin no matter how good its electronic receptors were. Danny knew the feeling. His hatch, too, was open, and his hand gripped the rounded metal of the powergun itself rather than the selsyn unit inside. They were climbing sharply now, the back end hopping and skittering as the driver fed more juice to the rear fans in trying to level the vehicle. The bow skirts grounded briefly, the blades spitting out a section of hillside as pebbles.

For nearly a minute the sky slammed and raved. Slender, clipped-off vapor trails of counter-battery fire streamed from the defiladed artillery. Half a minute after they ceased fire, the drumbeat of shells bursting on the rebels continued. No further incoming rounds fell.

Two Star lurched over the rim of the hill. Seconds later the lead blowers of K and M bucked in turn onto the flatter area. Smoke and ash from the gun-lit brushfire shoomped out in their downdrafts. There was no sign of the enemy, either Densonite rebels or Foster's crew—though if the mercenaries were involved, they would be bunkered beyond probable notice until they popped the cork themselves.

"Tank Section, ground! Ground in place and prepare for director control."

Danny hunched, bracing his palms against the hatch coaming. Inside the turret the movement and firing controls of the main gun glowed red, indicating that they had been locked out of Pritchard's command. Kowie lifted the bow to kill the tank's immense inertia. There was

always something spooky about feeling the
turret purr beneath you, watching the big gun
snuffle the air with deadly precision on its own.
Danny gripped his tribarrel, scanning the
horizon nervously. It was worst when you didn't
know what Central had on its mind . . . and you
did know that the primary fire control computer
was on the fritz—they always picked the
damnedest times!

"Six aircraft approaching from two-eight-
three degrees," Central mumbled. "Distance
seven point ought four kays, closing at one one
ought ought."

Pritchard risked a quick look away from
where the gun pointed toward a ridgeline
northwest of them, an undistinguished swelling
half-obscured by the heat-wavering pall of
smoke. Thirteen other tanks had crested the hill
before Central froze them, all aiming in the same
direction. Danny dropped below his hatch rim,
counting seconds.

The sky roared cyan. The tank's vision blocks
blanked momentarily, but the dazzle reflected
through the open hatch was enough to make
Pritchard's skin tingle. The smoke waved and
rippled about the superheated tracks of gunfire.
The horizon to the northwest was an expanding
orange dome that silently dominated the sky.

"Resume advance." Then, "Spectroanalysis
indicates five hostiles were loaded with chemical
explosives, one was carrying fissionables."

Danny was trembling worse than before the
botched attack. The briefing cubes had said the
Densonites were religious nuts, sure. But to use

unsupported artillery against a force whose satellite spotters would finger the guns before the
first salvo landed; aircraft—probably converted
cargo haulers—thrown against director-con-
trolled powerguns that shot light swift and line
straight; and then nukes, against a regiment
more likely to advance stark naked than without
a nuclear-damper up! They weren't just nuts—
Thrush central government was that, unwilling
to have any of its own people join the fighting—
they were as crazy as if they thought they could
breathe vacuum and live. You didn't play that
sort of game with the Regiment.

They'd laager for the night on the hilltop, the
rest of the outfit rumbling in through the afternoon and early evening hours. At daybreak
they'd leapfrog forward again, deeper into the
Star Plain, closer to whatever it was the
Densonites wanted to hold. Sooner or later, the
rebels and Foster's Infantry—a good outfit but
not good enough for this job—were going to have
to make a stand. And then the Regiment would
go out for contact again, because they'd have run
out of work on Thrush.

"She'll be in looking for you pretty soon,
won't she, handsome?"

"Two bits to stay."

"Check. Sure, Danny-boy, you Romeos from
Dunstan, you can pick up a slot anywhere,
huh?"

A troop of combat cars whined past, headed
for their position in the laager. Pritchard's hole
card, a jack, flipped over. He swore, pushed in

his hand. "I was folding anyway. And cut it out, will you? I didn't go looking for her. I didn't tell her to come back. And she may as well be the Colonel for all my chance of putting her flat."

Wanatamba, the lean, black Terran who drove Fourteen, laughed and pointed. A gold-spangled skimmer was dropping from the east, tracked by the guns of two of the blowers on that side. Everybody knew what it was, though. Pritchard grimaced and stood. "Seems that's the game for me," he said.

"Hey Danny," one of the men behind him called as he walked away. "Get a little extra for us, hey?"

The skimmer had landed in front of Command Central, at rest an earth-blended geodesic housing the staff and much of the commo hardware. Wearing a wrist-to-ankle sunsuit, yellow where it had tone, she was leaning on the plex windscreen. An officer in fatigues with unlatched body armor stepped out of the dome and did a double take. He must have recollected, though, because he trotted off toward a bunker before Danny reached the skimmer.

"Hey!" the girl called brightly. She looked about seventeen, her hair an unreal cascade of beryl copper over one shoulder. "We're going on a trip."

"Uh?"

The dome section flipped open again. Pritchard stiffened to attention when he saw the short, mustached figure who exited. "Peace, Colonel," the girl said.

"Peace, Sonna. You're such an ornament to a firebase that I'm thinking of putting you on requisition for our next contract."

Laughing cheerfully, the girl gestured toward the rigid sergeant. "I'm taking Danny to the Hamper Shrine this afternoon."

Pritchard reddened. "Sir, Sergeant-Commander Daniel Pritchard—"

"I know you, trooper," the Colonel said with a friendly smile. "I've watched Two Star in action often enough, you know." His eyes were blue.

"Sir, I didn't request—that is . . ."

"And I also know there's small point in arguing with our girl, here, hey Sonna? Go see your shrine, soldier, and worst comes to worst, just throw your hands up and yell 'Exchange.' You can try Col. Foster's rations for a week or two until we get this little business straightened out." The Colonel winked, bowed low to Sonna, and reentered the dome.

"I don't figure it." Danny said as he settled into the passenger seat. The skimmer was built low and sleek as if a racer, though its top speed was probably under a hundred kays. Any more would have put too rapid a drain of the rechargables packed into the decimeter-thick floor—a fusion unit would have doubled the flyer's bulk and added 400 kilos right off the bat. At that, the speed and an operating altitude of thirty meters were more than enough for the tanker. You judge things by what you're used to, and the blower chief who found himself that far above the cold, hard ground—it could happen on a narrow switchback—had seen his last action.

While the wind whipped noisily about the open cockpit, the girl tended to her flying and ignored Danny's curiosity. It was a hop rather than a real flight, keeping over the same hill at all times and circling down to land scarcely a minute after takeoff. On a field of grass untouched by the recent fire rose the multi-tented crystalline structure Pritchard had glimpsed during the assault. With a neat spin and a brief whine from the fans, the skimmer settled down.

Sonna grinned. Her sunsuit, opaquing completely in the direct light, blurred her outline in a dazzle of fluorescent saffron. "What don't you figure?"

"Well, ah . . ." Danny stumbled, his curiosity drawn between the girl and the building. "Well, the Colonel isn't that, ah, easy to deal with usually. I mean . . ."

Her laugh bubbled in the sunshine. "Oh, it's because I'm an Advisor, I'm sure."

"Excuse?"

"An Advisor. You know, the . . . well, a representative. Of the government, if you want to put it that way."

"My Lord!" the soldier gasped. "But you're so young."

She frowned. "You really don't know much about us, do you?" she reflected.

"Umm, well, the briefing cubes mostly didn't deal with the friendlies this time because we'd be operating without support . . . Anything was going to look good after Emporion, that was for sure. All desert there—you should've heard the cheers when the Colonel said that we'd lift.''

She combed a hand back absently through her hair. It flowed like molten bronze. "You won on Emporion?" she asked.

"We could've," Danny explained, "even though it was really a Lord-stricken place, dust and fortified plateaus and lousy recce besides because the government had two operating spacers. But the Monarchists ran out of money after six months and that's one sure rule for Hammer's Slammers—no pay, no play. Colonel yanked their bond so fast their ears rang. And we hadn't orbited before offers started coming in.''

"And you took ours and came to a place you didn't know much about," the girl mused. "Well, we didn't know much about you either.''

"What do you need to know except we can bust anybody else in this business?" the soldier said with amusement. "Anybody, public or planet-tied. If you're worried about Foster, don't; he wouldn't back the freaks today, but when he has to, we'll eat him for breakfast.''

"Has to?" the girl repeated in puzzlement. "But he always has to—the Densonites hired him, didn't they?''

Strategy was a long way from Danny's training, but the girl seemed not to know that. And besides, you couldn't spend seven years with the Slammers and not pick up some basics. "OK," he began, "Foster's boys'll fight, but they're not crazy. Trying to block our advance in open land like this'd be pure suicide—as those coppy freaks

—pardon, didn't mean that—must've found out today. Foster likely got orders to support the civvies but refused. I know for a fact that his arty's better'n what we wiped up today, and those *planes* . . ."

"But his contract . . . ?" Sonna queried.

"Sets out the objectives and says the outfit'll obey civvie orders where it won't screw things up too bad," Danny said. "Standard form. The legal of it's different, but that's what it means."

The girl was nodding, eyes slitted, and in a low voice she quoted, ". . .'except in circumstances where such directions would significantly increase the risks to be undergone by the party of the second part without corresponding military advantage.'" She looked full at Danny. "Very . . . interesting. When we hired your colonel, I don't think any of us understood that clause."

Danny blinked, out of his depth and aware of it. "Well, it doesn't matter really. I mean, the Colonel didn't get his rep from ducking fights. It's just, well . . . say we're supposed to clear the Densonites off the, the Star Plain? Right?"

The girl shrugged.

"So that's what we'll do." Danny wiped his palms before gesturing with both hands. "But if your Advisors—"

"We Advisors," the girl corrected, smiling.

"Anyway," the tanker concluded, his enthusiasm chilled, "if you tell the Colonel to fly the whole Regiment up to ten thousand and jump it out, he'll tell you to go piss up a rope. Sorry, he wouldn't say that. But you know what

I mean. We know our job, don't worry."

"Yes, that's true," she said agreeably. "And we don't, and we can't understand it. We thought that—one to one, you know?—perhaps if I got to know you, one of you . . . They thought we might understand all of you a little."

The soldier frowned uncertainly.

"What we don't see," she finally said, "is how you—"

She caught herself. Touching her cold fingertips to the backs of the tanker's wrists, the girl continued, "Danny, you're a nice . . . you're not a, a sort of monster like we thought you all must be. If you'd been born of Thrush you'd have had a—different—education, you'd be more, forgive me, I don't mean it as an insult, sophisticated in some ways. That's all.

"But how can a nice person like you go out and kill?"

He rubbed his eyes, then laced together his long, brown fingers. "You . . . well, it's not like that. What I said the other night—look, the Slammers're a good outfit, the best, and I'm damned lucky to be with them. I do my job the best way I know. I'll keep on doing that. And if somebody gets killed, OK. My brother Jig stayed home and he's two years dead now. Tractor rolled on a wet field but Via, coulda been a tow-chain snapped or old age; doesn't matter. He wasn't going to live forever and neither is anybody else. And I haven't got any friends on the far end of the muzzle."

Her voice was very soft as she said, "Perhaps if I keep trying . . ."

Danny smiled. "Well, I don't mind," he lied, looking at the structure. "What is this place, anyhow?"

Close up, it had unsuspected detail. The sides were a hedge of glassy rods curving together to a series of peaks ten meters high. No finger-slim member was quite the thickness or color of any other, although the delicacy was subliminal in impact. In ground plan it was a complex oval thirty meters by ten, pierced by scores of doorways which were not closed off but were foggy to look at.

"What do you think of it?" the girl asked.

"Well, it's . . ." Danny temporized. A fragment of the briefing cubes returned to him. "It's one of the alien, the Gedel, artifacts, isn't it?"

"Of course," the girl agreed. "Seven hundred thousand years old, as far as we can judge. Only a world in stasis, like Thrush, would have let it survive the way it has. The walls are far tougher than they look, but seven hundred millenia of earthquakes and volcanoes . . ."

Danny stepped out of the skimmer and let his hand run across the building's cool surface. "Yeah, if they'd picked some place with a hotter core there wouldn't be much left but sand by now, would there?"

"Pick it? Thrush was their home," Sonna's voice rang smoothly behind him. "The Gedel chilled it themselves to make it suitable, to leave a signpost for the next races following the Way. We can't even imagine how they did it, but there's no question but that Thrush was normally tectonic up until the last million years or so."

"Via!" Danny breathed, turning his shocked face toward the girl. "No wonder those coppy fanatics wanted to control this place. Why, if they could figure out just a few of the Gedel tricks they'd . . . Lord, they wouldn't stop with Thrush, that's for sure."

"You still don't understand," the girl said. She took Danny by the hand and drew him toward the nearest of the misty doorways. "The Densonites have, well, quirks that make them hard for the rest of us on Thrush to understand. But they would no more pervert Gedel wisdom to warfare than you would, oh, spit on your colonel. Come here."

She stepped into the fuzziness and disappeared. The tanker had no choice but to follow or break her grip; though, oddly, she was no longer clinging to him on the other side of the barrier. She was not even beside him in the large room. He was alone at the first of a line of tableaux, staring at a group of horribly inhuman creatures at play. Their sharp-edged faces, scale-dusted but more avian than reptile, stared enraptured at one of their number who hung in the air. The acrobat's bare, claw-tipped legs pointed 180° apart, straight toward ground and sky.

Pritchard blinked and moved on. The next scene was only a dazzle of sunlight in a glade whose foliage was redder than that of Thrush or Dunstan. There was something else, something wrong or strange about the tableau. Danny felt it, but his eyes could not explain.

Step by step, cautiously, Pritchard worked his way down the line of exhibits. Each was different, centered on a group of the alien bipeds or a ruddy, seemingly empty landscape that hinted unintelligibly. At first, Danny had noticed the eerie silence inside the hall. As he approached the far end he realized he was conscious of music of some sort, very crisp and distant. He laid his bare palm on the floor and found, as he had feared, that it did not vibrate in the least. He ran the last twenty steps to plunge out into the sunlight. Sonna still gripped his hand, and they stood outside the doorway they had entered.

The girl released him. "Isn't it incredible?" she asked, her expression bright. "And every one of the doorways leads to a different corridor—recreation there, agriculture in another, history—everything. A whole planet in that little building."

"That's what the Gedel looked like, huh?" Danny said. He shook his head to clear the strangeness from it.

"The Gedel? Oh, no," the girl replied, surprised again at his ignorance. "These were the folk we call the Hampers. No way to pronounce their own language, a man named Hamper found this site is all. But their homeworld was Kalinga IV, almost three days transit from Thrush. The shrine is here, we think, in the same relation to Starhome as Kalinga was to Thrush.

"You still don't understand," she concluded aloud, watching Danny's expression. She sat on the edge of the flyer, crossing her hands on the lap of her sunsuit. In the glitter thrown by the structure the fabric patterned oddly across her lithe torso. "The Gedel association—it wasn't an empire, couldn't have been. But to merge, a group ultimately needs a center, physical and intellectual. And Thrush and the Gedel were that for twenty races.

"And they achieved genuine unity, not just within one race but among all of them, each as strange to the others as any one of them would have been to man, to us. The . . . power that gave them, over themselves as well as the universe, was incredible. This—even Starhome itself—is such a tiny part of what could be achieved by perfect peace and empathy."

Danny looked at the crystal dome and shivered at what it had done to him. "Look," he said, "peace is just great if the universe cooperates. I don't mean just my line of work, but it doesn't happen that way in the real world. There's no peace spending your life beating wheat out of Dunstan, not like I'd call peace. And what's happened to the Gedel and their buddies for the last half million years or so if things were so great?"

"We can't even imagine what happened to them," Sonna explained gently, "but it wasn't the disaster you imagine. When they reached what they wanted, they set up this, Starhome, the other eighteen shrines as . . . monuments. And then they went away, all together. But they're not wholly gone, even from here, you know. Didn't you feel them in the background inside, laughing with you?"

"I . . ." Danny attempted. He moved, less toward the skimmer than away from the massive crystal behind him. "Yeah, there was something. That's what you're fighting for?"

You couldn't see the laager from where the skimmer rested, but Danny could imagine the silvery glitter of tanks and combat cars between the sky and the raw yellow grass. Her eyes fixed on the same stretch of horizon, the girl said, "Someday men will be able to walk through Starhome and understand. You can't live on Thrush without feeling the impact of the Gedel. That impact has . . . warped, perhaps, the Densonites. They have some beliefs about the Gedel that most of us don't agree with. And they're actually willing to use force to prevent the artifacts from being defiled by anyone who doesn't believe as they do."

"Well, you people do a better job of using force," Danny said. His mind braced itself on its memory of the Regiment's prickly hedgehog.

"Oh, not us!" the girl gasped.

Suddenly angry, the tanker gestured toward the unseen firebase. "Not you? The Densonites don't pay us. And if force isn't what happened to those silly bastards today when our counter-battery hit them, I'd like to know what is."

She looked at him in a way that, despite her previous curiosity, was new to him. "There's much that I'll have to discuss with the other Advisors," she said after a long pause. "And I don't know that it will stop with us, we'll have to put out the call to everyone, the Densonites as well if they will come." Her eyes caught Danny's squarely again. "We acted with little time for deliberation when the Densonites hired Col. Foster and turned all the other pilgrims out of the Star Plain. And we acted in an area beyond our practice—thank the Lord! The key to understanding the Gedel and joining them, Lord willing and the Way being short, is Starhome. And nothing that blocks any man, all men, from Starhome can be . . . tolerated. But with what we've learned since . . . well, we have other things to take into account."

She broke off, tossed her stunning hair. In the flat evening sunlight her garment had paled to translucence. The late rays licked her body red and orange. "But now I'd better get you back to your colonel." She slipped into the skimmer.

Danny boarded without hesitation. After the Gedel building, the transparent skimmer felt almost comfortable. "Back to my tank," he corrected lightly. "Colonel may not care where I am, but he damn well cares if Two Star is combat ready." The sudden rush of air cut off thought of further conversation, and though Sonna smiled as she landed Danny beside his blower, there was a blankness in her expression that indicated her thoughts were far away.

Hell with her, Danny thought. His last night in the Rec Center on Emporion seemed a long time in the past.

At three in the morning the Regiment was almost 200 kilometers from the camp they had abandoned at midnight. There had been no

warning, only the low hoot of the siren followed
by the Colonel's voice rasping from every man's
lapel speaker, "Mount up and move, boys. Order seven, and your guides are set." It might
have loomed before another outfit as a sudden
catastrophe. After docking one trip with the
Slammers, though, a greenie learned that everything not secured to his blower had better be secured to him. Col. Hammer thought an armored
regiment's firepower was less of an asset than its
mobility. He used the latter to the full with ten
preset orders of march and in-motion recharging
for the infantry skimmers, juicing from the tanks
and combat cars.

Four pongoes were jumpered to Two Star
when Foster's outpost sprang its ambush.

The lead combat car, half a kay ahead,
bloomed in a huge white ball that flooded the
photon amplifiers of Danny's goggles. The
buzzbomb's hollow detonation followed a moment later while the tanker, cursing, simultaneously switched to infra-red and swung his turret
left at max advance. He ignored the head of the
column, where the heated-air thump of powerguns merged with the crackle of mines blasted
to either side by the combat cars; that was somebody else's responsibility. He ignored the two infantrymen wired to his tank's port side as well. If
they knew their business, they'd drop the
jumpers and flit for Two Star's blind side as
swiftly as Danny could spin his heavy turret. If
not, well, you don't have time for niceness when
somebody's firing shaped charges at you.

"Damp that ground-sender!" Central

snapped to the lead elements. Too quickly to be a response to the command, the grass trembled under the impact of a delay-fused rocket punching down toward the computed location of the enemy's subsurface signaling. The Regiment must have rolled directly over an outpost, either through horrendously bad luck or because Foster had sewn his vedettes very thickly.

The firing stopped. The column had never slowed and Michael, first of the heavy companies behind the screen of combat cars, fanned the grass fires set by the hoses. Pritchard scanned the area of the firefight as Two Star rumbled through it in turn. The antipersonal charges had dimpled the ground with shrapnel, easily identifiable among the glassy scars left by the powerguns. In the center of a great vitrified blotch lay a left arm and a few scraps of gray coverall. Nearby was the plastic hilt of a buzzbomb launcher. The other vedette had presumably stayed on the commo in his covered foxhole until the penetrator had scattered it and him over the landscape. If there had been a third bunker, it escaped notice by Two Star's echo sounders.

"Move it out, up front," Central demanded. "This cuts our margin."

The burned-out combat car swept back into obscurity as Kowie put on speed. The frontal surfaces had collapsed inward from the heat, leaving the driver and blower chief as husks of carbon. There was no sign of the wing gunners. Perhaps they had been far enough back and clear of the spurt of directed radiance to escape.

The ammo canister of the port tri-barrel had flash-ignited, though, and it was more likely that the men were wasted on the floor of the vehicle.

Another hundred and fifty kays to go, and now Foster and the Densonites knew they were coming.

There were no further ambushes to break the lightless monotony of gently rolling grassland. Pritchard took occasional sips of water and ate half a tube of protein ration. He started to fling the tube aside, then thought of the metal detectors on following units. He dropped it between his feet instead.

The metal-pale sun was thrusting the Regiment's shadow in long fingers up the final hillside when Central spoke again. You could tell it was the Colonel himself sending. "Everybody freeze but Beta-First, Beta-First proceed in column up the rise and in. Keep your intervals, boys, and don't try to bite off too much. Last data we got was Foster had his anti-aircraft company with infantry support holding the target. Maybe they pulled out when we knocked on the door tonight, maybe they got reinforced. So take it easy—and don't bust up anything you don't have to."

Pritchard dropped his seat back inside the turret. There was nothing to be seen from the hatch but the monochrome sunrise and armored vehicles grounded on the yellow background. Inside, the three vision blocks gave greater variety. One was the constant 360° display, better than normal eyesight according to the designers because the blower chief could see all around the tank without turning his head. Danny didn't care for it. Images were squeezed a good deal horizontally. Shapes weren't quite what you expected, so you didn't react quite as fast; and that was a good recipe for a dead trooper. The screen above the three-sixty was variable in light sensitivity and in magnification, useful for special illumination and first-shot hits.

The bottom screen was the remote rig; Pritchard dialed it for the forward receptors of Beta-First-Three. It was strange to watch the images of the two leading combat cars trembling as they crested the hill, yet feel Two Star as stable as 170 tonnes can be when grounded.

"Nothing moving," the platoon leader reported unnecessarily. Central had remote circuits too, as well as the satellite net to depend on.

The screen lurched as the blower Danny was slaved to boosted its fans to level the downgrade. Dust plumed from the leading cars, weaving across a sky that was almost fully light. At an unheard command, the platoon turned up the wick in unison and let the cars hurtle straight toward the target's central corridor. It must have helped, because Foster's gunners caught only one car when they loosed the first blast through their camouflage.

The second car blurred in a mist of vaporized armor plate. Incredibly, the right wing gunner shot back. The deadly flame-lash of his hose was pale against the richer color of the hostile fire. Foster had sited his calliopes, massive 3 cm guns whose nine fixed barrels fired extra-length charges. Danny had never seen a combat car turned into swiss cheese faster than the one now spiked on the muzzles of a pair of the heavy guns.

Gray-suited figures were darting from cover as if the cars' automatics were harmless for being outclassed. The damaged blower nosed into the ground. Its driver leaped out, running for the lead car which had spun on its axis and was hosing blue-green fire in three directions. One of Foster's troops raised upright, loosing a buzzbomb at the wreckage of the grounded car. The left side of the vehicle flapped like a batwing as it sailed across Danny's field of view. The concussion knocked down the running man. He rose to his knees, jumped for a handhold as the lead car accelerated past him. As he swung himself aboard, two buzzbombs hit the blower simultaneously. It bloomed with joined skullcaps of pearl and bone.

Pritchard was swearing softly. He had switched to a stern pickup already, and the tumbled wreckage in it was bouncing, fading swiftly. Shots twinkled briefly as the four escaping blowers dropped over the ridge.

"In column ahead," said the Colonel grimly, "Hotel, Kitchen, Michael. Button up and hose 'em out, you know the drill."

And then something went wrong. "Are you insane?" the radio marveled, and Danny recognized that voice too. "I forbid you!"

"You can't. Somebody get her out of here."

"Your contract is over, finished, do you hear?

Heavenly Way, we'll all become Densonites if we must. This horror must end!''

"Not yet. You don't see—"

"I've seen too—" The shouted words cut off.

"So we let Foster give us a bloody nose and back off? That's what you want? But it's bigger than what you want now, sister, it's the whole Regiment. It's never bidding another contract without somebody saying, 'Hey, they got sand-bagged on Thrush, didn't they?' And nobody re-membering that Foster figured the civvies would chill us—and he was right. Don't you see? They killed my boys, and now they're going to pay the bill.

''Tank Section, execute! Dig 'em out, panzers!''

Danny palmed the panic bar, dropping the seat and locking the hatch over it. The rushing-air snarl of the fans was deadened out by the armor, but a hot bearing somewhere filled the compartment with its high keening. Two Star hurdled the ridge. Its whole horizon flared with crystal dancing and scattering in sunlight and the reflected glory of automatic weapons firing from its shelter. Starhome was immensely larger than Danny had expected.

A boulevard twenty meters wide divided two ranks of glassy buildings, any one of which, tow-ers and pavillions, stood larger than the shrine Danny had seen the previous day. At a kilometer's distance it was a coruscating unity of parts as similar as the strands of a silken rope. Danny rapped up the magnification and saw the details spring out; rods woven into columns that

streaked skyward a hundred meters; translucent
sheets formed of myriads of pinhead beads, each
one glowing a color as different from the rest as
one star is from the remainder of those seen on a
moonless night; a spiral column, free-standing
and the thickness of a woman's wrist, that
pulsed slowly through the spectrum as it
climbed almost out of sight. All the structures
seemed to front on the central corridor, with the
buildings on either side welded together by
tracery mazes, porticoes, arcades—a thousand
different plates and poles of glass.

A dashed cyan line joined the base of an up-
swept web of color to the tank. Two Star's hull
thudded to the shock of vaporizing metal. The
stabilizer locked the blower's pitching out of
Danny's sight picture. He swung the glowing orange bead onto the source of fire and kicked the
pedal. The air rang like a carillon as the whole
glassy facade sagged, then avalanched into the
street. There was a shock of heat in the closed
battle compartment as the breech flicked open
and belched out the spent case. The plastic
hissed on the floor, outgassing horribly while the
air-conditioning strained to clear the chamber.
Danny ignored the stench, nudged his sights
onto the onrushing splendor of the second structure on the right of the corridor. The breech of
the big powergun slapped again and again,
recharging instantly as the tanker worked the
foot trip.

Blue-green lightning scattered between the
walls as if the full power of each bolt was flashing
the length of the corridor. Two Star bellowed in

on the wake of its fire, and crystal flurried under
the fans. Kowie leveled their stroke slightly, cutting speed by a 'fraction but lifting the tank
higher above the abrasive litter. The draft hurled
glittering shards across the corridor, arcs of cold
fire in the light of Two Star's gun and those of
the blowers following. Men in gray were running
from their hiding places to avoid the sliding
crystal masses, the iridescent rain that pattered
on the upper surfaces of the tanks but
smashed jaggedly through the infantry's body
armor.

Danny set his left thumb to rotate the turret
counter-clockwise, held the gun-switch down
with his foot. The remaining sixteen rounds of
his basic load blasted down the right half of
Starhome, spread by the blower's forward motion and the turret swing. The compartment was
gray with fumes. Danny slammed the hatch
open and leaned out. His hands went to the 2 cm
as naturally as a calf turns to milk. The wind
was cold on his face. Kowie slewed the blower
left to avoid the glassy wave that slashed into the
corridor from one of the blasted structures. The
scintillance halted, then ground a little further as
something gave way inside the pile.

A soldier in gray stepped from an untouched
archway to the left. The buzzbomb on his shoulder was the size of a landing vessel as it swung
directly at Danny. The tri-barrel seemed to traverse with glacial slowness. It was too slow. Danny saw the brief flash as the rocket leaped from
the shoulder of the other mercenary. It whirred
over Two Star and the sergeant, exploded

cataclysmically against a spike of Starhome still rising on the other side.

The infantryman tossed the launcher tube aside. He froze, his arms spread wide, and shouted, "Exchange!"

"Exchange yourself, mother!" Danny screamed back white-faced. He triggered his hose. The gray torso exploded. The body fell backward in a mist of blood, chest and body armor torn open by four hits that shriveled bones and turned fluids to steam.

"Hard left and goose it, Kowie," the sergeant demanded. He slipped the panic bar again. As the hatch clanged shut over his head, Danny caught a momentary glimpse of the vision blocks, three soldiers with powerguns leaping out of the same towering structure from which the rocketeer had come. Their faces were blankly incredulous as they saw the huge blower swinging toward them at full power. The walls flexed briefly under the impact of the tank's frontal slope, but the filigree was eggshell thin. The structure disintegrated, lurching toward the corridor while Two Star plowed forward within it. A thousand images kaleidoscoped in Danny's skull, sparkling within the windchime dissonance of the falling tower.

The fans screamed as part of the structure's mass collapsed onto Two Star. Kowie rocked the tank, raising it like a submarine through a sea of ravaged glass. The gentle, green-furred humanoids faded from Danny's mind. He threw the hatch open. Kowie gunned the fans, reversing the blower in a polychrome shower. Several

tanks had moved ahead of Two Star, nearing the
far end of the corridor. Gray-uniformed soldiers
straggled from the remaining structures, hands
empty, eyes fixed on the ground. There was very
little firing. Kowie edged into the column and
followed the third tank into the laager forming
on the other side of Starhome. Pritchard was
drained. His throat was dry, but he knew from
past experience that he would vomit if he swallowed even a mouthful of water before his
muscles stopped trembling. The blower rested
with its skirts on the ground, its fans purring
gently as they idled to a halt.

Kowie climbed out of the driver's hatch, moving stiffly. He had a powergun in his hand, a
pistol he always carried for moral support. Two
Star's bow compartment was frequently nearer
the enemy than anything else in Hammer's
Slammers.

Several towers still stood in the wreckage of
Starhome. The nearest one wavered from orange
to red and back in the full blaze of sunlight. Danny watched it in the iridium mirror of his tank's
deck, the outline muted by the hatchwork of
crystal etching on the metal.

Kowie shot off-hand. Danny looked up in irritation. The driver shot again, his light charge
having no discernable effect on the structure.

"Shut it off." Danny croaked. "These're
shrines."

The ground where Starhome had stood blazed
like the floor of Hell.

INTERLUDE: THE CHURCH OF THE LORD'S UNIVERSE

PERHAPS THE MOST surprising thing about the faith that men took to the stars—and vice versa —was that it appeared to differ so little from the liturgical protestantism of the Nineteenth and Twentieth Centuries. Indeed, services of the Church of the Lord's Universe—almost always, except by Unitarians, corrupted to "Universal Church"—so resembled those of a high-flying Anglican parish of 1920 that a visitor from the past would have been hard put to believe that he was watching a sect as extreme in its own way as the Society for Krishna Consciousness was in its.

The Church of the Lord's Universe was officially launched in 1985 in Minneapolis, Minnesota, by the merger of 230 existing protestant congregations—Methodist, Presbyterian, Episcopalian, and Lutheran. In part the new church was a revolt against the extreme fundamentalism peaking at that time. The Universalists sought converts vigorously from the start. Their liturgy obviously attempted to recapture the traditional beauty of Christianity's greatest age, but there is reason to believe that the extensive use of Latin in the service was part of a design to avoid giving doctrinal offense as well.

Anyone who has attended both Presbyterian and
Methodist services has felt uneasiness at the line,
"Forgive us our debts/trespasses . . ." St
Jerome's Latin version of the Lord's Prayer flows
smoothly and unnoticed from the tongue of one
raised in either sect.

But the Church of the Lord's Universe had a
mission beyond the entertainment of its congregations for an hour every Sunday. The priests
and laiety alike preached the salvation of Mankind through His works. To Universalists, however, the means and the end were both secular.
The Church taught that Man must reach the
stars and there, among infinite expanses, find
room to live in peace. This temporal paradise
was one which could be grasped by all men. It
did not detract from spiritual hopes; but heaven
is in the hands of the Lord, while the stars were
not beyond Man's own strivings.

The Doctrine of Salvation through the Stars—
it was never labeled so bluntly in Universalist
writings, but the peevish epithet bestowed by a
Baptist theologian was not inaccurate—gave the
Church of the Lord's Universe a dynamism un-
known to the Christian center since the days of
Archbishop Laud. It was a naive doctrine, of
course. Neither the stars nor anything else
brought peace to Man; but realists did not bring
men to the stars, either, while the hopeful ro-
mantics of the Universal Church certainly
helped.

The Universalist credo was expressed most
clearly in the BOOK OF THE WAY, a slim volume commissioned at the First Consensus and

adopted after numerous emendations by the
Tenth. The BOOK OF THE WAY never officially replaced the Bible, but the committee of
laymen which framed it struck a chord in the
hearts of all Universalists. Despite its heavily
Eastern leanings (including suggestions of rein-
carnation), the BOOK spoke in an idiom in-
telligible and profoundly moving to men and
women who in another milieu would have been
Technocrats.

While the new faith appealed to men and
women everywhere, it by no means appealed to
every man and woman. By their uncompromis-
ing refusal to abandon future dreams to cope
with present disasters—the famines, pollution,
and pogroms of every day—the Universalists
faced frequent hatred. During the Food Riots of
2039, three hundred Universalists were ceremo-
nially murdered and eaten in a packed am-
phitheatre in Dacca, and there were other martyrs as well. But the survivors and their faith
drove on. Their ranks swelled every time
catastrophe proved Man was incapable of solving his problems on Earth alone.

Thus, when Man did reach the stars, the ships
were crewed in large measure by Universalists.
Those who had prayed for, worked for, and even
sworn by the Way of the Stars, *Via Stellarum,*
were certain to be among the first treading it. On
Earth, the Church of the Lord's Universe had
been a vocal minority; in the colonies spreading
like a bacterial culture through the galaxy, Universalists were frequently in the majority.

There were changes. Inevitably, fragmentation followed success as centuries and the high cost of interstellar communication made each congregation a separate entity. But the basic thrust of the Church, present peace and safety for Mankind, remained even when reality diluted it to lip service or less. Mercenaries were recruited mostly from rural cultures which were used to privation—and steeped in religion as well. Occasionally a trooper might feel uneasy as he swore, "Via!," for the Way had been a way of peace.

But mercs swore by blood and the martyrs as well; and few had better knowledge of either blood or innocent victims than the gunmen of the mercenary companies.

UNDER THE HAMMER

"THINK you're going to like killing, boy?" asked the old man on double crutches.

Rob Jenne turned from the streams of moving cargo to his unnoticed companion in the shade of the starship's hull. His own eyes were pale gray, suited like his dead-white skin to Burlage, whose ruddy sun could raise a blush but not a tan. When they adjusted, they took in the clerical collar which completed the other's costume. The smooth, black synthetic contrasted oddly with the coveralls and shirt of local weave. At that, the Curwinite's outfit was a cut above Rob's own, the same worksuit of Burlage sisal that he had worn as a quarryhand at home. Uniform issue would come soon.

At least, he hoped and prayed it would.

When the youth looked away after an embarrassed grin, the priest chuckled. "Another damned old fool, hey boy? There were a few in your family, weren't there . . . the ones who'd quote the Book of the Way saying not to kill—and here you go off for a hired murderer.

Right?" He laughed again, seeing he had the younger man's attention. "But that by itself wouldn't be so hard to take—you were leaving your family anyway, weren't you, nobody really believes they'll keep close to their people after five years, ten years of star hopping. But your mates, though, the team you worked with . . . how did you explain to them why you were leaving a good job to go on contract? 'Via!' " the priest mimicked, his tones so close to those of Barney Larsen, the gang boss, that Rob started in surprise, "you get your coppy ass shot off, lad, and it'll serve you right for being a fool!"

"How do you know I signed for a mercenary?" Jenne asked, clenching his great, calloused hands on the handle of his carry-all. It was everything he owned in the universe in which he no longer had a home. "And how'd you know about my Aunt Gudrun?"

"Haven't I seen a thousand of you?" the priest blazed back, his eyes like sparks glinting from the drill shaft as the sledge drove it deeper into the rock. "You're young and strong and bright enough to pass Alois Hammer's tests—you be proud of that, boy, few enough are fit for Hammer's Slammers. There you were, a man grown who'd read all the cop about mercenaries, believed most of it . . . more'n ever you did the Book of the Way, anyhow. Sure, I know. So you got some off-planet factor to send your papers in for you, for the sake of the bounty he'll get from the Colonel if you make the grade—"

The priest caught Rob's blink of surprise. He chuckled again, a cruel, unpriestly sound, and said, "He told you it was for friendship? One a these days you'll learn what friendship counts, when you get an order that means the death of a friend—and you carry it out."

Rob stared at the priest in repulsion, the grizzled chin resting on interlaced fingers and the crutches under either armpit supporting most of his weight. "It's my life," the recruit said with sulky defiance. "Soon as they pick me up here, you can go back to living your own. 'Less you'd be willing to do that right now?"

"They'll come soon enough, boy," the older man said in a milder voice. "Sure, you've been ridden by everybody you know . . . now that you're alone, here's a stranger riding you too. I don't mean it like I sound . . . wasn't born to the work, I guess. There's priests—and maybe the better ones—who'd say that signing on with mercenaries means so long a spiral down that maybe your soul won't come out of it in another life or another hundred. But I don't see it like that.

"Life's a forge, boy, and the purest metal comes from the hottest fire. When you've been under the hammer a few times, you'll find you've been beaten down to the real, no lies, no excuses. There'll be a time, then, when you got to look over the product . . . and if you don't like what you see, well, maybe there's time for change, too."

The priest turned his head to scan the half of the horizon not blocked by the bellied-down bulk of the starship. Ant columns of stevedores manhandled cargo from the ship's rollerway into

horse and oxdrawn wagons in the foreground:
like most frontier worlds, Burlage included, self-
powered machinery was rare in the backcountry.
Beyond the men and draft animals stretched the
fields, studded frequently by orange-golden
clumps of native vegetation.

"Nobody knows how little his life's worth till
he's put it on the line a couple times," the old
man said. "For nothing. Look at it here on
Curwin—the seaboard taxed these uplands into
revolt, then had to spend what they'd robbed
and more to hire an armored regiment. So boys
like you from—Scania? Felsen?—"

"Burlage, sir."

"Sure, a quarryman, should have known from
your shoulders. You come in to shoot farmers for
a gang of coastal moneymen you don't know and
wouldn't like if you did." The priest paused, less
for effect than to heave in a quick, angry breath
that threatened his shirt buttons. "And maybe
you'll die, too; if the Slammers were immortal,
they wouldn't need recruits. But some that die
will die like saints, boy, die martyrs of the Way,
for no reason, for no reason . . .

"Your ride's here, boy."

The suddenly emotionless words surprised
Rob as much as a scream in a silent prayer
would have. Hissing like a gun-studded dragon,
a gray-metal combat car slid onto the landing
field from the west. Light dust puffed from beneath it: although the flat-bed trailer behind was
supported on standard wheels, the armored vehicle itself hovered a hand's-breadth above the

surface at all points. A dozen powerful fans on the underside of the car kept it floating on an invisible bubble of air, despite the weight of the fusion power unit and the iridium-ceramic armor. Rob had seen combat cars on the entertainment cube occasionally, but those skittering miniatures gave no hint of the awesome power that emanated in reality from the machines. This one was seven meters long and three wide at the base, the armored sides curving up like a turtle's back to the open fighting compartment in the rear.

From the hatch in front of the powerplant stuck the driver's head, a blank-mirrored ball in a helmet with full face-shield down. Road dust drifted away from the man in a barely-visible haze, cleaned from the helmet's optics by a static charge. Faceless and terrible to the unfamiliar Burlager, the driver guided toward the starship a machine that appeared no more inhuman than did the man himself.

"Undercrewed," the priest murmured. "Two men on the back deck aren't enough for a car running single."

The older man's jargon was unfamiliar but Rob could follow his gist by looking at the vehicle. The two men standing above the waist-high armor of the rear compartment were clearly fewer than had been contemplated when the combat car was designed. Its visible armament comprised a heavy powergun forward to fire over the head of the driver, and similar weapons, also swivel-mounted, on either side to command the flanks and rear of the vehicle. But with only two men in the compartment there was a dangerous gap in the circle of fire the car could lay down if ambushed. Another vehicle for escort would have eased the danger, but this one was alone save for the trailer it pulled.

Though as the combat car drew closer, Rob began to wonder if the two soldiers present couldn't handle anything that occurred. Both were in full battle dress, wearing helmets and laminated back and breast armor over their khaki. Their faceplates were clipped open. The one at the forward gun, his eyes as deep-sunken and deadly as the three revolving barrels of his weapon, was in his forties and further aged by the dust sweated into black grime in the creases of his face. His head rotated in tiny jerks, taking in every nuance of the sullen crowd parting for his war-car. The other soldier was huge by comparison with the first and lounged across the back in feigned leisure: feigned, because either hand was within its breadth of a powergun's trigger, and his limbs were as controlled as spring steel.

With careless expertise, the driver backed his trailer up to the conveyor line. A delicate hand with the fans allowed him to angle them slightly, drifting the rear of the combat car to edge the trailer in the opposite direction. The larger soldier contemptuously thumbed a waiting horse and wagon out of its slot. The teamster's curse brought only a grin and a big hand rested on a powergun's receiver, less a threat than a promise. The combat car eased into the space.

"Wait for an old man," the priest said as Rob

lifted his carry-all, "and I'll go with you." Glad
even for that company, the recruit smiled nervously, fitting his stride to the other's surprisingly nimble swing-and-pause, swing-and-
pause.

The driver dialed back minusculy on the
power and allowed the big vehicle to settle to the
ground without a skip or a tremor. One hand
slid back the face shield to a high, narrow nose
and eyes that alertly focused on the two men approaching. "The Lord and his martyrs!" the
driver cried in amazement. "It's Blacky himself
come in with our newbie!"

Both soldiers on the back deck slewed their
eyes around at the cry. The smaller one took one
glance, then leaped the two meters to the ground
to clasp Rob's companion. "Hey!" he shouted,
oblivious to the recruit shifting his weight uncertainly. "Via, it's good to see you! But what're you
doing on Curwin?"

"I came back here afterwards," the older man
answered with a smile. "Born here, I must've
told you . . . though we didn't talk a lot. I'm a
priest now, see?"

"And I'm a flirt like the load we're supposed
to pick up," the driver said, dismounting with
more care than his companion. Abreast of the
first soldier, he too took in the round collar and
halted gapemouthed. "Lord, I'll be a coppy rag
if you ain't," he breathed. "Whoever heard of a
blower chief taking the Way?"

"Shut up, Jake," the first soldier said without
rancor. He stepped back from the priest to take
a better look, then seemed to notice Rob.

"Umm," he said, "you the recruit from Burlage?"

"Yessir. M-my name's Rob Jenne, sir."

"Not 'sir,' there's enough sirs around already," the veteran said. "I'm Chero, except if there's lots of brass around, then make it Sergeant-Commander Worzer. Look, take your gear back to the trailer and give Leon a hand with the load.

"Hey, Blacky," he continued with concern, ignoring Rob again, "what's wrong with your legs? We got the best there was."

"Oh, they're fine," Rob heard the old man reply, "but they need a weekly tuning. Out here we don't have the computers, you know; so I get the astrogation boys to sync me up on the ships' hardware whenever one docks in—just waiting for a chance now. But in six months the servos are far enough out of line that I have to shut off the power till the next ship arrives. You'd be surprised how well I get around on these pegs, though . . ."

Leon, the huge third crew member, had loosed the top catches of his body armor for ventilation. From the look of it, the laminated casing should have been a size larger; but Rob wasn't sure anything larger was made. The gunner's skin where exposed was the dense black of a basalt outcropping. "They'll be a big crate to go on, so just set your gear down till we get it loaded," he said. Then he grinned at Rob, teeth square and slightly yellow against his face. "Think you can take me?"

That was a challenge the recruit could under-

stand, the first he could meet fairly since board-
ing the starship with a one-way ticket to a planet
he had never heard of. He took in the waiting
veteran quickly but carefully, proud of his own
rock-hardened muscles but certain the other
man had been raised just as hard. "I give you
best," the blond said. "Unless you feel you got to
prove it?"

The grin broadened and a great black hand
reached out to clasp Rob's. "Naw," the soldier
said, "just like to clear the air at the start. Some
of the big ones; Lord, testy ain't the word. All
they can think about's what they want to prove
with me . . . so they don't watch their side of the
car, and then there's trouble for everybody."

"Hammer's Regiment?" called an unfamiliar
voice. Both men looked up. Down the conveyor
rode a blue-tunicked ship's man in front of what
first appeared to be a huge crate. At second
glance Rob saw that it was a cage of light alloy
holding four . . . "Dear Lord!" the recruit
gasped.

"Roger, Hammer's," Leon agreed, handing
the crewman a plastic chit while the latter cut
power to the rollers to halt the cage. The chit
slipped into the computer linkage on the
crewman's left wrist, lighting a green indicator
when it proved itself a genuine bill of lading.

There were four female humanoids in the cage
—stark naked except for a dusting of fine blue
scales. Rob blinked. One of the near-women
stood with a smile—Lord, she had no teeth!
—and rubbed her groin deliberately against one
of the vertical bars.

"First quality Genefran flirts," Leon chuckled. "Ain't human, boy, but the next best thing."

"Better," threw in Jake, who had swung himself into the fighting compartment as soon as the cage arrived. "I tell you, kid, you never had it till you had a flirt. Surgically modified and psychologically prepared. Rowf!"

"N-not human?" Rob stumbled, unable to take his eyes off the cage, "you mean like *monkeys?*"

Leon's grin lit his face again, and the driver cackled, "Well, don't know about monkeys, but they're a whole lot like sheep."

"You take the left side and we'll get this aboard," Leon directed. The trailer's bed was half a meter below the rollerway so that the cage, though heavy and awkward, could be slid without much lifting.

Rob gripped the bars numbly, turning his face down from the tittering beside him. "Amazing what they can do with implants and a wig," Jake was going on, "though a course there's a lot of cutting to do first, but those ain't the differences you see, if you follow. The scales, now—they have a way—"

"Lift!" Leon ordered, and Rob straightened at the knees. They took two steps backward with the cage wobbling above them as the girls—the flirts!—squealed and hopped about. "Down!" and cage clashed on trailer as the two big men moved in unison.

Rob stepped back, his mouth working in distaste, unaware of the black soldier's new look of respect. Quarry work left a man used to awkward weights. "This is foul," the recruit marveled. "Are those really going back with us for, for . . ."

"Rest'n relaxation," Leon agreed, snapping tie-downs around the bars.

"But how . . ." Rob began, looking again at the cage. When the red-wigged flirt fondled her left breast upward, he could see the implant scars pale against the blue. The scales were more thinly spread where the skin had been stretched in molding it. "I'll *never* touch something like that. Look, maybe Burlage is pretty backward about . . . things, about sex, I don't know. But I don't see how anybody could . . . I mean—"

"Via, wait till you been here as long as we have," Jake gibed. He clenched his right hand and pumped it suggestively. "Field expedients, that's all."

"On this kinda contract," Leon explained, stepping around to get at the remaining tie-downs, "you can't trust the local girls. Least not in the field, like we are. The Colonel likes to keep us patrol sections pretty much self-contained."

"Yeah," Jake broke in—would his cracked tenor never cease? "Why, some of these whores, they take a razor blade, see—in a cork you know?—and, well, never mind." He laughed, seeing Rob's face.

"Jake," Sgt. Worzer called, "Shut up and hop in."

The driver slipped instantly into his hatch. Disgusting as Rob found the little man, he recognized his ability. Jake moved with lethal certainty and a speed that belied the weight of his body armor.

"Ready to lift, Chero?" he asked.

The priest was levering himself toward the starship again. Worzer watched him go for a moment, shook his head. "Just run us out to the edge of the field," he directed. "I got a few things to show our recruit before we head back; nobody rides in my car without knowing how to work the guns." With a sigh he hopped into the fighting compartment. Leon motioned Rob in front of him. Gingerly, the recruit stepped onto the trailer hitch, gripped the armored rim with both hands, lifted himself aboard. Leon followed. The trailer bonged as he pushed off from it, and his bulk cramped the littered compartment as soon as he grunted over the side.

"Put this on," Worzer ordered, handing Rob a dusty, bulbous helmet like the others wore. "Brought a battle suit for you, too," he said, kicking the jointed armor leaning against the back of the compartment, "but it'd no more fit you than it would Leon there."

The black laughed. "Gonna be tight back here till the kid or me gets zapped."

"Move 'er out," Worzer ordered. The words came through unsuspected earphones in Rob's helmet, although the sergeant had simply spoken, without visibly activating a pick up.

The car vibrated as the fans revved, then lifted with scarcely a jerk. From behind came the squeals and chirrups of the flirts as the trailer rocked over the irregularities in the field.

Worzer looked hard at the starship's open crew portal as they hissed past it. "Funny what folks go an' do," he said to no one in particular. "Via, wonder what I'll be in another ten years."

"Pet food, likely," joked the driver, taking part in the conversation although physically separated from the other crewmen.

"Shut up, Jake," repeated the blower captain. "And you can hold it up here, we're out far enough."

The combat car obediently settled on the edge of the stabilized area. The port itself had capacity for two ships at a time; the region it served did not. Though with the high cost of animal transport many manufactures could be star-hopped to Curwin's back country more cheaply than they could be carried from the planet's own more urbanized areas, the only available exchange was raw agricultural produce—again limited to the immediate locality by the archaic transport. Its fans purring below audibility, the armored vehicle rested on an empty area of no significance to the region—unless the central government should choose to land another regiment of mercenaries on it.

"Look," the sergeant said, his deep-set eyes catching Rob's, "we'll pass you on to the firebase when we take the other three flirts in next week. They got a training section there. We got six cars in this patrol, that's not enough margin to fool with training a newbie. But neither's it enough to keep somebody useless underfoot for a week, so we'll give you some basics. Not so you can wise-ass when you get to training section, just so you don't get somebody killed if it drops in the pot. Clear?"

"Yessir." Rob broke his eyes away, then realized how foolish he must look staring at his own clasped hands. He looked back at Worzer.

"Just so it's understood," the sergeant said with a nod. "Leon, show him how the gun works."

The big black rotated his weapon so that the muzzles faced forward and the right side was toward Rob and the interior of the car. The mechanism itself was encased in dull-enameled steel ornamented with knobs and levers of unguessable intent. The barrels were stubby iridium cylinders with smooth, two-centimeter bores. Leon touched one of the buttons, then threw a lever back. The plate to which the barrels were attached rotated 120 degrees around their common axis, and a thick disk of plastic popped out into the gunner's hand.

"When the bottom barrel's ready to fire, the next one clockwise is loading one a these"— Leon held up the 2 cm disk—"and the other barrel, the one that's just fired, blows out the empty."

"There's a liquid nitrogen ejector," Worzer put in. "Cools the bore same time it kicks out the empty."

"She feeds up through the mount," the big soldier went on, his index finger tracing the path of the energized disks from the closed hopper bulging in the sidewall, through the ball joint and into the weapon's receiver. "If you try to fire and she don't, check this." The columnar finger

indicated but did not move the stud it had first
pressed on the side of the gun. "That's the safety. She still doesn't fire, pull this"—he clacked
the lever, rotating the barrel cluster another one-
third turn and catching the loaded round that
flew out. "Maybe there was a dud round. She
still don't go, just get down outa the way. We
start telling you about second-order malfunc-
tions and you won't remember where the trigger
is."

"Ah, where is the trigger?" Rob asked dif-
fidently.

Jake's laughter rang through the earphones
and Worzer himself smiled for the first time. The
sergeant reached out and rotated the gun. "See
the grips?" he asked, pointing to the double han-
dles at the back of the receiver. Rob nodded.

"Okay," Worzer continued, "you hold it
there"—he demonstrated—"and to fire, you just
press your thumbs against the trigger plate
between 'em. Let up and it quits. Simple."

"You can clear this field as quick as you can
spin this little honey," Leon said, patting the
gun with affection. "The hicks out there"—his
arm swept the woods and cultivated fields pro-
miscuously—"got some rifles, they hunted 'fore
the trouble started, but no powerguns to men-
tion. About all they do since we moved in is maybe pop a shot or two off, and hide in their holes."

"They've got some underground stockpiles,"
Worzer said, amplifying Leon's words, "explosives, maybe some factories to make rifle
ammo. But the Colonel set up a recce net—spy
satellites, you know—as part a the contract. Any

funny movement day or night, a signal goes
down to whoever's patrolling there. A couple
calls and we check out the area with ground sensors . . . anything funny then—vibration,
hollows showing up on the echo sounder, mag-
netics—anything!—and bam! we call in the artillery."

"Won't take much of a jog on the way back,"
Leon suggested, "and we can check out that report from last night."

"Via, that was just a couple dogs," Jake objected.

"Okay, so we prove it was a couple dogs,"
rumbled the gunner. "Or maybe the hicks got
smart and they're shielding their infra-red now.
Been too damn long since anything popped in
this sector."

"Thing to remember, kid," Worzer summed
up, "is never get buzzed at this job. Stay cool,
you're fine. This car's got more firepower'n
everything hostile in fifty kilos. One call to the
firebase brings in our arty, anything from smoke
shells to a nuke. The rest of our section can be
here in twenty minutes, or a tank platoon from
the firebase in two hours. Just stay cool."

Turning forward, the sergeant said, "Okay,
take her home. Jake. We'll try that movement
report on the way."

The combat car shuddered off the ground, the
flirts shrieking. Rob eyed them, blushed, and
turned back to his powergun, feeling con-
spicuous. He took the grips, liking the deliberate
way the weapon swung. The safety button was

glowing green, but he suddenly realized that he
didn't know the color code. Green for safe? Or
green for ready? He extended his index finger to
the switch.

"Whoa, careful, kid!" Leon warned. "You cut
fifty civvies in half your first day and the Colonel
won't like it one bit."

Sheepishly, Rob drew back his finger. His ears
burned, mercifully hidden beneath the helmet.

They slid over the dusty road in a flat, white
cloud at about forty kph. It seemed shockingly
fast to the recruit, but he realized that the car
could probably move much faster were it not for
the live cargo behind. Even as it was, the trailer
bounced dangerously from side to side.

The road led through a gullied scattering of
grain plots, generally fenced with withes rather
than imported metal. Houses were relatively un-
common. Apparently each farmer plowed several separate locations rather than trying to work
the rugged or less productive areas. Occasionally
they passed a rough-garbed local at work. The
scowls thrown up at the smoothly-running war
car were hostile, but there was nothing more
overt.

"Okay," Jake warned, "here's where it gets
interesting. Sure you still want this half-assed
check while we got the trailer hitched?"

"It won't be far," Worzer answered. "Go
ahead." He turned to Rob, touching the
recruit's shoulder and pointing to the lighted
map panel beside the forward gun. "Look,
Jenne," he said, keeping one eye on the coun-
tryside as Jake took the car off the road in a

sweeping turn, "if you need to call in a location to the firebase, here's the trick. The red dot"— it was in the center of the display and remained there although the map itself seemed to be flowing kitty-corner across the screen as the combat car moved—"that's us. The black dot"—the veteran thumbed a small wheel beside the display and the map, red dot and all, shifted to the right on the panel, leaving a black dot in the center— "that's your pointer. The computer feeds out the grid coordinates here"—his finger touched the window above the map display. Six digits, changing as the map moved under the centered black dot, winked brightly. "You just put the black dot on a bunker site, say, and read off the figures to Fire Central. The arty'll do all the rest."

"Ah," Rob murmured, "ah . . . sergeant, how do you get the little dot off that and onto a bunker like you said?"

There was a moment's silence. "You know how to read a map, don't you, kid?" Worzer finally asked.

"What's that, sir?"

The earphones boomed and cackled with raucous laughter. "Oh my coppy ass!" the sergeant snarled. He snapped the little wheel back, re-centering the red dot. "Lord, I don't know how the training cadre takes it!"

Rob hid his flaming embarrassment by staring over his gunsights. He didn't really know how to use them, either. He didn't know why he'd left Conner's Stoneworks, where he was the cleanest, fastest driller on the whole coppy crew.

His powerful hands squeezed at the grips as if they were the driver's throat through which bubbles of laughter still burst.

"Shut up, Jake," the sergeant finally ordered. "Most of us had to learn something new when we joined. Remember how the ol' man found you your first day, pissing up against the barracks?"

Jake quieted.

They had skirted a fence of cane palings, brushing it once without serious effect. Russet grass flanking the fence flattened under the combat car's downdraft, then sprang up unharmed as the vehicle moved past. Jake seemed to be following a farm track leading from the field to a rambling, substantially-constructed building on the near hilltop. Instead of running with the ground's rise, however, the car cut through brush and down a half-meter bank into a broad-based arroyo. The bushes were too stiff to lie down under the fans. They crunched and howled in the blades, making the car buck, and ricocheted wildly from under the skirts. The bottom of the arroyo was sand, clean-swept by recent run-off. It boiled fiercely as the car first shoomped into it, then ignored the fans entirely. Somehow Jake had managed not to overturn the trailer, although its cargo had been screaming with fear for several minutes.

"Hold up," Worzer ordered suddenly as he swung his weapon toward the left-hand bank. The wash was about thirty meters wide at that point, sides sheer and a meter high. Rob glanced forward to see that a small screen to Worzer's left on the bulkhead, previously dark, was now crossed by three vari-colored lines. The red one was bouncing frantically.

"They got an entrance, sure 'nough," Leon said. He aimed his powergun at the same point, then snapped his face shield down. "Watch it, kid," he said. The black's right hand fumbled in a metal can welded to the blower's side. Most of the paint had chipped from the stencilled legend: GRENADES. What appeared to be a lazy overarm toss snapped a knobby ball the size of a child's fist straight and hard against the bank.

Dirt and rock fragments shotgunned in all directions. The gully side burst in a globe of black streaked with garnet fire, followed by a shock wave that was a physical blow.

"Watch your side, kid!" somebody shouted through the din, but Rob's bulging eyes were focused on the collapsing bank, the empty triangle of black gaping suddenly through the dust —the two ravening whiplashes of directed lightning ripping into it to blast and scatter.

The barrel clusters of the two veterans' powerguns spun whining, kicking gray, eroded disks out of their mechanisms in nervous arcs. The bolts they shot were blue-green flashes barely visible until they struck a target and exploded it with transferred energy. The very rocks burst in droplets of glassy slag splashing high in the air and even back into the war-car to pop against the metal.

Leon's gun paused as his fingers hooked another grenade. "Hold it!" he warned. The sergeant, too, came off the trigger, and the bomb arrowed into the now-vitrified gap in the tunnel mouth. Dirt and glass shards blew straight back at the bang. A stretch of ground sagged for twenty meters beyond the gully wall, closing the tunnel the first explosion had opened.

Then there was silence. Even the flirts, huddled in a terrified heap on the floor of their cage, were soundless.

Glowing orange specks vibrated on Rob's retinas; the cyan bolts had been more intense than he had realized. "Via," he said in awe, "how do they dare . . . ?"

"Bullet kills you just as dead," Worzer grunted. "Jake, think you can climb that wall?"

"Sure. She'll buck a mite in the loose stuff." The gully side was a gentle declivity, now, where the grenades had blown it in. "Wanna unhitch the trailer first?"

"Negative, nobody gets off the blower till we cleaned this up."

"Umm, don't want to let somebody else in on the fun, maybe?" the driver queried. If he was tense, his voice did not indicate it. Rob's palms were sweaty. His glands had understood before his mind had that his companions were considering smashing up, unaided, a guerrilla stronghold.

"Cop," Leon objected determinedly. "We found it, didn't we?"

"Let's go," Worzer ordered. "Kid, watch your side. They sure got another entrance, maybe a couple."

The car nosed gently toward the subsided bank, wallowed briefly as the driver fed more power to the forward fans to lift the bow. With a surge and a roar, the big vehicle climbed. Its fans caught a few pebbles and whanged them around inside the plenum chamber like a rattle of sudden gunfire. At half speed, the car glided toward another fenced grainplot, leaving behind it a rising pall of dust.

"Straight as a plumb line," Worzer commented, his eyes flicking his sensor screen. "Bastards'll be waiting for us."

Rob glanced at him—a mistake. The slam-spang! of shot and ricochet were nearly simultaneous. The recruit whirled back, bawling in surprise. The rifle pit had opened within five meters of him, and only the haste of the dark-featured guerrilla had saved Rob from his first shot. Rob pivoted his powergun like a hammer, both thumbs mashing down the trigger. Nothing happened. The guerrilla ducked anyway, the black circle of his foxhole shaped into a thick crescent by the lid lying askew.

Safety, *safety!* Rob's mind screamed and he punched the button fat-fingered. The rifleman raised his head just in time to meet the hose of fire that darted from the recruit's gun. The guerrilla's head exploded. His brains, flash-cooked by the first shot, changed instantly from a colloid to a blast of steam that scattered itself over a three-meter circle. The smouldering fragments of the rifle followed the torso as it slid downward.

The combat car roared into the field of waist-high grain, ripping down twenty meters of woven fencing to make its passage. Rob, vaguely aware of other shots and cries forward, vomited onto the floor of the compartment. A colossal explosion nearby slewed the car sideways. As Rob raised his eyes, he noticed three more swarthy riflemen darting through the grain from the right rear of the vehicle.

"Here!" he cried. He swiveled his weapon blindly, his hips colliding with Worzer in the cramped space. A rifle bullet cracked past his helmet. He screamed something again but his own fire was too high, blue-green droplets against the clear sky, and the guerrillas had grabbed the bars while the flirts jumped and blatted.

The rifles were slamming but the flirts were in the way of Rob's gun. "Down! Down!" he shouted uselessly, and the red-haired flirt pitched across the cage with one synthetic breast torn away by the bullet she had leaped in front of. Leon cursed and slumped against Rob's feet, and then it was Chero Worzer shouting, "Hard left, Jake," and leaning across the fallen gunner to rotate his weapon. The combat car tilted left as the bow came around, pinching the trailer against the left rear of the vehicle—in the path of Worzer's powergun. The cage's light alloy bloomed in superheated fireballs as the cyan bolts ripped through it. Both tires exploded together, and there was a red mist of blood in the air. The one guerrilla who had ducked under the burst dropped his rifle and ran.

Worzer cut him in half as he took his third step.

The sergeant gave the wreckage only a glance, then knelt beside Leon. "Cop, he's gone," he said. The bullet had struck the big man in the neck between helmet and body armor, and there was almost a gallon of blood on the floor of the compartment.

"Leon?" Jake asked.

"Yeah. Lord, there musta been twenty kilos of explosive in that satchel charge. If he hadn't hit it in the air . . ." Worzer looked back at the wreck of the trailer, then at Rob. "Kid, can you unhitch that yourself?"

"You just *killed* them," Rob blurted. He was half blinded by tears and the after-image of the gunfire.

"Via, they did their best on us, didn't they?" the sergeant snarled. His face was tiger striped by dust and sweat.

"No, not them!" the boy cried. "Not them— the girls. You just—"

Worzer's iron fingers gripped Rob by the chin and turned the recruit remorselessly toward the carnage behind. The flirts had been torn apart by their own fluids, some pieces flung through gaps in the mangled cage. "Look at 'em, Jenne!" Worzer demanded. "They ain't human but if they was, if it was *Leon* back there, I'd a done it."

His fingers uncurled from Rob's chin and slammed in a fist against the car's armor. "This ain't heroes, it ain't no coppy game you play when you want to! You do what you got to do, 'cause if you don't, some poor bastard gets killed later when he tries to.

"Now get down there and unhitch us."

"Yes, sir." Rob gripped the lip of the car for support.

Worzer's voice, more gentle, came through the haze of tears: "And watch it, kid. Just because they're keeping their heads down don't mean they're all gone." Then, "Wait." Another pause while the sergeant unfastened the belt and holstered handgun from his waist and handed it to Rob. Leon wore a similar weapon, but Worzer did not touch the body. Rob wordlessly clipped the belt, loose for not being fitted over armor, and swung down from the combat car.

The hitch had a quick-release handle, but the torqueing it had received in the last seconds of battle had jammed it. Nervously aware that the sergeant's darting-eyed watchfulness was no pretense, that the shot-scythed grainfield could hide still another guerrilla, or a platoon of them, Rob smashed his boot heel against the catch. It held. Wishing for his driller's sledge, he kicked again.

"Sarge!" Jake shouted. Grain rustled on the other side of the combat car, and against the sky beyond the scarred armor loomed a parcel. Rob threw himself flat.

The explosion picked him up from the ground and bounced him twice, despite the shielding bulk of the combat car. Stumbling upright, Rob steadied himself on the armored side.

The metal felt odd. It no longer trembled with the ready power of the fans. The car was dead, lying at rest on the torn-up soil. With three quick strides, the recruit rounded the bow of the vehicle. He had no time to inspect the dished-in metal, because another swarthy guerrilla was approaching from the other side.

Seeing Rob, the ex-farmer shouted something and drew a long knife. Rob took a step back, remembered the pistol. He tugged at its unfamiliar grip and the weapon popped free into his hand. It seemed the most natural thing in the world to finger the safety, placed just as the tribarrel's had been, then trigger two shots into the face of the lunging guerrilla. The snarl of hatred blanked as the body tumbled face-down at Rob's feet. The knife had flown somewhere into the grain.

"Ebros?" a man called. Another lid had raised from the ground ten meters away. Rob fired at the hole, missed badly. He climbed the caved-in bow, clumsily one-handed, keeping the pistol raised. There was nothing but twisted metal where the driver had been. Sgt. Worzer was still semi-erect, clutched against his powergun by a length of structural tubing. It had curled around both his thighs, fluid under the stunning impact of the satchel charge. The map display was a pearly blank, though the window above it still read incongruously 614579 and the red line on the detector screen blipped in nervous solitude. Worzer's helmet was gone, having flayed a bloody track across his scalp as it sailed away. His lips moved, though, and when Rob put his face near the sergeant's he could hear. "The red . . . pull the red tab . . ."

Over the left breast of each set of armor were a blue and a red tab. Rob had assumed they were decorations of some sort. He shifted the sergeant gently. The tab was locked down by a cotter pin which he yanked out. Something hissed in the armor as he pulled the tab, and Sgt. Worzer murmured, "Oh Lord. Oh Lord." Then, "Now the stimulant, the blue tab."

After the second injection sped into his system, the sergeant opened his eyes. Rob was already trying to straighten the entrapping tube. "Forget it," Worzer ordered weakly. "It's inside, too . . . damn armor musta flexed. Oh Lord." He closed his eyes, opened them in time to see another head peak cautiously from the tunnel mouth. "Bastard!" he rasped, and faster than he spoke he triggered his powergun. Its motor whined spitefully though the burst went wide. The head disappeared.

"I want you to run back to the gully," the sergeant said, resting his eyes again. "You get there, you say 'Fire Central.' That cuts in the arty frequency automatic. Then you say, 'Bunker complex . . .'" Worzer looked down. "'Six-one-four, five-seven-nine.' Stay low and wait for a patrol."

"It won't bend!" Rob snarled in frustration as his fingers slid again from the blood-slick tubing.

"Jenne, get your ass out of here, *now*."

"Sergeant—"

"Lord curse your soul, get out or I'll call it in myself! Do I look like I wanna live?"

"Oh, Via . . ." Rob tried to reholster the pistol he had set on the bloody floor. It slipped back with a clang. He left it, gripping the sidewall again.

"Maybe tell Dad it was good to see him," Worzer whispered. "You lose touch in this business, Lord knows you do."

"Sir?"

"The priest . . . you met him. Sergeant-Major Worzer, he was. Oh Lord, *move it*—"

At the muffled scream, the recruit leaped from the smashed war-car and ran blindly back the way they had come. He did not know he had reached the gully until the ground flew out from under him and he pitched spread-eagled onto the sand. "Fire Central," he sobbed through strangled breaths, "Fire Central."

"Clear," a strange voice snapped crisply. "Data?"

"Wh-what?"

"Lord and martyrs," the voice blasted, "if you're screwing around on firing channels, you'll wish you never saw daylight!"

"S-six . . . oh Lord, yes, six one four, five seven nine," Rob sing-songed. He was staring at the smooth sand. "Bunkers, the sergeant says it's bunkers."

"Roger," the voice said, businesslike again. "Ranging in fifteen."

Could they really swing those mighty guns so swiftly, those snub-barrelled rocket howitzers whose firing looked so impressive on the entertainment cube?

"On the way," warned the voice.

The big tri-barrel whined again from the combat car, the silent lash of its bolts answered this time by a crash of rifle shots. A flattened bullet burred through the air over where Rob lay. It was lost in the eerie, thunderous shriek from the northwest.

"Splash," the helmet said.

The ground bucked. From the grainplot spouted rock, smoke and metal fragments into a black column fifty meters high.

"Are we on?" the voice demanded.

"Oh Lord," Rob prayed, beating his fists against the sand, "Oh Lord."

"Via, what is this?" the helmet wondered aloud. Then, "All guns, battery five."

And the earth began to ripple and gout under the hammer of the guns.

INTERLUDE:
POWERGUNS

By THE 21st Century, missile-firing small arms appeared to have reached the pinnacle of their development, and there was nothing on hand to replace them. The mass and velocity of projectiles could be juggled, but they could not be increased in sum without a corresponding increase in recoil or backblast. Explosive bullets were very destructive on impact, but they had no penetration beyond the immediate blast radius. An explosive bullet might vaporize a leaf it hit near the muzzle as easily as the intended target down-range, and using explosives in heavy brush was worse than useless because it endangered the shooter.

Lasers, though they had air-defense applications, were not the infantryman's answer either. The problem with lasers was the power source. Guns store energy in the powder charge. A machinegun with one cartridge is just as effective— once—as it is with a thousand round belt, so the ammunition load can be tailored to circumstances. Man-killing lasers required a 400-kilo fusion unit to drive them. Hooking a laser on line with any less bulky energy source was of zero military effectiveness rather than lesser effectiveness.

Science lent Death a hand in this impasse—as Science has always done, since the day the first wedge became the first knife. Thirty thousand residents of St. Pierre, Martinique, had been killed on May 8, 1902. The agent of their destruction was a "burning cloud" released during an eruption of Mt. Pelee. Popular myth had attributed the deaths to normal volcanic phenomena, hot gases or ash like that which buried Pompeii; but even the most cursory examination of the evidence indicated that direct energy release had done the lethal damage. In 2073, Dr. Marie Weygand, heading a team under contract to Olin-America, managed to duplicate the phenomenon.

The key had come from spectroscopic examination of pre-1902 lavas from Pelee's crater. The older rocks had showed inexplicable gaps among the metallic elements expected there. A year and a half of empirical research followed, guided more by Dr. Weygand's intuition than by the battery of scientific instrumentation her employers had rushed out at the first signs of success. The principle ultimately discovered was of little utility as a general power source—but then, Olin-America had not been looking for a way to heat homes.

Weygand determined that metallic atoms of a fixed magnetic orientation could be converted directly into energy by the proper combination of heat, pressure, and intersecting magnetic fields. Old lava locks its rich metallic burden in a pattern dictated by the magnetic ambience at the time the flow cools. At Pelee in 1902, the heavy Gauss loads of the new eruption made a chance alignment with the restressed lava of the crater's rim. Matter flashed into energy in a line dictated by the intersection, ripping other atoms free of the basalt matrix and converting them in turn. Below in St. Pierre, humans burned.

When the principle had been discovered, it remained only to refine its destructiveness. Experiments were held with different fuel elements and matrix materials. A copper-cobalt charge in a wafer of microporous polyurethane became the standard, since it appeared to give maximum energy release with the least tendency to scatter. Because the discharge was linear, there was no need of a tube to channel the force as a rifle's barrel does; but some immediate protection from air-induced scatter was necessary for a hand-held weapon. The best barrel material was iridium. Tungsten and osmium were even more refractory, but those elements absorbed a large component of the discharge instead of reflecting it as the iridium did.

To function in service, the new weapons needed to be cooled. Even if a white-hot barrel did not melt, the next charge certainly would vaporize before it could be fired. Liquified gas, generally nitrogen or one of the noble gases which would not themselves erode the metal, was therefore released into the bore after every shot. Multiple barrels, either rotating like those of a Gatling gun or fixed like those of the mitrailleuse, the Gatling's French contemporary, were used to achieve high rates of fire or to fire very high intensity charges. Personal weapons were generally semi-automatic to keep weight and bulk within manageable limits. Submachineguns with large gas reservoirs to fire pistol charges had their uses and advocates, as their bullet-firing predecessors had.

Powerguns—the first usage of the term is as uncertain as that of "gun" itself, though the derivation is obvious—greatly increased the range and destructiveness of the individual soldier. The weapons were so destructive, in fact, that even on most frontier planets their use was limited to homicide. Despite that limited usefulness, factories for the manufacture of powerguns and their ammunition would probably have been early priority items on most worlds—had not that manufacture been utterly beyond the capacity of all but the most highly industrialized planets.

Precision forming of metal as hard as iridium is an incredible task. Gas reservoirs required a nul-conductive sheath if they were not to bleed empty before they even reached the field. If ammunition wafers were rolled out in a fluctuating electrical field, they were as likely to blow out the breech of a weapon or gang-fire in the loading tube as they were to injure a foe. All the planetary pride in the cosmos would not change laws of physics.

Of course, some human cultures preferred alternate weaponry. The seven worlds of the Gorgon Cluster equipped their armies—and a number of mercenary units—with flechette guns, for instance. Their hypervelocity osmium projectiles had better short-range penetration than 2 cm powerguns, and they cycled at a very high rate. But the barrels of flechette guns were of synthetic diamond, making them at least as difficult to manufacture as the more common energy weapons.

Because of the expense of modern weapons, would-be combatants on rural worlds often delayed purchasing guns until fighting was inevitable. Then it became natural to consider buying not only the guns but men who were used to them—for powerguns were no luxury to the mercenaries whose lives and pay depended on their skill with the best possible equipment. The gap between a citizen-soldier holding a powergun he had been issued a week before, and the professional who had trained daily for years with the weapon, was a wide one.

Thus if only one side on a poor world hired mercenaries, its victory was assured—numbers and ideology be damned. That meant, of course, that both sides had to make the investment even if it meant mortgaging the planetary income for a decade. Poverty was preferable to what came with defeat.

All over the galaxy, men with the best gifts of Science and no skills but those of murder looked for patrons who would hire them to bring down civilization. Business was good.

CULTURAL CONFLICT

PLATOON SERGEANT HORTHY stood with his right arm—his only arm—akimbo, surveying the rippling treetops beneath him and wishing they really were the waves of a cool, gray ocean. The trees lapped high up the sides of the basalt knob that had become Firebase Bolo three weeks before when a landing boat dropped them secretly onto it. Now, under a black plastic ceiling that mimicked the basalt to the eye of the Federation spy satellite, nestled a command car, a rocket howitzer with an air cushion truck to carry its load of ammunition, and Horthy's three combat cars.

Horthy's cars—except on paper. There Lt. Simmons-Brown was listed as platoon leader.

One of the long-limbed native reptiles suddenly began to gesture and screech up at the sergeant. The beasts occasionally appeared on the treetops, scurrying and bounding like fleas in a dog's fur. Recently their bursts of rage had become more common—and more irritating. Horthy was a short, wasp-waisted man who wore a spiky goatee and a drum-magazined powergun slung beneath his shoulder. His hand now moved to its grip . . . but shooting meant giving in to frustration and instead Horthy only muttered a curse.

"You say something, Top?" asked a voice behind him. He turned without speaking and saw Jenne and Scratchard, his two gunners, with a lanky howitzer crewman whose name escaped him.

"Nothing that matters," Horthy said.

Scratchard's nickname was Ripper Jack because he carried a long knife in preference to a pistol. He fumbled a little nervously with its hilt as he said, "Look, Top, ah . . . we been talking and Bonmarcher here—" he nodded at the artilleryman—"he says we're not supporting the rest of the Regiment, we're stuck out here in the middle of nowhere to shoot up Federation ships when the war starts."

The sergeant looked sharply at Bonmarcher, then said, "*If* the war starts. Yeah, that's pretty much true. We're about the only humans on South Continent, but if the government decides it still wants to be independent and the Federation decides it's gotta have Squire's World as a colony—well, Fed supply routes pass through two straits within hog shot of this rock." Simmons-Brown would cop a screaming worm if he heard Horthy tell the men a truth supposed to be secret, but one way or another it wasn't going to matter very long.

"But Lord and *Martyrs,* Top," Bonmarcher burst out, "how long after we start shooting is it gonna be before the Feds figure out where the shells're coming from? Sure, this cap—" he thumbed toward the plastic supported four meters over the rock by thin pillars— "hides us now. But sure as death, we'll loose one off while the satellite's still over us, or the Feds'll triangulate radar tracks as the shells come over the horizon at them. Then what'll happen?"

"That's what our combat cars are for," Horthy said wearily, knowing that the Federation would send not troops but a salvo of their own shells to deal with the thorn in their side. "We'll worry about that when it happens. Right now—" He broke off. Another of those damned, fluffy reptiles was shrieking like a cheated whore not twenty meters from him.

"Bonmarcher," the sergeant said in sudden inspiration, "you want to go down there and do something about that noisemaker for me?" Two noisemakers, actually—the beast and the artilleryman himself for as long as the hunt kept him out of the way.

"Gee, Top, I'd sure love to get outa this oven, but I heard the Lieutenant order . . ." Bonmarcher began, looking sidelong at the command car fifty meters away in the center of the knob. Its air conditioner whined, cooling Simmons-Brown and the radioman on watch within its closed compartment.

"Look, you just climb down below the leaf cover and don't loose off unless you've really got a target," said Horthy. "I'll handle the Lieutenant."

Beaming with pleasure, Bonmarcher patted his sidearm to make sure it was snapped securely in its holster. "Thanks, Top," he said and began to descend by the cracks and shelvings that eternity had forged even into basalt.

Horthy ignored him, turning instead to the pair of his own men who had waited in silent concern during the exchange. "Look, boys," the one-armed sergeant said quietly, "I won't give you a load of cop about this being a great vacation for us. But you keep your mouths shut and do your jobs, and I'll do my damnedest to get us all out of here in one piece." He looked away from his listeners for a moment, up at the dull iridium vehicles and the stripped or khaki crewmen lounging over them. "Anyhow, neither the Feds or the twats that hired us have any guts. I'll give you even money that one side or the other backs down before anything drops in the pot."

Scratchard, as lean and dark as Horthy, looked at the huge, blond Jenne. There was no belief on either face. Then the rear hatch of the command car flung open and the communications sergeant stepped out whooping with joy. "They've signed a new treaty!" he shouted. "We're being recalled!"

Horthy grinned, punched each of his gunners lightly in the stomach. "See?" he said. "You listen to Top and he'll bring you home."

All three began to laugh with released tension.

Hilf, Caller of the Moon Sept, followed his sept-brother Seida along the wire-thin filaments of the canopy. Their black footpads flashed a rare primary color as they leaped. The world was slate-gray bark and huge pearly leaves sprouting on flexible tendrils, raised to a sky in which the sun was a sizzling platinum bead.

Both runners were lightly dusted with the pollen they had shaken from fruiting bodies in their course. The Tree, though an entity, required cross-fertilization among its segments for healthy growth. The mottled gray-tones of Seida's feathery scales blended perfectly with his surroundings, and his strength was as smooth as the Tree's. Hilf knew the young male hoped to become Caller himself in a few years, knew also that Seida lacked the necessary empathy with the Tree and the sept to hold the position. Besides, his recklessness was no substitute for intelligence.

But Seida was forcing Hilf to act against his better judgment. The creatures on the bald, basalt knob were clearly within the sept's territory; but what proper business had any of the Folk with rock-dwellers? Still, knowing that token activity would help calm his brothers, Hilf had let Seida lead him to personally view the situation. At the back of the Caller's mind was the further realization that the Mothers were sometimes swayed by the "maleness" of action as opposed to intelligent lethargy.

Poised for another leap, Hilf noticed the black line of a worm track on the bark beside him. He halted, instinctively damping the springiness of his perch by flexing his hind legs. Seida shrieked but fell into lowering silence when he saw what his Caller was about. Food was an immediate need. As Hilf had known, Seida's unfitness for leadership included his inability to see beyond the immediate.

The branch was a twenty-centimeter latticework of intergrown tendrils, leapfrogging kilometers across the forest. In its career it touched and fused with a dozen trunks, deep-rooted pillars whose tendrils were of massive cross section. Hilf blocked the worn track with a spike-clawed, multi-jointed thumb twice the length of the three fingers on each hand. His other thumb thrust into the end of the track and wriggled. The bark split, baring the hollowed pith and the worm writhing and stretching away from the impaling claw. Hilf's esophagus spasmed once to crush the soft creature. He looked up. Seida stuttered an impoliteness verging on command: he had not forgotten his self-proclaimed mission. The Caller sighed and followed him.

The ancient volcanic intrusion was a hundred-meter thumb raised from the forest floor. The Tree crawled partway up the basalt, but the upper faces of the rock were steep and dense enough to resist attachments by major branches. Three weeks previously a huge ball had howled out of the sky and poised over the rock, discharging other silvery beasts shaped like great sowbugs and guided by creatures not too dissimilar to the Folk. These had quickly raised the black cover which now hung like an optical illusion to the eyes of watchers in the highest nearby branches. The unprecedented event had sparked the hottest debate of the Caller's memory. Despite opposition from Seida and a few other hotheads, Hilf had finally convinced his sept that the rock was not their affair.

Now, on the claim that one of the brown-coated invaders had climbed out onto a limb, Seida was insisting that he should be charged at once with leading a war party. Unfortunately, at least the claim was true.

Seida halted, beginning to hoot and point. Even without such notice the interloper would have been obvious to Hilf. The creature was some fifty meters away—three healthy leaps, the Caller's mind abstracted—and below the observers. It was huddled on a branch which acted as a flying buttress for the high towers of the Tree. At near view it was singularly unattractive: appreciably larger than one of the septbrothers, it bore stubby arms and a head less regular than the smooth bullets of the Folk.

As he pondered, the Caller absently gouged a feather of edible orange fungus out of the branch. The rest of the aliens remained under their roof, equally oblivious to the Folk and their own sept-brother. The latter was crawling a little closer on his branch, manipulating the object he carried while turning his lumpy face toward Seida.

Hilf, blending silently into the foliage behind his brother, let his subconscious float and merge while his surface mind grappled with the unpalatable alternatives. The creature below was technically an invader, but it did not seem the point of a thrust against the Moon Sept. Tradition did not really speak to the matter. Hilf could send out a war party, losing a little prestige to Seida since the younger brother had cried for that course from the beginning. Far worse than the loss of prestige was the risk to the sept which war involved. If the interlopers were as strong as they were big, the Folk would face a grim battle.

In addition, the huge silver beasts which had whined and snarled as they crawled onto the rock were a dangerous uncertainty, though they had been motionless since their appearance.

But the only way to avoid war seemed to be for Hilf to kill his sept-brother. Easy enough to do—a sudden leap and both thumbs rammed into the brainbox. The fact Seida was not prepared for an attack was further proof of his unfitness to lead. No one would dispute the Caller's tale of a missed leap and a long fall. . . .Hilf poised as Seida leaned out to thunder more abuse at the creature below.

The object in the interloper's hand flashed. The foliage winked cyan and Seida's head blew apart. Spasming muscles threw his body forward, following its fountaining blood in an arc to the branch below. The killer's high cackles of triumph pursued Hilf as he raced back to the Heart.

He had been wrong: the aliens *did* mean war.

Simmons-Brown broke radio contact with a curse. His khakis were sweatstained and one of the shoulder-board chevrons announcing his lieutenancy was missing. "Top," he whined to Sergeant Horthy who stood by the open hatch of the command car, "Command Central won't send a space boat to pick us up, they want us to *drive* all the way to the north coast for surface pick-up to Johnstown. That's 1200 kilometers and anyhow, we can't even get the cars *down* off this Lord-stricken rock!"

"Sure we can," Horthy said, planning aloud

rather than deigning to contradict the wispy
lieutenant. Simmons-Brown was a well-con-
nected incompetent whose approach to problem
solving was to throw a tantrum while other people tried to work around him. "We'll link tow
cables and . . . no, a winch won't hold but we
can blast-set an eyebolt, then rappel the cars
down one at a time. How long they give us till
pick-up?"

"Fifteen days, but—"

A shot bumped the air behind the men. Both
whipped around. Horthy's hand brushed his
submachinegun's grip momentarily before he relaxed. He said, "It's all plus, just Bonmarcher. I
told him he could shut up a couple of the local
noisemakers if he stayed below the curve of the
rock and didn't put a hole in our camouflage.
The fed satellite isn't good enough to pick up
small arms fire in this jungle."

"I distinctly ordered that no shots be fired
while we're on detached duty!" snapped
Simmons-Brown, his full moustache trembling
like an enraged caterpillar. "Distinctly!"

Sergeant Horthy looked around the six
blowers and twenty-three men that made up
Firebase Bolo. He sighed. Waiting under commo
security, between bare rock and hot plastic,
would have been rough at the best of times. With
Simmons-Brown added. . . . "Sorry, sir," the
sergeant lied straight-faced, "I must have forgotten."

"Well, get the men moving," Simmons-Brown
ordered, already closing the hatch on his air con-
ditioning. "Those bastards at Central might just

leave us if we missed pick-up. They'd like that."

"Oh, we'll make it fine," Horthy said to himself, his eyes already searching for a good place to sink the eyebolt. "Once we get off the rock there won't be any problem. The ground's flat, and with all the leaves up here cutting off light we won't have under-growth to bother about. Just set the compasses on north and follow our noses."

"Hey, Top," someone called. "Look what I got!" Bonmarcher had clambered back onto the rock. Behind him, dragged by its lashed ankles, was a deep-chested reptile that had weighed about forty kilos before being decapitated. "Blew this monkey away my first shot," the artileryman bragged.

"Nice work," Horthy replied absently. His mind was on more important things.

The world of the Moon Sept was not a sphere but a triangular section of forest. That wedge, like those of each of the twenty-eight other septs, was dominated by the main root of a Tree. The ground at the center was thin loam over not subsoil but almost a hectare of ancient root. The trunks sprouting from the edge of this mass were old, too, but not appreciably thicker than the other pillars supporting the Tree for hundreds of kilometers in every direction. Interwoven stems and branches joined eighty meters in the air, roofing the Heart in a quivering blanket of leaves indistinguishable from that of the rest of the forest. The hollow dome within was an awesome thing even without its implications, and few of the Folk cared to enter it.

Hilf himself feared the vast emptiness and the power it focused, but he had made his decision three years before when the Mothers summoned the previous Caller to the Nest and a breeder's diet. Hilf had thrust forward and used the flowing consciousness of the whole sept to face down his rivals for the Callership. Now he thumped to the hard floor without hesitation and walked quickly on feet and knuckles to the pit worn in the center of the root by millenia of Callers. His body prone below the lips of the blond rootwood, Hilf's right claw gashed sap from the Tree and then nicked his own left wrist. Sap and pale blood oozed together, fusing Caller and Tree physically in a fashion dictated by urgency. The intense wood grain rippled from in front of Hilf's eyes and his mind began to fill with shattered, spreading images of the forest. Each heartbeat sent Hilf out in a further surge and blending until every trunk and branch-bundle had become the Tree, each member of the Moon Sept had blurred into the Folk. A black warmth beneath the threshold of awareness indicated that even the Mothers had joined.

The incident trembled through the sept, a kaleidoscope more of emotion than pictures. Seida capered again, gouted and died in the invader's raucous laughter. Reflex stropped claws on the bark of a thousand branches. Response was the Caller's to suggest and guide, not to determine. The first blood-maddened reply by the sept almost overwhelmed Hilf. But his response had been planned, stamped out on the template of experience older than that of any living sept-brother—as old, perhaps, as the joinder of Folk and Tree. The alien nature of the invaders would not be allowed to pervert the traditional response: the remainder of Seida's hatching would go out to punish the death of their brother.

The pattern of the root began to reimpose itself on Hilf's eyes. He continued to lie in the hollow, logy with reaction. Most of the sept were returning to their foraging or play, but there were always eyes trained on the knob and the activity there. And scattered throughout the wedge of the Tree were thirty-seven of the Folk, young and fierce in their strength, who drifted purposefully together.

At the forest floor the raindrops, scattered by the triple canopy, were a saturated fog that clung and made breath a struggle. Horthy ignored it, letting his feet and sinewed hand mechanically balance him against the queasy ride of the air-cushion vehicle. His eyes swept the ground habitually. When reminded by his conscious mind, they took in the canopies above also.

The rain had slowed the column. The strangely-woven tree boles were never spaced too closely to pass the armored vehicles between them, but frequent clumps of spire-pointed fungus thrust several meters in the air and confused the aisles. Experience had shown that when struck by a car the saprophytes would collapse in a cloud of harmless spores, but in the

fog-blurred dimness they sometimes hid an unyielding trunk behind them. The lead car had its
driving lights on though the water dazzle made
them almost useless, and all six vehicles had
closed up more tightly than Horthy cared to see.
There was little chance of a Federation ambush,
but even a sudden halt would bring on a multiple collision.

The brassy trilling that had grown familiar in
the past several hours sounded again from somewhere in the forest. Just an animal, though. The
war on Squire's World was over for the time, and
whether the Regiment's employers had won or
lost there was no reason for Horthy to remain as
tense as he was. Simmons-Brown certainly was
unconcerned, riding in the dry cabin of his command car. That was the second vehicle, just
ahead of Horthy's. The sergeant's wing gunners
huddled in the fighting compartment to either
side of him. They were miserable and bored,
their minds as empty as their slack, dripping
faces.

Irritated but without any real reason to slash
the men to vigilance, Horthy glared back along
his course. The stubby 150 mm howitzer, the
cause of the whole Lord-accursed operation, was
the fourth vehicle. Only its driver, his head a
mirroring ball behind its face shield, was visible.
The other five men of the crew were within the
open-backed turret whose sheathing was poor
protection against hostile fire but enough to keep
the rain out.

The ammo transporter was next, sandwiched
between the hog and the combat car which

brought up the rear of the column. Eighty-kilo shells were stacked ten high on its flat bed, their noses color coded with incongruous gaiety. The nearby mass of explosive drew a wince from Horthy, who knew that if it went off together it could pulverize the basalt they had been emplaced on. On top of the front row of shells where its black fuse winked like a cyclops's eye was the gas round, a thin-walled cylinder of K3 which could kill as surely by touch as by inhalation. Everyone in the Regiment respected K3, but Horthy was one of the few who understood it well enough to prefer the gas to conventional weapons in some situations.

In part, that was a comment on his personality as well.

To Horthy's right, Rob Jenne began to shrug out of his body armor. "Keep it on, trooper," the sergeant said.

"But Top," Jenne complained, "it rubs in this wet." His fingers lifted the segmented porcelain to display the weal chafed over his floating ribs.

"Leave it on," Horthy repeated, gesturing about the fighting compartment crowded with ammunition and personal gear. "There's not enough room here for us, even without three suits of armor standing around empty. Besides—"

The gray creature's leap carried it skimming over Horthy to crash full into Jenne's chest. Man and alien pitched over the bulkhead. Horthy leaned forward and shot by instinct, using his sidearm instead of the powerful, less handy, tribarrel mounted on the car. His light finger

pressure clawed three holes in the creature's
back as it somersaulted into the ground with
Jenne.

The forest rang as the transporter plowed into
the stern of the grounded howitzer. The gun vehicle seemed to crawl with scores of the scale-
dusted aliens, including the one whose spear-
sharp thumbs had just decapitated the driver.
Horthy twisted his body to spray the mass with
blue-green fire. The hog's bow fulcrumed in the
soil as the transporter's impact lifted its stern. The
howitzer upended, its gun tube flopping freely in
an arc while inertia vomited men from the turret.

"Watch the bloody ammo!" Horthy shouted
into his intercom as a tribarrel hosed one of the
aliens off the transporter in a cloud of gore and
vaporized metal. Ahead, the command car
driver had hit his panic bar in time to save
himself, but one of the long-armed creatures was
hacking at the vision-blocs as though they were
the vehicle's eyes. The rear hatch opened and
Simmons-Brown flung himself out screaming
with fear. Horthy hesitated. The alien gave up
its assault on the optical fibers and sprang on the
lieutenant's back.

Horthy's burst chopped both of them to death
in a welter of blood.

Only body armor saved the sergeant from the
attack that sledged his chest forward into the
iridium bulkhead. He tried to rise but could not
against the weight and the shocks battering both
sides of his thorax like paired trip-hammers.

The blows stopped and the weight slid from
Horthy's back and down his ankles. He levered

himself upright, gasping with pain as intense as that of the night a bullet-firing machinegun had smashed across his armor. Scratchard, the left gunner, grinned at him. The man's pale skin was spattered with the same saffron blood that covered his knife.

"They've gone off, Top," Scratchard said. "Didn't like the tribarrels—even though we didn't hit much but trees. Didn't like this, neither." He stropped his blade clean on the thighs of the beast he had killed with it.

"Bleeding martyrs," Horthy swore under his breath as he surveyed the damage. The platoon's own four blowers were operable, but the overturned hog was a total loss and the transporter's front fan had disintegrated when the steel ground-effect curtain had crumpled into its arc. If there was any equipment yard on Squire's World that could do the repairs, it sure as cop was too far away from this stretch of jungle to matter. Five men were dead and another, his arm ripped from shoulder to wrist, was comatose under the effects of sedatives, clotting agents, antibiotics, and shock.

"All plus," Horthy began briskly. "We leave the bodies, leave the two arty blowers too; and I just hope our scaly friends get real curious about them soon. Before we pull out, I want ten of the high explosive warheads unscrewed and loaded into the command car—yeah, and the gas shell too."

"Via, Top," one of the surviving artillerymen muttered, "why we got to haul that stuff around?"

"Cause I said so," Horthy snarled, "and ain't I in charge?" His hand jerked the safety pin from one of the delay-fused shells, then spun the dial to one hour. "Now get moving, because we want to be a long way away in an hour."

The platoon was ten kilometers distant when the shock wave rippled the jungle floor like the head of a drum. The jungle had blown skyward in a gray puree, forming a momentary bubble over a five-hectare crater.

The Moon Sept waited for twilight in a ring about the shattered clearing in which the invaders were halted. The pain that had slashed through every member of the sept at the initial explosion was literally beyond comparison: when agony gouged at the Tree, the brothers had collapsed wherever they stood, spewing waste and the contents of their stomach uncontrollably. Hours later the second blast tore away ten separate trunks and brought down a hectare of canopy. The huge silver beasts had shoved the debris to the side before they settled down in the new clearing. That explosion was bearable on top of the first only because of the black rage of the Mothers now insulating the Moon Sept from full empathy with their Tree; but not even the Mothers could accept further punishment at that level. Hilf moaned in the root-alcove, only dimly aware that he had befouled it in reaction. He was a conduit now, not the Caller in fact, for the eyeless ones had assumed control. The Mothers had made a two-dimensional observation which the males, to whom up and down were more important than horizontal direction, had missed: the invaders were proceeding toward the Nest. They must be stopped.

The full thousand of the Moon Sept blended into the leaves with a perfection achieved in the days in which there had been carnivores in the forest. When one of the Folk moved it was to ease cramps out of a muscle or to catch the sun-pearl on the delicate edge of a claw. They did not forage; the wracking horror of the explosions had left them beyond desire for food.

The effect on the Tree had been even worse. In multi-kilometer circles from both blast sites the wood sagged sapless and foliage curled around its stems. The powerguns alone had been devastating to the Tree's careful stasis, bolts that shattered the trunks they clipped and left the splinters ablaze in the rain. Only the lightning could compare in destructiveness, and the charges building in the uppermost branches gave warning enough for the Tree to minimize lightning damage.

There would be a further rain of cyan charges, but that could not be helped. The Mothers were willing to sacrifice to necessity, even a Tree or a sept.

The four silvery beasts lay nose to tail among the craters, only fifty meters from the standing trunks in which the Folk waited. Hilf watched from a thousand angles. Only the rotating cones on the foreheads of each of the beasts seemed to be moving. Their riders were restive, however, calling to one another in low voices whose alien nature could not disguise their tension. The sun

that had moments before been a spreading blob
on the western horizon was now gone; invisible
through the clouds but a presence felt by the
Folk, the fixed Moon now ruled the sky alone. It
was the hour of the Moon Sept, and the command of the Mothers was the loosing of a blood-
mad dog to kill.

"Death!" screamed the sept-brothers as they
sprang into the clearing.

There was death in plenty awaiting them.

The antipersonnel strips of the cars were live.
Hilf was with the first body when it hurtled to
within twenty meters of a car and the strips
began to fire on radar command. Each of the
white flashes that slammed and glared from just
above the ground-effect curtains was fanning out
a handful of tetrahedral pellets. Where the
energy released by the power-guns blasted flesh
into mist and jelly, the projectiles ripped like
scythes over a wide area. Then the forest blazed
as flickering cyan hosed across it.

The last antipersonnel charge went off, leaving screams and the thump of powerguns that
were almost silence after the rattling crescendo
of explosions.

The sept, the surprising hundreds whom the
shock had paralyzed but not slain, surged forward again. The three-limbed Caller of the invaders shouted orders while he fired. The huge
silver beasts howled and spun end for end even
as Hilf's brothers began to leap aboard—then
the port antipersonnel strips cut loose in a pointblank broadside. For those above the plane of
the discharges there was a brief flurry of claws

aimed at neck joints and gun muzzles tight against flesh as they fired. Then a grenade, dropped or jarred from a container, went off in the blood-slick compartment of number one car. Mingled limbs erupted. The sides blew out and the bins of ready ammunition gang-fired in a fury of light and gobbets of molten iridium.

The attack was over. The Mothers had made the instant assumption that the third explosion would be on the order of the two previous—and blocked their minds off from a Tree-empathy that might have been lethal. Without their inexorable thrusting, the scatter of sept-brothers fled like grubs from the sun. They had fought with the savagery of their remote ancestors eliminating the great Folk-devouring serpents from the forest.

And it had not been enough.

"Cursed right we're staying here," Horthy said in irritation. "This is the only high ground in 500 kilometers. If we're going to last out another attack like yesterday's, it'll be by letting our K3 roll downhill into those apes. And the Lord help us if a wind comes up."

"Well, I still don't like it, Top," Jenne complained. "It doesn't look natural."

Horthy fully agreed with that, though he did so in silence. Command Central had used satellite coverage to direct them to the hill, warning again that even in their emergency it might be a day before a landing boat could be cleared to pick them up. From above, the half-kilometer dome of laterite must have been as obvious as a

baby in the wedding party, a gritty red pustule
on the gray hide of the continent. From the forest
edge it was even stranger, and strange meant
deadly to men in Horthy's position. But only the
antipersonnel strips had saved the platoon the
night before, and they were fully discharged.
They were left with the gas or nothing.

The hill was as smooth as the porous stone
allowed it to be and rose at a gentle 1:3 ratio.
The curve of its edge was broken by the great
humped roots that lurched and knotted out of
the surrounding forest, plunging into the hill at
angles that must lead them to its center. As
Jenne had said, it wasn't natural. Nothing about
this cursed forest was.

"Let's go," Horthy ordered. His driver
boosted the angle and power of his drive fans
and they began to slide up the hill, followed by
the other two cars. Strange that the trees hadn't
covered the hill with a network of branches, even
if their trunks for some reason couldn't seat in
the rock. Enough ground was clear for the powerguns alone to mince an attack, despite the
awesome quickness of the gray creatures. Except
that the powerguns were low on ammo too.

Maybe there wouldn't be a third attack.

An alien appeared at the hillcrest fifty meters
ahead. Horthy killed it by reflex, using a single
shot from his tribarrel. There was an opening
there, a cave or tunnel mouth, and a dozen more
of the figures spewed from it. "Watch the sides!"
Horthy roared at Jenne and Scratchard, but all
three powerguns were ripping the new targets.
Bolts that missed darted off into the dull sky like

brief, blue-green suns.

Jenne's grenade spun into the meter-broad hole as the car overran it. If anything more had planned to come out, that settled it. Scratchard jiggled the controls of the echo sounder, checked the read-out again, and swore, "Via! I don't see any more surface openings, Top, but this whole mound's like a fencepost in termite country!"

The three blowers were pulled up close around the opening, the crews awaiting orders. Horthy toothed his lower lip but there was no hesitation in his voice after he decided. "Wixom and Chung," he said, "get that gas shell out and bring it over here. The rest of you cover the forest —I'll keep this hole clear."

The two troopers wrestled the cylinder out of the command car and gingerly carried it to the lip of the opening. The hill was reasonably flat on top and the laterite gave good footing, but the recent shooting had left patches glazed by the powerguns and a film of blood over the whole area. The container should not have ruptured if dropped, but no one familiar with K3 wanted to take the chance.

"All plus," Horthy said. "Fuse it for ten seconds and drop it in. As soon as that goes down, we're going to hover over the hole with our fans on max, just to make sure all the gas goes in the right direction. If we can do them enough damage, maybe they'll leave us alone."

The heavy shell clinked against something as it disappeared into the darkness but kept falling in the passage cleared by the grenade. It was well below the surface when the bursting charge

tore the casing open. That muted *whoomp* was
lost in the shriek of Horthy's fans as his car wob-
bled on a column of air a meter above the hilltop.
K3 sank even in still air, pooling in invisible
deathtraps in the low spots of a battlefield.
Rammed by the drive fans, it had permeated the
deepest tunnels of the mound in less than a
minute.

The rioting air blew the bodies and body parts
of the latest victims into a windrow beside the
opening. Horthy glanced over them with a professional concern for the dead as he marked
time. These creatures had the same long limbs
and smooth-faced features as the ones which had
attacked in the forest, but there was a difference
as well. The genitals of the earlier-seen aliens
had been tiny, vestigial or immature, but each of
the present corpses carried a dong the length
and thickness of a forearm. Bet their girlfriends
walk bow-legged, Horthy chuckled to himself.

The hill shook with an impact noticeable even
through the insulating air. "Top, they're tunnel-
ing out!" cried the command car's driver over
the intercom.

"Hold your distance!" Horthy commanded as
five meters of laterite crumbled away from the
base of the hill. The thing that had torn the gap
almost filled it. Horthy and every other gunman
in the platoon blasted at it in a reaction that
went deeper than fear. Even as it gouted fluids
under the multiple impacts, the thing managed
to squirm completely out. The tiny head and the
limbs that waved like broomstraws thrust into a
watermelon were the only ornamentation on the

slug-white torso. The face was blind, but it was the face of the reptiloids of the forest until a burst of cyan pulped its obscenity. Horthy's tribarrel whipsawed down the twenty-meter belly. A sphincter convulsed in front of the line of shots and spewed a mass of eggs in jelly against the unyielding laterite. The blackening that K3 brought to its victims was already beginning to set in before the platoon stopped firing.

Nothing further attempted to leave the mound.

"Wh-what do we do now, Top?" Jenne asked.

"Wait for the landing boat," answered Horthy. He shook the cramp out of his hand and pretended that it was not caused by his panicky deathgrip on the tribarrel moments before. "And we pray that it comes before too bleeding long."

The cold that made Hilf's body shudder was the residue of the Mothers' death throes deep in the corridors of the Nest. No warmth remained in a universe which had seen the last generation of the Folk. The yellow leaf-tinge of his blast-damaged Tree no longer concerned Hilf. About him, a psychic pressure rather than a message, he could feel the gathering of the other twenty-eight septs—just too late to protect the Mothers who had summoned them. Except for the Moon Sept's, the Trees were still healthy and would continue to be so for years until there were too few of the Folk scampering among the branches to spread their pollen. Then, with only the infrequent wind to stimulate new growth, the Trees as well would begin to die.

Hilf began to walk forward on all fours, his knuckles gripping firmly the rough exterior of the Nest. "Top!" cried one of the invaders, and Hilf knew that their eyes or the quick-darting antennae of their silver beasts had discovered his approach. He looked up. The three-limbed Caller was staring at him, his stick extended to kill. His eyes were as empty as Hilf's own.

The bolt hammered through Hilf's lungs and he pitched backwards. Through the bloodroar in his ears he could hear the far-distant howl that had preceded the invader's appearance in the forest.

As if the landing boat were their signal, the 30,000 living males of the Folk surged forward from the Trees.

INTERLUDE: BACKDROP TO CHAOS

THE MERCENARY COMPANIES of the late Third Millenium were both a result of and a response to a spurt of empire-building among the new industrial giants of the human galaxy. Earth's first flash of colonization had been explosive. Transit was an expensive proposition for trade or tourism; but on a national scale, a star colony was just as possible as the high-rise Palace of Government which even most of the underdeveloped countries had built for the sake of prestige.

And colonies were very definitely a matter of prestige. The major powers had them. So, just as Third World countries had squandered their resources on jet fighters in the Twentieth Century (and on ironclads in the Nineteenth), they bought or leased or even built starships in the Twenty-First. These colonies were almost invariably mono-national, under-capitalized, and stratified by class even more rigidly than were their mother countries. All of those factors affected later galactic history. There was a plethora of suitable worlds on which to plant colonies, however, so that even the most ineptly-handled groups of settlers generally managed to survive. Theirs was a hand-to-mouth survival of farming and barter, though, not of spaceports shipping vast quanties of minerals and protein back to Earth.

A few of the better-backed colonies did become very successful. Most of them had been spawned by the larger nations, though a few were private ventures (including that of the Dutch consortium which founded Friesland). Success left their backers in the same situation of those whose colonies were barely surviving, however, since the first result of planetary self-sufficiency was invariably to cut ties and find the best prices available for manufactures on the open market.

There followed a spate of secondary colonization from the successful colony worlds. These new colonies were planted with a specific product in mind: a mineral; a drug; sometimes simply agriculture, freeing more valuable real estate on the homeworlds. Even a planet could be filled in a few centuries by the asymtotic population growth which empty spaces seem to engender in human beings. Secondary colonies were frequently joint efforts, combining settlers and capital from several worlds. They were a business proposition, after all, not matters of national honor.

Unfortunately for the concept, the newly-mixed national and racial groups got along just as badly as their ancestors had a few centuries earlier on Earth. The planetary governments of Hiroseke and Stewart, for instance, conferred placidly with each other; but in the iridium-mining colony they had founded together on Kalan,

Japanese and Scotsmen were shooting at each other within five years.

The new colonizers had thought they would be able to control their colonies without military force. Their own experience had taught them to control space transport to the new colonies. Without the ability to sell its produce in markets of its own choice, a colony could not strike off on its own—as the homeworlds had themselves done.

But a colony could be forced into a pattern of logical subservience only if its populace were willing to be logical. If instead the settlers decided to eat their own guts out through internal warfare, the colony would become as commercially valueless as Germany in 1648. Inevitably, homeworlds attempted through military force to control and unify their colonies; also inevitably, they generally increased the disruption by their activities.

And even if some sort of a military solution *was* imposed, there remained the question of how to deal with the defeated troublemakers—however they were defined—to avoid a new outbreak of fighting. Ideally, they could be used as expendables in battles elsewhere. It was a course which had been followed with success often in the past—Germans in French Indo-China in 1948, and Scots borderers in Ulster in 1605, for two examples. The course required that there be other battles to fight—but there were other unruly colonies as well as backwater worlds whose produce would be useful if it could be controlled at acceptable cost. Perhaps the first case of this occurred in 2414 when Monument equipped 4,000 Sikh rebels from Ramadan and shipped them to Portales to take over that planet's tobacco trade, but there were many other examples later.

And in any case, there was always someone willing to hire soldiers, somewhere. World after world armed its misfits and sent them off to someone else's back yard, to attack or defend, to kill or die—so long as they were not doing it at home. Because of the pattern of colonization, there were only a few planets that were not so tense that they might snap into bloody war if mercenaries from across the galaxy were available.

Even for the stable elite of worlds, Friesland and Kronstad, Ssu-ma and Wylie, the system was a losing proposition. Wars and the warriors they spawned were short-term solutions, binding the industrial worlds into a fabric of short-term solutions. In the long run, off-world markets were destroyed, internal investment was channelled into what were basically non-productive uses, and the civil populace became restive in the omnipresence of violence and a foreign policy directed toward its continuance.

On rural worlds, the result was nothing so subtle as decay. It was life and society shattered forever by the sledge of war.

CAUGHT IN THE CROSSFIRE

MARGRITTE GRAPPLED with the nearest soldier in the instant her husband broke for the woods. The man in field-gray cursed and tried to jerk his weapon away from her, but Margritte's muscles were young and taut from shifting bales. Even when the mercenary kicked her ankles from under her, Margritte's clamped hands kept the gun barrel down and harmless.

Neither of the other two soldiers paid any attention to the scuffle. They clicked off the safety catches of their weapons as they swung them to their shoulders. Georg was running hard, fresh blood from his retorn calf muscles staining his bandages. The double slap of automatic fire caught him in mid-stride and whipsawed his slender body. His head and heels scissored to the ground together. They were covered by the mist of blood that settled more slowly.

Sobbing, Margritte loosed her grip and fell back on the ground. The man above her cradled his flechette gun again and looked around the village. "Well, aren't you going to shoot me too?" she cried.

"Not unless we have to," the mercenary replied quietly. He was sweating despite the stiff breeze, and he wiped his black face with his sleeve. "Helmuth," he ordered, "start setting up in the building. Landschein, you stay out with me, make sure none of these women try the same damned thing." He glanced out to where Georg lay, a bright smear on the stubbled, golden earth. "Best get that out of sight too," he added. "The convoy's due in an hour."

Old Leida had frozen to a statue in ankle-length muslin at the first scream. Now she nodded her head of close ringlets. "Myrie, Della," she called, gesturing to her daughters, "bring brush hooks and come along." She had not lost her dignity even during the shooting.

"Hold it," said Landschein, the shortest of the three soldiers. He was a sharp-featured man who had grinned in satisfaction as he fired. "You two got kids in there?" he asked the younger women. The muzzle of his flechette gun indicated the locked door to the dugout which normally stored the crop out of sun and heat; today it imprisoned the village's twenty-six children. Della and Myrie nodded, too dry with fear to speak.

"Then you go drag him into the woods," Landschein said, grinning again. "Just remember—you might manage to get away, but you won't much like what you'll find when you come back. I'm sure some true friend'll point your brats out to us quick enough to save her own."

Leida nodded a command, but Landschein's freckled hand clamped her elbow as she turned to follow her daughters. "Not you, old lady. No need for you to get that near to cover."

"Do you think *I* would run and risk—everyone?" Leida demanded.

"Curst if I know what you'd risk," the soldier said. "But we're risking plenty already to ambush one of Hammer's convoys. If anybody gets loose ahead of time to warn them, we can kiss our butts goodbye."

Margritte wiped the tears from her eyes, using her palms because of the gritty dust her thrashings had pounded into her knuckles. The third soldier, the broad-shouldered blond named Helmuth, had leaned his weapon beside the door of the hall and was lifting bulky loads from the nearby air cushion vehicle. The settlement had become used to whining gray columns of military vehicles, cruising the road at random. This truck, however, had eased over the second canopy of the forest itself. It was a flimsy cargo-hauler like the one in which Krauder picked up the cotton at season's end, harmless enough to look at. Only Georg, left behind for his sickle-ripped leg when a government van had carried off the other males the week before as "recruits," had realized what it meant that the newcomers wore field-gray instead of khaki.

"Why did you come here?" Margritte asked in a near-normal voice.

The black mercenary glanced at her as she rose, glanced back at the other women obeying orders by continuing to pick the iridescent boles of Terran cotton grown in Pohweil's soil. "We had the capital under siege," he said, "until Hammer's tanks punched a corridor through. We can't close the corridor, so we got to cut your boys off from supplies some other way. Otherwise the Cartel'll wish it had paid its taxes instead of trying to take over. You grubbers may have been pruning their wallets, but Lord! they'll be flayed alive if your counter-attack works."

He spat a thin, angry stream into the dust. "The traders hired us and four other regiments, and you grubbers sank the whole treasury into bringing in Hammer's armor. Maybe we can prove today those cocky bastards aren't all they're billed as. . . ."

"We didn't care," Margritte said. "We're no more the Farm Bloc than Krauder and his truck is the Trade Cartel. Whatever they do in the capital—*we* had no choice. I hadn't even seen the capital . . . oh dear Lord, Georg would have taken me there for our honeymoon except that there was fighting all over. . . ."

"How long we got, Sarge?" the blond man demanded from the stark shade of the hall.

"Little enough. Get those bloody sheets set up or we'll have to pop the cork bare-ass naked; and we got enough problems." The big non-com shifted his glance about the narrow clearing, wavering rows of cotton marching to the edge of the forest's dusky green. The road, an unsurfaced track whose ruts were not a serious hindrance to air cushion traffic, was the long axis. Beside it stood the hall, twenty meters by five and the only above-ground structure in the settlement. The battle with the native vegetation made dug-outs beneath the cotton preferable to cleared land wasted for dwellings. The hall be-

came more than a social center and common re-
fectory: it was the gaudiest of luxuries and a
proud slap to the face of the forest.

Until that morning, the forest had been the
village's only enemy.

"Georg only wanted—"

"God *damn* it!" the sergeant snarled. "Will
you shut it off? Every man but your precious
husband gone off to the siege—no, shut it off till
I finish!—and him running to warn the convoy.
If you'd wanted to save his life, you should've
grabbed him, not me. Sure, all you grubbers,
you don't care about the war—not much! It's all
one to you whether you kill us yourselves or your
tankers do it, those bastards so high and mighty
for the money they've got and the equipment. I
tell you, girl, I don't take it personal that people
shoot at me, it's just the way we both earn our
livings. But it's fair, it's even . . . and Hammer
thinks he's the Way made Flesh because nobody
can bust his tanks."

The sergeant paused and his lips sucked in
and out. His thick, gentle fingers rechecked the
weapon he held. "We'll just see," he whispered.

"Georg said we'd all be killed in the crossfire
if we were out in the fields when you shot at the
tanks."

"If Georg had kept his face shut and his ass in
bed, he'd have lived longer than he did. Just shut
if off!" the non-com ordered. He turned to his
blond underling, fighting a section of sponge
plating through the door. "Via, Bornzyk!" he
shouted angrily. "Move it!"

Helmuth flung his load down with a hollow

clang. "Via, then lend a hand! The wind catches these and—"

"I'll help him," Margritte offered abruptly. Her eyes blinked away from the young soldier's weapon where he had forgotten it against the wall. Standing, she far lacked the bulk of the sergeant beside her, but her frame gave no suggestion of weakness. Golden dust soiled the back and sides of her dress with butterfly scales.

The sergeant gave her a sharp glance, his left hand spreading and closing where it rested on the black barrel-shroud of his weapon. "All right," he said, "you give him a hand and we'll see you under cover with us when the shooting starts. You're smarter than I gave you credit."

They had forgotten Leida was still standing beside them. Her hand struck like a spading fork. Margritte ducked away from the blow, but Leida caught her on the shoulder and gripped. When the mercenary's reversed gun-butt cracked the older woman loose, a long strip of Margritte's blue dress tore away with her. "Bitch," Leida mumbled through bruised lips. "You'd help these beasts after they killed your own man?"

Margritte stepped back, tossing her head. For a moment she fumbled at the tear in her dress; then, defiantly, she let it fall open. Landschein turned in time to catch the look in Leida's eyes. "Hey, you'll give your friends more trouble," he stated cheerfully, waggling his gun to indicate Della and Myrie as they returned gray-faced from the forest fringe. "Go on, get out and pick some cotton."

When Margritte moved, the white of her loose shift caught the sun and the small killer's stare. "Landschein!" the black ordered sharply, and Margritte stepped very quickly toward the truck and the third man struggling there.

Helmuth turned and blinked at the girl as he felt her capable muscles take the windstrain off the panel he was shifting. His eyes were blue and set wide in a face too large-boned to be handsome, too frank to be other than attractive. He accepted the help without question, leading the way into the hall.

The dining tables were hoisted against the rafters. The windows, unshuttered in the warm autumn and unglazed, lined all four walls at chest height. The long wall nearest the road was otherwise unbroken; the one opposite it was pierced in the middle by the single door. In the center of what should have been an empty room squatted the mercenaries' construct. The metal-ceramic panels had been locked into three sides of a square, a pocket of armor open only toward the door. It was hidden beneath the lower sills of the windows; nothing would catch the eye of an oncoming tanker.

"We've got to nest three layers together," the soldier explained as he swung the load, easily managed within the building, "or they'll cut us apart if they get off a burst this direction."

Margritte steadied a panel already in place as Helmuth mortised his into it. Each sheet was about five centimeters in thickness, a thin plate of gray metal on either side of a white porcelain sponge. The girl tapped it dubiously with a blunt finger. "This can stop bullets?"

The soldier—he was younger than his size suggested, no more than eighteen. Younger even than Georg, and he had a smile like Georg's as he raised his eyes with a blush and said, "P-pow-erguns, yeah; three layers of it ought to. . . . It's light, we could carry it in the truck where iridium would have bogged us down. But look, there's another panel and the rockets we still got to bring in."

"You must be very brave to fight tanks with just—this," Margritte prompted as she took one end of the remaining armor sheet.

"Oh, well, Sgt. Counsel says it'll work," the boy said enthusiastically. "They'll come by, two combat cars, then three big trucks, and another combat car. Sarge and Landschein buzzbomb the lead cars before they know what's happening. I reload them and they hit the third car when it swings wide to get a shot. Any shooting the blower jocks get off, they'll spread because they won't know—oh, cop I said it. . . ."

"They'll think the women in the fields may be firing, so they'll kill us first," Margritte reasoned aloud. The boy's neck beneath his helmet turned brick red as he trudged into the building.

"Look," he said, but he would not meet her eyes, "we got to do it. It'll be fast—nobody much can get hurt. And your . . . the children, they're all safe. Sarge said that with all the men gone, we wouldn't have any trouble with the women if we kept the kids safe and under our thumbs."

"We didn't have time to have children," Margritte said. Her eyes were briefly unfocused.

"You didn't give Georg enough time before you killed him."

"He was. . . ," Helmuth began. They were outside again and his hand flicked briefly toward the slight notch Della and Myrie had chopped in the forest wall. "I'm sorry."

"Oh, don't be sorry," she said. "He knew what he was doing."

"He was—I suppose you'd call him a patriot?" Helmuth suggested, jumping easily to the truck's deck to gather up an armload of cylindrical bundles. "He was really against the Cartel?"

"There was never a soul in this village who cared who won the war," Margritte said. "We have our own war with the forest."

"They joined the siege!" the boy retorted. "They cared that m-much, to fight us!"

"They got in the vans when men with guns told them to get in," the girl said. She took the gear Helmuth was forgetting to hand to her and shook a lock of hair out of her eyes. "Should they have run? Like Georg? No, they went off to be soldiers; praying like we did that the war might end before the forest had eaten up the village again. Maybe if we were really lucky, it'd end before this crop had spoiled in the fields because there weren't enough hands left here to pick it in time."

Helmuth cleared the back of the truck with his own load and stepped down. "Well, just the same your, your husband tried to hide and warn the convoy," he argued. "Otherwise why did he run?"

"Oh, he loved me—you know?" said Margritte. "Your sergeant said all of us should be out picking as usual. Georg knew, he *told* you, that the crossfire would kill everybody in the fields as sure as if you shot us deliberately. And when you wouldn't change your plan . . . well, if he'd gotten away you would have had to give up your ambush, wouldn't you? You'd have known it was suicide if the tanks learned that you were waiting for them. So Georg ran."

The dark-haired woman stared out at the forest for a moment. "He didn't have a prayer, did he? You could have killed him a hundred times before he got to cover."

"Here, give me those," the soldier said, taking the bundles from her instead of replying. He began to unwrap the cylinders one by one on the wooden floor. "We couldn't let him get away," he said at last. He added, his eyes still down on his work, "Flechettes when they hit . . . I mean, sh-shooting at his legs wouldn't, wouldn't have been a kindness, you see?"

Margritte laughed again. "Oh, I saw what they dragged into the forest, yes." She paused, sucking at her lower lip. "That's how we always deal with our dead, give them to the forest. Oh, we have a service; but we wouldn't have buried Georg in the dirt, if . . . if he'd died. But you didn't care, did you? A corpse looks bad, maybe your precious ambush, your own lives. . . . Get it out of the way, toss it in the woods."

"We'd have buried him afterwards," the soldier mumbled as he laid a fourth thigh-thick projectile beside those he had already unwrapped.

"Oh, of *course*," Margritte said. "And me, and all the rest of us murdered out there in the cotton. Oh, you're gentlemen, you are."

"Via!" Helmuth shouted, his flush mottling as at last he lifted his gaze to the girl's. "We'd have b-buried him. *I'd* have buried him. You'll be safe in here with us until it's all over, and by the Lord, then you can come back with us too! You don't have to stay here with these hard-faced bitches."

A bitter smile tweaked the left edge of the girl's mouth. "Sure, you're a good boy."

The young mercenary blinked between protest and pleasure, settled on the latter. He had readied all six of the finned, gray missles; now he lifted one of the pair of launchers. "It'll be really quick," he said shyly, changing the subject. The launcher was an arm-length tube with double handgrips and an optical sight. Helmuth's big hands easily inserted one of the buzzbombs to lock with a faint snick.

"Very simple," Margritte murmured.

"Cheap and easy," the boy agreed with a smile. "You can buy a thousand of these for what a combat car runs—Hell, maybe more than a thousand. And it's one for one today, one bomb to one car. Landschein says the crews are just a little extra, like weevils in your biscuit."

He saw her grimace, the angry tensing of a woman who had just seen her husband blasted into a spray of offal. Helmuth grunted with his own pain, his mouth dropping open as his hand stretched to touch her bare shoulder. "Oh, Lord —didn't mean to say . . ."

She gently detached his fingers. His breath caught and he turned away. Unseen, her look of hatred seared his back. His hand was still stretched toward her and hers toward him, when the door scraped to admit Landschein behind them.

"Cute, oh bloody cute," the little mercenary said. He carried his helmet by its strap. Uncovered, his cropped gray hair made him an older man. "Well, get on with it, boy—don't keep me 'n Sarge waiting. He'll be mad enough about getting sloppy thirds."

Helmuth jumped to his feet. Landschein ignored him, clicking across to a window in three quick strides. "Sarge," he called, "we're all set. Come on, we can watch the women from here."

"I'll run the truck into the woods," Counsel's voice burred in reply. "Anyhow, I can hear better from out here."

That was true. Despite the open windows, the wails of the children were inaudible in the hall. Outside, they formed a thin backdrop to every other sound.

Landschein set down his helmet. He snapped the safety on his gun's sideplate and leaned the weapon carefully against the nest of armor. Then he took up the loaded launcher and ran his hands over its tube and grips. Without changing expression, he reached out to caress Margritte through the tear in her dress.

Margritte screamed and clawed her left hand as she tried to rise. The launcher slipped into Landschein's lap and his arm, far swifter, locked hers and drew her down against him. Then the little mercenary himself was jerked upward. Helmuth's hand on his collar first broke Landschein's grip on Margritte, then flung him against the closed door.

Landschein rolled despite the shock and his glance flicked toward his weapon, but between gun and gunman crouched Helmuth, no longer a red-faced boy but the strongest man in the room. Grinning, Helmuth spread fingers that had crushed ribs in past rough and tumbles. "Try it, little man," he said. "Try it and I'll rip your head off your shoulders."

"You'll do wonders!" Landschein spat, but his eyes lost their glaze and his muscles relaxed. He bent his mouth into a smile. "Hey, kid, there's plenty of slots around. We'll work out something afterwards, no need to fight."

Helmuth rocked his head back in a nod of acceptance with nothing of friendship in it. "You lay another hand on her," he said in a normal voice, "and you'd best have killed me first." He turned his back deliberately on the older man and the nearby weapons. Landschein clenched his left fist once, twice, but then he began to load the remaining launcher.

Margritte slipped the patching kit from her belt pouch. Her hands trembled, but the steel needle was already threaded. Her whip-stitches tacked the torn piece top and sides to the remaining material, close enough for decency. Pins were a luxury that a cotton settlement could well do without. Landschein glanced back at her once, but at the same time the floor creaked as Helmuth's weight shifted to his other leg. Neither man spoke.

Sgt. Counsel opened the door. His right arm cradled a pair of flechette guns and he handed one to Helmuth. "Best not to leave it in the dust," he said. "You'll be needing it soon."

"They coming, Sarge?" Landschein asked. He touched his tongue to thin, pale lips.

"Not yet." Counsel looked from one man to the other. "You boys get things sorted out?"

"All green here," Landschein muttered, smiling again but lowering his eyes.

"That's good," the big black said, "because we got a job to do and we're not going to let anything stop us. Anything."

Margritte was putting away her needle. The sergeant looked at her hard. "You keep your head down, hear?"

"It won't matter," the girl said calmly, tucking the kit away. "The tanks, they won't be surprised to see a woman in here."

"Sure, but they'll shoot your bleeding head off," Landschein snorted.

"Do you think I care?" she blazed back. Helmuth winced at the tone; Sgt. Counsel's eyes took on an undesirable shade of interest.

"But you're helping us," the big non-com mused. He tapped his fingertips on the gun in the crook of his arm. "Because you like us so much?" There was no amusement in his words, only a careful mind picking over the idea, all ideas.

She stood and walked to the door, her face as composed as a priest's at the gravesite. "Have your ambush," she said. "Would it help us if the convoy came through before you were ready for it?"

"The smoother it goes, the faster. . ." Counsel agreed quietly, "then the better for all of you."

Margritte swung the door open and stood looking out. Eight women were picking among the rows east of the hall. They would be relatively safe there, not caught between the ambushers' rockets and the raking powerguns of their quarry. Eight of them safe and fourteen sure victims on the other side. Most of them could have been out of the crossfire if they had only let themselves think, only considered the truth that Georg had died to underscore.

"I keep thinking of Georg," Margritte said aloud. "I guess my friends are just thinking about their children, they keep looking at the storage room. But the children, they'll be all right; it's just that most of them are going to be orphans in a few minutes."

"It won't be that bad," Helmuth said. He did not sound as though he believed it either.

The older children had by now ceased the screaming begun when the door shut and darkness closed in on them. The youngest still wailed and the sound drifted through the open door.

"I told her we'd take her back with us, Sarge," Helmuth said.

Landschein chortled, a flash of instinctive humor he covered with a raised palm. Counsel shook his head in amazement. "You were wrong, boy. Now, keep watching those women or we may not be going back ourselves."

The younger man reddened again in frustration. "Look, we've got women in the outfit now, and I don't mean the rec troops. Capt. Denzil told me there's six in Bravo Company alone—"

"Hoo, little Helmuth wants his own girlie friend to keep his bed warm," Landschein gibed.

"Landschein, I—" Helmuth began, clenching his right hand into a ridge of knuckles.

"Shut if off!"

"But Sarge—"

"Shut it off, boy, or you'll have me to deal with!" roared the black. Helmuth fell back and rubbed his eyes. The non-com went on more quietly, "Landschein, you keep your tongue to yourself, too."

Both big men breathed deeply, their eyes shifting in concert toward Margritte who faced them in silence. "Helmuth," the sergeant continued, "some units take women, some don't. We've got a few, damned few, because not many women have the guts for our line of work."

Margritte's smile flickered. "The hardness, you mean. The callousness."

"Sure, words don't matter," Counsel agreed mildly. He smiled back at her as one equal to another. "This one, yeah; she might just pass. Via, you don't have to look like Landschein there to be tough. But you're missing the big point, boy."

Helmuth touched his right wrist to his chin. "Well, what?" he demanded.

Counsel laughed. "She wouldn't go with us. Would you, girl?"

Margritte's eyes were flat, and her voice was dead flat. "No," she said, "I wouldn't go with you."

The non-com grinned as he walked back to a window vantage. "You see, Helmuth, you want her to give up a whole lot to gain you a bunkmate."

"It's not like that," Helmuth insisted, thumping his leg in frustration. "I just mean—"

"Oh, *Lord!*" the girl said loudly, "can't you just get on with your ambush?"

"Well, not till Hammer's boys come through," chuckled the sergeant. "They're so good, they can't run a convoy to schedule."

"S-sergeant," the young soldier said, "she doesn't understand." He turned to Margritte and gestured with both hands, forgetting the weapon in his left. "They won't take you back, those witches out there. The . . . the rec girls at Base Denzil don't go home, they can't. And you know damned well that s-somebody's going to catch it out there when it drops in the pot. They'll crucify you for helping us set up, the ones that're left."

"It doesn't matter what they do," she said. "It doesn't matter at all."

"Your life matters!" the boy insisted.

Her laughter hooted through the room. "My life?" Margritte repeated. "You splashed all that across the field an hour ago. You didn't give a damn when you did it, and I don't give one now —but I'd only follow you to Hell and hope your road was short."

Helmuth bit his knuckle and turned, pinched over as though he had been kicked. Sgt. Counsel grinned his tight, equals grin. "You're wasted here, you know," he said. "And we could use you. Maybe if—"

"Sarge!" Landschein called from his window. "Here they come."

Counsel scooped up a rocket launcher, probing its breech with his fingers to make finally sure of its load. "Now you keep down," he repeated to Margritte. "Backblast'll take your head off if their shooting don't." He crouched below the sill and the rim of the armor shielding him, peering through a periscope whose button of optical fibers was unnoticeable in the shadow. Faced inward toward the girl, Landschein hunched over the other launcher in the right corner of the protected area. His flechette gun rested beside him and one hand curved toward it momentarily, anticipating the instant he would raise it to spray the shattered convoy. Between them Helmuth knelt as stiffly as a statue of gray-green jade. He drew a buzzbomb closer to his right knee where it clinked against the barrel of his own weapon. Cursing nervously, he slid the flechette gun back out of the way. Both his hands gripped reloads, waiting.

The cars' shrill whine trembled in the air.

Margritte stood up by the door, staring out through the windows across the hall. Dust plumed where the long, straight roadway cut the horizon into two blocks of forest. The women in the fields had paused, straightening to watch the oncoming vehicles. But that was normal, nothing to alarm the khaki men in the bellies of their war cars; and if any woman thought of falling to hug the earth, the fans' wailing too nearly approximated that of the imprisoned children.

"Three hundred meters," Counsel reported

softly as the blunt bow of the lead car gleamed through the dust. "Two fifty." Landschein's teeth bared as he faced around, poised to spring.

Margritte swept up Helmuth's flechette gun and leveled it at waist height. The safety clicked off. Counsel had dropped his periscope and his mouth was open to cry an order. The deafening muzzle blast lifted him out of his crouch and pasted him briefly, voiceless, against the pocked inner face of the armor. Margritte swung her weapon like a flail into a triple splash of red. Helmuth died with only a reflexive jerk, but Landschein's speed came near to bringing his launcher to bear on Margritte. The stream of flechettes sawed across his throat. His torso dropped, headless but still clutching the weapon.

Margritte's gun silenced when the last needle slapped out of the muzzle. The aluminum barrel shroud had softened and warped during the long burst. Eddies in the fog of blood and propellant smoke danced away from it. Margritte turned as if in icy composure, but she bumped the door jamb and staggered as she stepped outside. The racket of the gun had drawn the sallow faces of every woman in the fields.

"It's over!" Margritte called. Her voice sounded thin in the fresh silence. Three of the nearer mothers ran toward the storage room.

Down the road, dust was spraying as the convoy skidded into a herringbone for defense. Gun muzzles searched: the running women; Margritte armed and motionless; the sudden eruption of children from the dugout. The men in the cars waited, their trigger fingers partly tensed.

Bergen, Della's six-year-old, pounded past Margritte to throw herself into her mother's arms. They clung together, each crooning to the other through their tears. "Oh, we were so afraid!" Bergen said, drawing away from her mother. "But now it's all right." She rotated her head and her eyes widened as they took in Margritte's tattered figure. "Oh, Margi," she gasped, "whatever happened to *you?*"

Della gasped and snatched her daughter back against her bosom. Over the child's loose curls, Della glared at Margritte with eyes like a hedge of pikes. Margritte's hand stopped half way to the child. She stood—gaunt, misted with blood as though sunburned. A woman who had blasted life away instead of suckling it. Della, a frightened mother, snarled at the killer who had been her friend.

Margritte began to laugh. She trailed the gun three steps before letting it drop unnoticed. The captain of the lead car watched her approach over his gunsights. His short, black beard fluffed out from under his helmet, twitching as he asked, "Would you like to tell us what's going on, honey, or do we got to comb it out ourselves?"

"I killed three soldiers," she answered simply. "Now there's nothing going on. Except that wherever you're headed, I'm going along. You can use my sort, soldier."

Her laughter was a crackling shadow in the sunlight.

INTERLUDE: THE BONDING AUTHORITY

Wars result when one side either misjudges its chances or wishes to commit suicide; and not even Masada *began* as a suicide attempt. In general, both warring parties expect to win. In the event, they are wrong more than half the time.

Employing mercenaries adds new levels of uncertainty to the already risky business of war. Too often in history a mercenary force has disappeared a moment before the battle; switched sides for a well-timed bribe; or even conquered its employer and brought about the very disasters it was hired to prevent.

Mercenaries, for their part, face the chances common to every soldier of being killed by the enemy. In addition, however, they must reckon with the possibility of being bilked of their pay or massacred to avoid its payment; of being used as cannon fodder by an employer whose distaste for "money-grubbing aliens" may exceed the enemy's; or of being abandoned far from home when defeat or political change erases their employer or his good will. As Xenophon and the Ten Thousand learned, in such circumstances the road home may be long—or as short as a shallow grave.

A solution to both sets of special problems was
made possible by the complexity of galactic com-
merce. The recorded beginnings came early in
the 27th Century when several planets caught up
in the Confederation Wars used the Terran firm
of Felchow und Sohn as an escrow agent for their
mercenaries' pay. Felchow was a commercial
banking house which had retained its pre-
eminence even after Terran industry had been in
some measure supplanted by that of newer
worlds. Neither Felchow nor Terra herself had
any personal stake in the chaotic rise and fall of
the Barnard Confederation; thus the house was
the perfect neutral to hold the pay of the condot-
tieri being hired by all parties. Payment was
scrupulously made to mercenaries who performed according to their contracts. This included the survivors of the Dalhousie debacle
who were able to buy passage off that ravaged
world, despite the fact that less than 10% of the
populace which had hired them was still alive.
Conversely, the pay of Wrangel's Legion, which
had refused to assault the Confederation drop
zone on Montauk, was forfeited to the Montauk
government. The Third Armistice intervened
and Wrangel's troops were hunted across the
face of the planet by both sides; too faithless to
use and too dangerous to ignore.

Felchow und Sohn had performed to the satisfaction of all honest parties when first used as an
intermediary. Over the next three decades the
house was similarly involved in other conflicts, a
passive escrow agent and paymaster. It was only
after the Ariete Incident of 2662 that the concept

coalesced into the one stable feature of a galaxy at war.

The Ariete, a division recruited mostly from among the militias of the Aldoni System, was hired by the rebels on Paley. Their pay was banked with Felchow, since the rebels very reasonably doubted that anyone would take on the well-trained troops of the Republic of Paley if they had already been handed the carrot. But the Ariete fought very well indeed, losing an estimated 30% of its effectives before surrendering in the final collapse of the rebellion. The combat losses have to be estimated because the Republican forces, in defiance of the "Laws of War" and their own promises before the surrender, butchered all their fifteen or so thousand mercenary prisoners.

Felchow und Sohn, seeing an excuse for an action which would raise it to incredible power, reduced Paley to Stone Age savagry.

An industrialized world (as Paley was) is an interlocking whole. Off-planet trade may amount to no more than 5% of its GNP; but when that trade is suddenly cut off, the remainder of the economy resembles a car lacking two pistons. It may make whirring sounds for a time, but it isn't going anywhere.

Huge as Felchow was, a single banking house could not have cut Paley off from the rest of the galaxy. When Felchow, however, offered other commercial banks membership in a cartel and a share of the lucrative escrow business, the others joined gladly and without exception. No one would underwrite cargoes to or from Paley; and

Paley, already wracked by a war and its aftermath, shuddered down into the slag heap of history.

Lucrative was indeed a mild word for the mercenary business. The escrowed money itself could be put to work, and the escrowing bank was an obvious agent for the other commercial transactions needed to run a war. Mercenaries replaced equipment, recruited men, and shipped themselves by the thousands across the galaxy. The new banking cartel served those needs smoothly—and maximized its own profits.

With the banks' new power came a new organization. The expanded escrow operations were made the responsibility of a Bonding Authority, still based in Bremen but managed independently of the cartel itself. The Authority's fees were high. In return, its Contracts Department was expert in preventing expensive misunderstandings from arising, and its investigative staff could neither be bribed nor deluded by a violator. Under the Authority's ruthless nurture, the business of war became as regular as any other commercial endeavor; and more profitable than most.

HANGMAN

THE LIGHT in the kitchen alcove glittered on Lt. Schilling's blond curls; glittered also on the frost-spangled window beside her and from the armor of the tank parked outside. All the highlights looked cold to Capt. Danny Pritchard as he stepped closer to the infantry lieutenant.

"Sal—" Pritchard began. From the orderly room behind them came the babble of the radios ranked against one wall and, less muted, the laughter of soldiers waiting for action. "You can't think like a Dutchman any more. We're Hammer's Slammers, all of us. We're mercs. Not Dutch, not Frisians—"

"You're not," Lt. Schilling snapped, looking up from the cup of bitter chocolate she had just drawn from the urn. She was a short woman and lightly built, but she had the unerring instinct of a bully who is willing to make a scene for a victim who is not willing to be part of one. "You're a farmer from Dunstan, what d'you care about Dutch miners, whatever these bleeding French do to them. But a lot of us do care, Danny, and if you had a little compassion—"

"But Sal—" Pritchard repeated, only his right

165

arm moving as he touched the blonde girl's shoulder.

"Get your hands off me, Captain!" she shouted, "That's over!" She shifted the mug of steaming chocolate in her hand. The voices in the orderly room stilled. Then, simultaneously, someone turned up the volume of the radios and at least three people began to talk loudly on unconnected subjects.

Pritchard studied the back of his hand, turned it over to examine the calloused palm as well. He smiled. "Sorry, I'll remember that," he said in a normal voice. He turned and stepped back into the orderly room, a brown-haired man of 34 with a good set of muscles to cover his moderate frame and nothing at all to cover his heart. Those who knew Danny Pritchard slightly thought him a relaxed man, and he looked relaxed even now. But waiting around the electric grate were three troopers who knew Danny very well indeed: The crew of the Plow, Pritchard's command tank.

Kowie drove the beast, a rabbit-eyed man whose fingers now flipped cards in another game of privy solitaire. His deck was so dirty that only familiarity allowed him to read the pips. Kowie's hands and eyes were just as quick at the controls of the tank, sliding its bulbous hundred and fifty metric tons through spaces that were only big enough to pass it. When he had to, he drove nervelessly through objects instead of going around. Kowie would never be more than a tank driver; but he was the best tank driver in the Regiment.

Rob Jenne was big and as blond as Lt. Schilling. He grinned up at Pritchard, his expression changing from embarrassment to relief as he saw that his captain was able to smile also. Jenne had transferred from combat cars to tanks three years back, after the Slammers had pulled out of Squire's World. He was sharp-eyed and calm in a crisis. Twice after his transfer Jenne had been offered a blower of his own to command if he would return to combat cars. He had refused both promotions, saying he would stay with tanks or buy back his contract, that there was no way he was going back to those open-topped coffins again. When a tank commander's slot came open, Jenne got it; and Pritchard had made the blond sergeant his own blower chief when a directional mine had retired the previous man. Now Jenne straddled a chair backwards, his hands flexing a collapsible torsion device that kept his muscles as dense and hard as they had been the day he was recruited from a quarry on Burlage.

Line tanks carry only a driver and the blower chief who directs the tank and its guns when they are not under the direct charge of the Regiment's computer. In addition to those two and a captain, command tanks have a Communications Technician to handle the multiplex burden of radio traffic focused on the vehicle. Pritchard's commo tech was Margritte DiManzo, a slender widow who cropped her lustrous hair short so that it would not interfere with the radio helmet she wore most of her waking hours. She was off-duty now, but she had not

removed the bulky headgear which linked her to
the six radios in the tank parked outside. Their
simultaneous sound would have been unin-
telligible babbling to most listeners. The black-
haired woman's training, both conscious and
hypnotic, broke that babbling into a set of dis-
crete conversations. When Pritchard reentered
the room, Margritte was speaking to Jenne. She
did not look up at her commander until Jenne's
brightening expression showed her it was safe to
do so.

Two commo people and a sergeant with Intelligence tabs were at consoles in the orderly
room. They were from the Regiment's HQ Battalion, assigned to Sector Two here on Kobold
but in no sense a part of the sector's combat
companies: Capt. Riis' S Company—infantry—
and Pritchard's own tanks.

Riis was the senior captain and in charge of
the sector, a matter which neither he nor
Pritchard ever forgot. Sally Schilling led his first
platoon. Her aide, a black-haired corporal, sat
with his huge boots up, humming as he polished
the pieces of his field-stripped powergun. Its barrel gleamed orange in the light of the electric
grate. Electricity was more general on Kobold
than on some wealthier worlds, since mining and
copper smelting made fusion units a practical
necessity. But though the copper in the transmission cable might well have been processed on
Kobold, the wire had probably been drawn off-
world and shipped back here. Aurore and
Friesland had refused to allow even such simple
manufactures here on their joint colony. They

had kept Kobold a market and a supplier of raw materials, but never a rival.

"Going to snow tonight?" Jenne asked.

"Umm, too cold," Pritchard said, walking over to the grate. He pretended he did not hear Lt. Schilling stepping out of the alcove. "I figure—"

"Hold it," said Margritte, her index finger curling out for a volume control before the duty man had time to react. One of the wall radios boomed loudly to the whole room. Prodding another switch, Margritte patched the signal separately through the link implanted in Pritchard's right mastoid. "—guns and looks like satchel charges. There's only one man in each truck, but they've been on the horn too and we can figure on more Frenchies here any—"

"Red Alert," Pritchard ordered, facing his commo tech so that she could read his lips. "Where is this?"

The headquarters radiomen stood nervously, afraid to interfere but unwilling to let an outsider run their equipment, however ably. "Red Alert," Margritte was repeating over all bands. Then, through Pritchard's implant, she said, "It's Patrol Sigma three-nine, near Haacin. Dutch civilians've stopped three outbound provisions trucks from Barthe's Company."

"Scramble First Platoon," Pritchard said, "but tell 'em to hold for us to arrive." As Margritte coolly passed on the order, Pritchard picked up the commo helmet he had laid on his chair when he followed Lt. Schilling into the kitchen. The helmet gave him automatic switching and greater range than the bio-electric unit behind his ear.

The wall radio was saying, "—need some big friendlies fast or it'll drop in the pot for sure."

"Sigma three-niner," Pritchard said, "this is Michael One."

"Go ahead, Michael One," replied the distant squad leader. Pritchard's commo helmet added an airy boundlessness to his surroundings without really deadening the ambient noise.

"Hold what you've got, boys," the tank captain said. "There's help on the way."

The door of the orderly room stood ajar the way Pritchard's crewmen had left it. The captain slammed it shut as he too ran for his tank. Behind in the orderly room, Lt. Schilling was snapping out quick directions to her own platoon and to her awakened commander.

The Plow was already floating when Danny reached it. Ice crystals, spewed from beneath the skirts by the lift fans, made a blue-white dazzle in the vehicle's running lights. Frost whitened the ladder up the high side of the tank's plenum chamber and hull. Pritchard paused to pull on his gloves before mounting. Sgt. Jenne, anchoring himself with his left hand on the turret's storage rack, reached down and lifted his captain aboard without noticeable effort. Side by side, the two men slid through the hatches to their battle stations.

"Ready," Pritchard said over the intercom.

"Movin' on," replied Kowie, and with his words the tank slid forward over the frozen ground like grease on a hot griddle.

The command post had been a district road-maintenance center before all semblance of central government on Kobold had collapsed. The orderly room and officers' quarters were in the supervisor's house, a comfortable structure with shutters and mottoes embroidered in French on the walls. Some of the hangings had been defaced by short-range gunfire. The crew barracks across the road now served the troopers on headquarters duty. Many of the Slammers could read the Dutch periodicals abandoned there in the break-up. The equipment shed beside the barracks garaged the infantry skimmers because the battery-powered platforms could not shrug off the weather like the huge panzers of M Company. The shed doors were open, pluming the night with heated air as the duty platoon ran for its mounts. Some of the troopers had not yet donned their helmets and body armor. Jenne waved as the tank swept on by; then the road curved and the infantry was lost in the night.

Kobold was a joint colony of Aurore and Friesland. When eighty years of French oppression had driven the Dutch settlers to rebellion, their first act was to hire Hammer's Slammers. The break between Hammer and Friesland had been sharp, but time has a way of blunting anger and letting old habits resume. The Regimental language was Dutch, and many of the Slammers' officers were Frisians seconded from their own service. Friesland gained from the men's experience when they returned home; Hammer gained company officers with excellent training from the Gröningen Academy.

To counter the Slammers, the settlers of Auroran descent had hired three Francophone regiments. If either group of colonists could have af-
forded to pay its mercenaries unaided, the fighting would have been immediate and brief.
Kobold had been kept deliberately poor by its
homeworlds, however; so in their necessities the
settlers turned to those homeworlds for financial
help.

And neither Aurore nor Friesland wanted a
war on Kobold.

Friesland had let its settlers swing almost from
the beginning, sloughing their interests for a half
share of the copper produced and concessions
elsewhere in its sphere of influence. The arrangement was still satisfactory to the Council of
State, if Frisian public opinion could be mollified
by apparent activity. Aurore was on the brink of
war in the Zemla System. Her Parlement feared
another proxy war which could in a moment explode full-fledged, even though Friesland had
been weakened by a decade of severe internal
troubles. So Aurore and Friesland reached a
compromise. Then, under threat of abandonment, the warring parties were forced to transfer
their mercenaries' contracts to the home worlds.
Finally, Aurore and Friesland mutually hired
the four regiments: the Slammers; Compagnie
de Barthe; the Alaudae; and Phenix Moirots.
Mercs from either side were mixed and divided
among eight sectors imposed on a map of in-
habited Kobold. There the contract ordered
them to keep peace between the factions; prevent

the importation of modern weapons to either side; and—wait.

But Col Barthe and the Auroran leaders had come to a further, secret agreement; and although Hammer had learned of it, he had informed only two men—Maj Steuben, his aide and bodyguard; and Capt Daniel Pritchard.

Pritchard scowled at the memory. Even without the details a traitor had sold Hammer, it would have been obvious that Barthe had his own plans. In the other sectors, Hammer's men and their French counterparts ran joint patrols. Both sides scattered their camps throughout the sectors, just as the villages of either nationality were scattered. Barthe had split his sectors in halves, brusquely ordering the Slammers to keep to the west of the River Aillet because his own troops were mining the east of the basin heavily. Barthe's Company was noted for its minefields. That skill was one of the reasons they had been hired by the French. Since most of Kobold was covered either by forests or by rugged hills, armor was limited to roads where well-placed mines could stack tanks like crushed boxes.

Hammer listened to Barthe's pronouncement and laughed, despite the anger of most of his staff officers. Beside him, Joachim Steuben had grinned and traced the line of his cut-away holster. When Danny Pritchard was informed, he had only shivered a little and called a vehicle inspection for the next morning. That had been three months ago. . . .

The night streamed by like smoke around the tank. Pritchard lowered his face shield, but he did not drop his seat into the belly of the tank. Vision blocks within gave a 360° view of the tank's surroundings, but the farmer in Danny could not avoid the feeling of blindness within the impenetrable walls. Jenne sat beside his captain in a cupola fitted with a three-barrelled automatic weapon. He too rode with his head out of the hatch, but that was only for comradeship. The sergeant much preferred to be inside. He would button up at the first sign of hostile action. Jenne was in no sense a coward; it was just that he had quirks. Most combat veterans do.

Pritchard liked the whistle of the black wind past his helmet. Warm air from the tank's resistance heaters jetted up through the hatch and kept his body quite comfortable. The vehicle's huge mass required the power of a fusion plant to drive its lift motors, and the additional burden of climate control was inconsequential.

The tankers' face shields automatically augmented the light of the moon, dim and red because the sun it reflected was dim and red as well. The boosted light level displayed the walls of forest, the boles snaking densely to either side of the road. At Kobold's perihelion, the thin stems grew in days to their full six-meter height and spread a ceiling of red-brown leaves the size of blankets. Now, at aphelion, the chilled, sapless trees burned with almost explosive intensity. The wood was too dangerous to use for heating, even if electricity had not been common; but it fueled the gasogene engines of most vehicles on the planet.

Jenne gestured ahead. "Blowers," he muttered on the intercom. His head rested on the gun switch though he knew the vehicles must be friendly. The Plow slowed.

Pritchard nodded agreement. "Michael First, this is Michael One," he said. "Flash your running lights so we can be sure it's you."

"Roger," replied the radio. Blue light flickered from the shapes hulking at the edge of the forest ahead. Kowie throttled the fans up to cruise, then chopped them and swung expertly into the midst of the four tanks of the outlying platoon.

"Michael One, this is Sigma One," Capt. Riis' angry voice demanded in the helmet.

"Go ahead."

"Barthe's sent a battalion across the river. I'm moving Lt. Schilling into position to block 'em and called Central for artillery support. You hold your first platoon at Haacin for reserve and any partisans up from Portela. I'll take direct command of the rest of—"

"Negative, negative, Sigma One!" Pritchard snapped. The Plow was accelerating again, second in the line of five tanks. They were beasts of prey sliding across the landscape of snow and black trees at 80 kph and climbing. "Let the French through, Captain. There won't be fighting, repeat, negative fighting."

"There damned well *will* be fighting, Michael One, if Barthe tries to shove a battalion into my sector!" Riis thundered back. "Remember, this isn't your command or a joint command. *I'm* in charge here."

"Margritte, patch me through to Battalion,"

Pritchard hissed on intercom. The Plow's turret was cocked 30° to the right. It covered the forest sweeping by to that side and anything which might be hiding there. Pritchard's mind was on Sally Schilling, riding a skimmer through forest like that flanking the tanks, hurrying with her fifty men to try to stop a battalion's hasty advance.

The commo helmet popped quietly to itself. Pritchard tensed, groping for the words he would need to convince Lt. Col. Miezierk. Miezierk, under whom command of Sectors One and Two was grouped, had been a Frisian regular until five years ago. He was supposed to think like a merc, now, not like a Frisian; but. . . .

The voice that suddenly rasped, "Override, override!" was not Miezierk's. "Sigma One, Michael One, this is Regiment."

"Go ahead," Pritchard blurted. Capt. Riis, equally rattled, said, "Yes *sir!*" on the three-way link.

"Sigma, your fire order is cancelled. Keep your troops on alert, but keep 'em the hell out of Barthe's way."

"But Col. Hammer—"

"Riis, you're not going to start a war tonight. Michael One, can your panzers handle whatever's going on at Haacin without violating the contract?"

"Yes, sir." Pritchard flashed a map briefly on his face shield to check his position. "We're almost there now."

"If you can't handle it, Captain, you'd better hope you're killed in action," Col. Hammer said bluntly. "I haven't nursed this regiment for twenty-three years to lose it because somebody forgets what his job is." Then, more softly—Pritchard could imagine the Colonel flicking his eyes side to side to gauge bystanders' reactions—he added, "There's support if you need it, Captain—if they're the ones who breach the contract."

"Affirmative."

"Keep the lid on, boy. Regiment out."

The trees had drunk the whine of the fans. Now the road curved and the tanks banked greasily to join the main highway from Dimo to Portela. The tailings pile of the Haacin Mine loomed to the right and hurled the drive noise back redoubled at the vehicles. The steel skirts of the lead tank touched the road metal momentarily, showering the night with orange sparks. Beyond the mine were the now-empty wheat fields and then the village itself.

Haacin, the largest Dutch settlement in Sector Two, sprawled to either side of the highway. Its houses were two- and three-story lumps of cemented mine tailings. They were roofed with tile or plastic rather than shakes of native timber, because of the wood's lethal flammability. The highway was straight and broad. It gave Pritchard a good view of the three cargo vehicles pulled to one side. Men in local dress swarmed about them. Across the road were ten of Hammer's khaki-clad infantry, patrol S-39, whose ported weapons half-threatened, half-protected the trio of drivers in their midst. Occasionally a civilian turned to hurl a curse at

Barthe's men, but mostly the Dutch busied themselves with off-loading cartons from the trucks.

Pritchard gave a brief series of commands. The four line tanks grounded in a hedgehog at the edge of the village. Their main guns and automatics faced outward in all directions. Kowie swung the command vehicle around the tank which had been leading it. He cut the fans' angle of attack, slowing The Plow without losing the ability to accelerate quickly. The command vehicle eased past the squad of infantry, then grounded behind the rearmost truck. Pritchard felt the fans' hum through the metal of the hull.

"Who's in charge here?" the captain demanded, his voice booming through the command vehicle's public address system.

The Dutch unloading the trucks halted silently. A squat man in a parka of feathery native fur stepped forward. Unlike many of the other civilians, he was not armed. He did not flinch when Pritchard pinned him with the spotlight of the tank. "I am Paul van Oosten," the man announced in the heavy Dutch of Kobold. "I am Mayor of Haacin. But if you mean who leads us in what we are doing here, well . . . perhaps Justice herself does. Klaus, show them what these trucks were carrying to Portela."

Another civilian stepped forward, ripping the top off the box he carried. Flat plastic wafers spilled from it, glittering in the cold light: powergun ammunition, intended for shoulder weapons like those the infantry carried.

"They were taking powerguns to the beasts of

Portela to use against us," van Oosten said. He
used the slang term, "skepsels" to name the
Francophone settlers. The Mayor's shaven jaw
was jutting out in anger.

"Captain!" called one of Barthe's truck
drivers, brushing forward through the ring of
Hammer's men. "Let me explain."

One of the civilians growled and lifted his
heavy musket. Rob Jenne rang his knuckles
twice on the receiver of his tribarrel, calling attention to the muzzles as he swept them down
across the crowd. The Dutchman froze. Jenne
smiled without speaking.

"We were sent to pick up wheat the regiment
had purchased," Barthe's man began. Pritchard
was not familiar with Barthe's insigniae, but
from the merc's age and bearing he was a senior
sergeant. An unlikely choice to be driving a provisions truck. "One of the vehicles happened to
be partly loaded. We didn't take the time to
empty it because we were in a hurry to finish the
run and go off duty—there was enough room
and lift to handle that little bit of gear and the
grain besides.

"In any case—" and here the sergeant began
pressing, because the tank captain had not cut
him off at the first sentence as expected—"you
do not, and these fools *surely* do not, have the
right to stop Col. Barthe's transport. If you have
questions about the way we pick up wheat,
that's between your CO and ours. Sir."

Pritchard ran his gloved index finger back and
forth below his right eyesocket. He was ice inside, bubbling ice that tore and chilled him and

had nothing to do with the weather. He turned back to Mayor van Oosten. "Reload the trucks," he said, hoping that his voice did not break.

"You can't!" van Oosten cried. "These powerguns are the only chance my village, my *people* have to survive whan you leave. You know that'll happen, don't you? Friesland and Aurore, they'll come to an agreement, a *trade-off,* they'll call it, and all the troops will leave. It's our lives they're trading! The beasts in Dimo, in Portela if you let these go through, they'll have powerguns that *their* mercenaries gave them. And we—"

Pritchard whispered a prepared order into his helmet mike. The rearmost of the four tanks at the edge of the village fired a single round from its main gun. The night flared cyan as the 200 mm bolt struck the middle of the tailings pile a kilometer away. Stone, decomposed by the enormous energy of the shot, recombined in a huge gout of flame. Vapor, lava, and cinders spewed in every direction. After a moment, bits of high-flung rock began pattering down on the roofs of Haacin.

The bolt caused a double thunder-clap, that of the heated air followed by the explosive release of energy at the point of impact. When the reverberations died away there was utter silence in Haacin. On the distant jumble of rock, a dying red glow marked where the charge had hit. The shot had also ignited some saplings rooted among the stones. They had blazed as white torches for a few moments but they were already collapsing as cinders.

"The Slammers are playing this by rules," Pritchard said. Loudspeakers flung his quiet words about the village like the echoes of the shot; but he was really speaking for the recorder in the belly of the tank, preserving his words for a later Bonding Authority hearing. "There'll be no powerguns in civilian hands. Load every bit of this gear back in the truck. Remember, there's satellites up there—" Pritchard waved generally at the sky—"that see everything that happens on Kobold. If one powergun is fired by a civilian in this sector, I'll come for him. I promise you."

The mayor sagged within his furs. Turning to the crowd behind him, he said, "Put the guns back on the truck. So that the Portelans can kill us more easily."

"Are you mad, van Oosten?" demanded the gunman who had earlier threatened Barthe's sergeant.

"Are *you* mad, Kruse?" the mayor shouted back without trying to hide his fury. "D'ye doubt what those tanks would do to Haacin? And do you doubt this butcher—" his back was to Pritchard but there was no doubt as to whom the mayor meant—"would use them on us? Perhaps tomorrow we could have. . . ."

There was motion at the far edge of the crowd, near the corner of a building. Margritte, watching the vision blocks within, called a warning. Pritchard reached for his panic bar—Rob Jenne was traversing the tribarrel. All three of them were too late. The muzzle flash was red and it expanded in Pritchard's eyes as a hammer blow smashed him in the middle of the forehead.

The bullet's impact heaved the tanker up and
backwards. His shattered helmet flew off into the
night. The unyielding hatch coaming caught
him in the small of the back, arching his torso
over it as if he were being broken on the wheel.
Pritchard's eyes flared with sheets of light. As
reaction flung him forward again, he realized he
was hearing the reports of Jenne's powergun and
that some of the hellish flashes were real.

If the tribarrel's discharges were less brilliant
than that of the main gun, then they were more
than a hundred times as close to the civilians.
The burst snapped within a meter of one
bystander, an old man who stumbled backward
into a wall. His mouth and staring eyes were
three circles of empty terror. Jenne fired seven
rounds. Every charge but one struck the sniper
or the building he sheltered against. Powdered
concrete sprayed from the wall. The sniper's
body spun backwards, chest gobbled away by
the bolts. His right arm still gripped the musket
he had fired at Pritchard. The arm had been
flung alone onto the snowy pavement. The electric bite of ozone hung in the air with the ghostly
afterimages of the shots. The dead man's clothes
were burning, tiny orange flames that rippled
into smoke an inch from their bases.

Jenne's big left hand was wrapped in the fabric of Pritchard's jacket, holding the dazed officer upright. "There's another rule you play
by," the sergeant roared to the crowd. "You
shoot at Hammer's Slammers and you get your
balls kicked between your ears. Sure as god,
boys; sure as death." Jenne's right hand swung

the muzzles of his weapon across the faces of the
civilians. "Now, load the bleeding trucks like the
captain said, heroes."

For a brief moment, nothing moved but the
threatening powergun. Then a civilian turned
and hefted a heavy crate back aboard the truck
from which he had just taken it. Empty-handed,
the colonist began to sidle away from the vehicle
—and from the deadly tribarrel. One by one the
other villagers reloaded the hijacked cargo, the
guns and ammunition they had hoped would
save them in the cataclysm they awaited. One by
one they took the blower chief's unspoken leave
to return to their houses. One who did not leave
was sobbing out her grief over the mangled body
of the sniper. None of her neighbors had gone to
her side. They could all appreciate—now—what
it would have meant if that first shot had led to
a general firefight instead of Jenne's selective response.

"Rob, help me get him inside," Pritchard
heard Margritte say.

Pritchard braced himself with both hands and
leaned away from his sergeant's supporting arm.
"No, I'm all right," he croaked. His vision was
clear enough, but the landscape was flashing
bright and dim with varicolored light.

The side hatch of the turret clanked. Margritte was beside her captain. She had stripped
off her cold weather gear in the belly of the tank
and wore only her khaki uniform. "Get back inside there," Pritchard muttered. "It's not safe."
He was afraid of falling if he raised a hand to
fend her away. He felt an injector prick the swell-

ing flesh over his cheekbones. The flashing colors
died away though Pritchard's ears began to ring.

"They carried some into the nearest building," the non-com from Barthe's Company was
saying. He spoke in Dutch, having sleep-trained
in the language during the transit to Kobold just
as Hammer's men had in French.

"Get it," Jenne ordered the civilians still near
the trucks. Three of them were already scurrying
toward the house the merc had indicated. They
were back in moments, carrying the last of the
arms chests.

Pritchard surveyed the scene. The cargo had
been reloaded, except for the few spilled rounds
winking from the pavement. Van Oosten and the
furious Kruse were the only villagers still in
sight. "All right," Pritchard said to the truck
drivers, "get aboard and get moving. And come
back by way of Bitzen, not here. I'll arrange an
escort for you."

The French non-com winked, grinned, and
shouted a quick order to his men. The infantrymen stepped aside silently to pass the
truckers. The French mercenaries mounted their
vehicles and kicked them to life. Their fans
whined and the trucks lifted, sending snow
crystals dancing. With gathering speed, they slid
westward along the forest-rimmed highway.

Jenne shook his head at the departing trucks,
then stiffened as his helmet spat a message.
"Captain," he said, "we got company coming."

Pritchard grunted. His own radio helmet had
been smashed by the bullet, and his implant
would only relay messages on the band to which

it had been verbally keyed most recently. "Margritte, start switching for me," he said. His slender commo tech was already slipping back inside through the side hatch. Pritchard's blood raced with the chemicals Margritte had shot into it. His eyes and mind worked perfectly, though all his thoughts seemed to have razor edges on them.

"Use mine," Jenne said, trying to hand the captain his helmet.

"I've got the implant," Pritchard said. He started to shake his head and regretted the motion instantly. "That and Margritte's worth a helmet any day."

"It's a whole battalion," Jenne explained quietly, his eyes scanning the Bever Road down which Command Central had warned that Barthe's troops were coming. "All but the artillery—that's back in Dimo, but it'll range here easy enough. Brought in anti-tank battery and a couple calliopes, though."

"Slide us up ahead of Michael First," Pritchard ordered his driver. As The Plow shuddered, then spun on its axis, the captain dropped his seat into the turret to use the vision blocks. He heard Jenne's seat whirr down beside him and the cupola hatch snick closed. In front of Pritchard's knees, pale in the instrument lights, Margritte DiManzo sat still and open-eyed at her communications console.

"Little friendlies," Pritchard called through his loudspeakers to the ten infantrymen, "find yourselves a quiet alley and hope nothing happens. The Lord help you if you fire a shot

without me ordering it." The Lord help us all,
Pritchard thought to himself.

Ahead of the command vehicle, the beetle
shapes of First Platoon began to shift position.
"Michael First," Pritchard ordered sharply,
"get back as you were. We're not going to en-
gage Barthe, we're going to meet him." Maybe.

Kowie slid them alongside, then a little forward of the point vehicle of the defensive
lozenge. They set down. All of the tanks were
buttoned up, save for the hatch over Pritchard's
head. The central vision block was a meter by 30
cm panel. It could be set for anything from a
360° view of the tank's surroundings to a one-to-
one image of an object a kilometer away.
Pritchard focused and ran the gain to ten magni-
fications, then thirty. At the higher power, motion curling along the snow-smoothed grainfields
between Haacin and its mine resolved into men.
Barthe's troops were clad in sooty-white coveralls and battle armor. The leading elements
were hunched low on the meager platforms of
their skimmers. Magnification and the
augmented light made the skittering images
grainy, but the tanker's practiced eye caught the
tubes of rocket launchers clipped to every one of
the skimmers. The skirmish line swelled at two
points where self-propelled guns were strung like
beads on the cord of men: anti-tank weapons, 50
mm powerguns firing high-intensity charges.
They were supposed to be able to burn through
the heaviest armor. Barthe's boys had come
loaded for bear; oh yes. They thought they knew
just what they were going up against. Well, the

Slammers weren't going to show them they were wrong. Tonight.

"Running lights, everybody," Pritchard ordered. Then, taking a deep breath, he touched the lift on his seat and raised himself head and shoulders back into the chill night air. There was a hand light clipped to Pritchard's jacket. He snapped it on, aiming the beam down onto the turret top so that the burnished metal splashed diffused radiance up over him. It bathed his torso and face plainly for the oncoming infantry. Through the open hatch, Pritchard could hear Rob cursing. Just possibly Margritte was mumbling a prayer.

"Batteries at Dimo and Harfleur in Sector One have received fire orders and are waiting for a signal to execute," the implant grated. "If Barthe opens fire, Command Central will not, repeat, negative, use Michael First or Michael One to knock down the shells. Your guns will be clear for action, Michael One."

Pritchard grinned starkly. His face would not have been pleasant even if livid bruises were not covering almost all of it. The Slammers' central fire direction computer used radar and satellite reconnaissance to track shells in flight. Then the computer took control of any of the Regiment's vehicle-mounted powerguns and swung them onto the target. Central's message notified Pritchard that he would have full control of his weapons at all times, while guns tens or hundreds of kilometers away kept his force clear of artillery fire.

Margritte had blocked most of the commo

traffic, Pritchard realized. She had let through only this message that was crucial to what they were about to do. A good commo tech; a very good person indeed.

The skirmish line grounded. The nearest infantrymen were within fifty meters of the tanks and their fellows spread off into the night like lethal wings. Barthe's men rolled off their skimmers and lay prone. Pritchard began to relax when he noticed that their rocket launchers were still aboard the skimmers. The anti-tank weapons were in instant reach, but at least they were not being leveled for an immediate salvo. Barthe didn't want to fight the Slammers. His targets were the Dutch civilians, just as Mayor van Oosten had suggested.

An air cushion jeep with a driver and two officers aboard drew close. It hissed slowly through the line of infantry, then stopped nearly touching the command vehicle's bow armor. One of the officers dismounted. He was a tall man who was probably very thin when he was not wearing insulated coveralls and battle armor. He raised his face to Pritchard atop the high curve of the blower, sweeping up his reflective face shield as he did so. He was Lt. Col. Benoit, commander of the French mercenaries in Sector Two; a clean-shaven man with sharp features and a splash of gray hair displaced across his forehead by his helmet. Benoit grinned and waved at the muzzle of the 200 mm powergun pointed at him. Nobody had ever said Barthe's chief subordinate was a coward.

Pritchard climbed out of the turret to the

deck, then slid down the bow slope to the
ground. Benoit was several inches taller than the
tanker, with a force of personality which was
daunting in a way that height alone could never
be. It didn't matter to Pritchard. He worked
with tanks and with Col.Hammer; nothing else
was going to face down a man who was ac-
customed to those.

"Sgt.Major Oberlie reported how well and . . .
firmly you handled their little affair, Captain,"
Benoit said, extending his hand to Pritchard.
"I'll admit that I was a little concerned that I
would have to rescue my men myself."

"Hammer's Slammers can be depended on to
keep their contracts," the tanker replied, smiling
with false warmth. "I told these squareheads
that any civilian caught with a powergun was
going to have to answer to me for it. Then we
made sure nobody thinks we were kidding."

Benoit chuckled. Little puffs of vapor spurted
from his mouth with the sounds. "You've been
sent to the Gröningen Academy, have you not,
Capt. Pritchard?" the older man asked. "You
understand that I take an interest in my opposite
numbers in this sector."

Pritchard nodded. "The Old Man picked me
for the two year crash course on Friesland, yeah.
Now and again he sends non-coms he wants to
promote."

"But you're not a Frisian, though you have
Frisian military training," the other mercenary
continued, nodding to himself. "As you know,
Captain, promotion in some infantry regiments
comes much faster than it does in the . . . Slam-

mers. If you feel a desire to speak to Col. Barthe some time in the future, I assure you this evening's business will not be forgotten."

"Just doing my job, Colonel," Pritchard simpered. Did Benoit think a job offer would make a traitor of him? Perhaps. Hammer had bought Barthe's plans for very little, considering their military worth. "Enforcing the contract, just like you'd have done if things were the other way around."

Benoit chuckled again and stepped back aboard his jeep. "Until we meet again, Capt. Pritchard," he said. "For the moment, I think we'll just proceed on into Portela. That's permissible under the contract, of course."

"Swing wide around Haacin, will you?" Pritchard called back. "The folks there're pretty worked up. Nobody wants more trouble, do we?"

Benoit nodded. As his jeep lifted, he spoke into his helmet communicator. The skirmish company rose awkwardly and set off in a counter-clockwise circuit of Haacin. Behind them, in a column reformed from their support positions at the base of the tailings heap, came the truck-mounted men of the other three companies. Pritchard stood and watched until the last of them whined past.

Air stirred by the tank's idling fans leaked out under the skirts. The jets formed tiny deltas of the snow which winked as Pritchard's feet caused eddy currents. In their cold precision, the tanker recalled Col. Benoit's grin.

"Command Central," Pritchard said as he

climbed his blower, "Michael One. Everything's smooth here. Over." Then, "Sigma One, this is Michael One. I'll be back as quick as fans'll moye me, so if you have anything to say we can discuss it then." Pritchard knew that Capt. Riis must have been burning the net up, trying to raise him for a report or to make demands. It wasn't fair to make Margritte hold the bag now that Pritchard himself was free to respond to the sector chief; but neither did the Dunstan tanker have the energy to argue with Riis just at the moment. Already this night he'd faced death and Col. Benoit. Riis could wait another ten minutes.

The Plow's armor was a tight fit for its crew, the radios, and the central bulk of the main gun with its feed mechanism. The command vehicle rode glass-smooth over the frozen roadway, with none of the jouncing that a rougher surface might bring even through the air cushion. Margritte faced Pritchard over her console, her seat a meter lower than his so that she appeared a suppliant. Her short hair was the lustrous purple-black of a grackle's throat in sunlight. Hidden illumination from the instruments brought her face to life.

"Gee, Captain," Jenne was saying at Pritchard's side, "I wish you'd a let me pick up that squarehead's rifle. I know those ground-pounders. They're just as apt as not to claim the kill credit themselves, and if I can't prove I stepped on the body they might get away with it. I remember on Paradise, me and Piet de Hagen

—he was left wing gunner, I was right—both shot at a partisan. And then damned if Central didn't decide the slope had blown herself up with a hand grenade after we'd wounded her. So *neither* of us got the credit. You'd think—"

"Lord's *blood*, sergeant," Pritchard snarled, "are you so damned proud of killing one of the poor bastards who hired us to protect them?"

Jenne said nothing. Pritchard shrank up inside, realizing what he had said and unable to take the words back. "Oh, Lord, Rob," he said without looking up, "I'm sorry. It . . . I'm shook, that's all."

After a brief silence, the blond sergeant laughed. "Never been shot in the head myself, Captain, but I can see it might shake a fellow, yeah." Jenne let the whine of the fans stand for a moment as the only further comment while he decided whether he would go on. Then he said, "Captain, for a week after I first saw action I meant to get out of the Slammers, even if I had to sweep floors on Curwin for the rest of my life. Finally I decided I'd stick it. I didn't like the . . . rules of the game, but I could learn to play by them.

"And I did. And one rule is, that you get to be as good as you can at killing the people Col. Hammer wants killed. Yeah, I'm proud about that one just now. It was a tough snap shot and I made it. I don't care why we're on Kobold or who brought us here. But I know I'm supposed to kill anybody who shoots at us, and I will."

"Well, I'm glad you did," Pritchard said evenly as he looked the sergeant in the eyes. "You

pretty well saved things from getting out of hand
by the way you reacted."

As if he had not heard his captain, Jenne went
on, "I was afraid if I stayed in the Slammers I'd
turn into an animal, like the dogs we trained
back home to kill rats in the quarries. And I was
right. But it's the way I am now, so I don't seem
to mind."

"You do care about those villagers, don't
you?" Margritte asked Pritchard unexpectedly.

The captain looked down and found her eyes
on him. They were the rich powder-blue of
chicory flowers. "You're probably the only person in the Regiment who thinks that," he said
bitterly. "Except for me. And maybe Col.
Hammer. . . ."

Margritte smiled, a quick flash and as quickly
gone. "There're rule-book soldiers in the Slammers," she said, "captains who'd never believe
Barthe was passing arms to the Auroran settle-
ments since he'd signed a contract that said he
wouldn't. You aren't that kind. And the Lord
knows Col. Hammer isn't, and he's backing you.
I've been around you too long, Danny, to believe
you like what you see the French doing."

Pritchard shrugged. His whole face was stiff
with bruises and the drugs Margritte had in-
jected to control them. If he'd locked the
helmet's chin strap, the bullet's impact would
have broken his neck even though the lead itself
did not penetrate. "No, I don't like it," the
brown-haired captain said. "It reminds me too
much of the way the Combine kept us so poor on
Dunstan that a thousand of us signed on for

birdseed to fight off-planet. Just because it *was* off-planet. And if Kobold only gets cop from the worlds who settled her, then the French skim the best of that. Sure, I'll tell the Lord I feel sorry for the Dutch here."

Pritchard held the commo tech's eyes with his own as he continued, "But it's just like Rob said, Margritte: I'll do my job, no matter who gets hurt. We can't do a thing to Barthe or the French until they step over the line in a really obvious way. That'll mean a lot of people get hurt too. But that's what I'm waiting for."

Margritte reached up and touched Pritchard's hand where it rested on his knee. "You'll do something when you can," she said quietly.

He turned his palm up so that he could grasp the woman's fingers. What if she knew he was planning an incident, not just waiting for one? "I'll do something, yeah," he said. "But it's going to be too late for an awful lot of people."

Kowie kept The Plow at cruising speed until they were actually in the yard of the command post. Then he cocked the fan shafts forward, lifting the bow and bringing the tank's mass around in a curve that killed its velocity and blasted an arc of snow against the building. Someone inside had started to unlatch the door as they heard the vehicle approach. The air spilling from the tank's skirts flung the panel against the inner wall and skidded the man within on his back.

The man was Capt. Riis, Pritchard noted without surprise. Well, the incident wouldn't make the infantry captain any angrier than the rest of the evening had made him already.

Riis had regained his feet by the time Pritchard could jump from the deck of his blower to the fan-cleared ground in front of the building. The Frisian's normally pale face was livid now with rage. He was of the same somatotype as Lt. Col. Benoit, his French counterpart in the sector: tall, thin, and proudly erect. Despite the fact that Riis was only 27, he was Pritchard's senior in grade by two years. He had kept the rank he held in Friesland's regular army when Col. Hammer recruited him. Many of the Slammers were like Riis, Frisian soldiers who had transferred for the action and pay of a fighting regiment in which their training would be appreciated.

"You cowardly filth!" the infantryman hissed as Pritchard approached. A squad in battle gear stood within the orderly room beyond Riis. He pursed his fine lips to spit.

"Hey Captain!" Rob Jenne called. Riis looked up. Pritchard turned, surprised that the big tank commander was not right on his heels. Jenne still smiled from The Plow's cupola. He waved at the officers with his left hand. His right was on the butterfly trigger of the tribarrel.

The threat, unspoken as it was, made a professional of Riis again. "Come on into my office," he muttered to the tank captain, turning his back on the armored vehicle as if it were only a part of the landscape.

The infantrymen inside parted to pass the captains. Sally Schilling was there. Her eyes were as hard as her porcelain armor as they raked over Pritchard. That didn't matter, he lied to himself tiredly.

Riis' office was at the top of the stairs, a narrow cubicle which had once been a child's bedroom. The sloping roof pressed in on the occupants, though a dormer window brightened the room during daylight. One wall was decorated with a regimental battle flag—not Hammer's rampant lion but a pattern of seven stars on a white field. It had probably come from the unit in which Riis had served on Friesland. Over the door hung another souvenir, a big-bore musket of local manufacture. Riis threw himself into the padded chair behind his desk. "Those bastards were carrying powerguns to Portela!" he snarled at Pritchard.

The tanker nodded. He was leaning with his right shoulder against the door jamb. "That's what the folks at Haacin thought," he agreed. "If they'll put in a complaint with the Bonding Authority, I'll testify to what I saw."

"Testify, *testify!*" Riis shouted. "We're not lawyers, we're soldiers! You should've seized the trucks right then and—"

"No I should *not* have, Captain!" Pritchard shouted back, holding up a mirror to Riis' anger. "Because if I had, Barthe would've complained to the Authority himself, and we'd at least've been fined. At least! The contract says the Slammers'll cooperate with the other three units in keeping peace on Kobold. Just because we suspect Barthe is violating the contract doesn't give us a right to violate it ourselves. Especially in a way any *simpleton* can see is a violation."

"If Barthe can get away with it, we can," Riis insisted, but he settled back in his chair. He was physically bigger than Pritchard, but the tanker had spent half his life with the Slammers. Years like those mark men; death is never very far behind their eyes.

"I don't think Barthe can get away with it," Pritchard lied quietly, remembering Hammer's advice on how to handle Riis and calm the Frisian without telling him the truth. Barthe's officers had been in on his plans; and one of them had talked. Any regiment might have one traitor.

The tanker lifted down the musket on the wall behind him and began turning it in his fingers. "If the Dutch settlers can prove to the Authority that Barthe's been passing out powerguns to the French," the tanker mused aloud, "well, they're responsible for half Barthe's pay, remember. It's about as bad a violation as you'll find. The Authority'll forfeit his whole bond and pay it over to whoever they decide the injured parties are. That's about three years' gross earnings for Barthe, I'd judge—he won't be able to replace it. And without a bond posted, well, he may get jobs, but they'll be the kind nobody else'd touch for the risk and the pay. His best troops'll sign on with other people. In a year or so, Barthe won't have a regiment any more."

"He's willing to take the chance," said Riis.

"Col. Hammer isn't!" Pritchard blazed back.

"You don't know that. It isn't the sort of thing the Colonel could say—"

"Say?" Pritchard shouted. He waved the

musket at Riis. Its breech was triple-strapped to take the shock of the industrial explosive it used for propellant. Clumsy and large, it was the best that could be produced on a mining colony whose home worlds had forbidden local manufacturing. "Say? I bet my life against one of these tonight that the Colonel wanted us to obey the contract. Do you have the guts to ask him flat out if he wants us to run guns to the Dutch?"

"I don't think that would be proper, Captain," said Riis coldly as he stood up again.

"Then try not to 'think it proper' to go do some bloody stupid stunt on your own—sir," Pritchard retorted. So much for good intentions. Hammer—and Pritchard—had expected Riis' support of the Dutch civilians. They had even planned on it. But the man seemed to have lost all his common sense. Pritchard laid the musket on the desk because his hands were trembling too badly to hang it back on the hooks.

"If it weren't for you, Captain," Riis said, "there's not a Slammer in this sector who'd object to our helping the only decent people on this planet the way we ought to. You've made your decision, and it sickens me. But I've made decisions too."

Pritchard went out without being dismissed. He blundered into the jamb, but he did not try to slam the door. That would have been petty, and there was nothing petty in the tanker's rage.

Blank-faced, he clumped down the stairs. His bunk was in a parlor which had its own door to the outside. Pritchard's crew was still in The Plow. There they had listened intently to his half

of the argument with Riis, transmitted by the
implant. If Pritchard had called for help, Kowie
would have sent the command vehicle through
the front wall buttoned up, with Jenne ready to
shoot if he had to, to rescue his CO. A tank looks
huge when seen close up. It is all howling steel
and iridium, with black muzzles ready to spew
death across a planet. On a battlefield, when the
sky is a thousand shrieking colors no god ever
made and the earth beneath trembles and gouts
in sudden mountains, a tank is a small world
indeed for its crew. Their loyalties are to nearer
things than an abstraction like "The Regiment."

Besides, tankers and infantrymen have never
gotten along well together.

No one was in the orderly room except two
radiomen. They kept their backs to the stairs.
Pritchard glanced at them, then unlatched his
door. The room was dark, as he had left it, but
there was a presence. Pritchard said, "Sal—" as
he stepped within and the club knocked him forward into the arms of the man waiting to catch
his body.

The first thing Pritchard thought as his mind
slipped toward oblivion was that the cloth rub-
bing his face was homespun, not the hard synthetic from which uniforms were made. The last
thing Pritchard thought was that there could
have been no civilians within the headquarters
perimeter unless the guards had allowed them;
and that Lt. Schilling was officer of the guard
tonight.

Pritchard could not be quite certain when he

regained consciousness. A heavy felt rug covered
and hid his trussed body on the floor of a clatter-
ing surface vehicle. He had no memory of being
carried to the truck, though presumably it had
been parked some distance from the command
post. Riis and his confederates would not have
been so open as to have civilians drive to the door
to take a kidnapped officer, even if Pritchard's
crew could have been expected to ignore the
breach of security.

Kidnapped. Not for later murder, or he would
already be dead instead of smothering under the
musty rug. Thick as it was, the rug was still inadequate to keep the cold from his shivering
body. The only lights Pritchard could see were
the washings of icy color from the night's
doubled shock to his skull.

That bone-deep ache reminded Pritchard of
the transceiver implanted in his mastoid. He
said in a husky whisper which he hoped would
not penetrate the rug, "Michael One to any unit,
any unit at all. Come in please, any Slammer."

Nothing. Well, no surprise. The implant had
an effective range of less than twenty meters,
enough for relaying to and from a base unit, but
unlikely to be useful in Kobold's empty
darkness. Of course, if the truck happened to be
passing one of M Company's night defensive
positions. . . . "Michael One to any unit," the
tanker repeated more urgently.

A boot slammed him in the ribs. A voice in
guttural Dutch snarled, "Shut up, you, or you
get what you gave Henrik."

So he'd been shopped to the Dutch, not that

there had been much question about it. And not that he might not have been safer in French hands, the way everybody on this cursed planet thought he was a traitor to his real employers. Well, it wasn't fair; but Danny Pritchard had grown up a farmer, and no farmer is ever tricked into believing that life is fair.

The truck finally jolted to a stop. Gloved hands jerked the cover from Pritchard's eyes. He was not surprised to recognise the concrete angles of Haacin as men passed him hand to hand into a cellar. The attempt to hijack Barthe's powerguns had been an accident, an opportunity seized; but the crew which had kidnapped Pritchard must have been in position before the call from S-39 had intervened.

"Is this wise?" Pritchard heard someone demand from the background. "If they begin searching, surely they'll begin in Haacin."

The two men at the bottom of the cellar stairs took Pritchard's shoulders and ankles to carry him to a spring cot. It had no mattress. The man at his feet called, "There won't be a search, they don't have enough men. Besides, the beasts'll be blamed—as they should be for so many things. If Pauli won't let us kill the turncoat, then we'll all have to stand the extra risk of him living."

"You talk too much," Mayor van Oosten muttered as he dropped Pritchard's shoulders on the bunk. Many civilians had followed the captive into the cellar. The last of them swung the door closed. It lay almost horizontal to the ground. When it slammed, dust sprang from the ceiling. Someone switched on a dim incandes-

cent light. The scores of men and women in the
storage room were as hard and fell as the bare
walls. There were three windows at street level,
high on the wall. Slotted shutters blocked most
of their dusty glass.

"Get some heat in this hole or you may as well
cut my throat," Pritchard grumbled.

A woman with a musket cursed and spat in his
face. The man behind her took her arm before
the gunbutt could smear the spittle. Almost in
apology, the man said to Pritchard, "It was her
husband you killed."

"You're being kept out of the way," said a
husky man—Kruse, the hothead from the hijack
scene. His facial hair was pale and long, merging
indistinguishably with the silky fringe of his
parka. Like most of the others in the cellar, he
carried a musket. "Without your meddling,
there'll be a chance for us to . . . get ready to
protect ourselves, after the tanks leave and the
beasts come to finish us with their powerguns."

"Does Riis think I won't talk when this is
over?" Pritchard asked.

"I told you—" one of the men shouted at van
Oosten. The heavy-set mayor silenced him with
a tap on the chest and a bellowed, "Quiet!" The
rising babble hushed long enough for van
Oosten to say, "Captain, you will be released in
a very few days. If you—cause trouble, then, it
will only be an embarrassment to yourself. Even
if your Colonel believes you were doing right, he
won't be the one to bring to light a violation
which was committed with—so you will claim—
the connivance of his own officers."

The mayor paused to clear his throat and glower around the room. "Though in fact we had no help from any of your fellows, either in seizing you or in arming ourselves for our own protection."

"Are you all blind?" Pritchard demanded. He struggled with his elbows and back to raise himself against the wall. "Do you think a few lies will cover it all up? The only ships that've touched on Kobold in three months are the ones supplying us and the other mercs. Barthe maybe's smuggled in enough guns in cans of lube oil and the like to arm some civilians. He won't be able to keep that a secret, but maybe he can keep the Authority from proving who's responsible.

"That's with three months and pre-planning. If Riis tries to do anything on his own, that many of his own men are going to be short sidearms—they're all issued by serial number, Lord take it!—and a blind Mongoloid could get enough proof to sink the Regiment."

"You think we don't understand," said Kruse in a quiet voice. He transferred his musket to his left hand, then slapped Pritchard across the side of the head. "We understand very well," the civilian said. "All the mercenaries will leave in a few days or weeks. If the French have powerguns and we do not, they will kill us, our wives, our children. . . . There's a hundred and fifty villages on Kobold like this one, Dutch, and as many French ones scattered between. It was bad before, with no one but the beasts allowed any real say in the government; but now if they win,

there'll be French villages and French mines—
and slave pens. Forever."

"You think a few guns'll save you?" Pritchard
asked. Kruse's blow left no visible mark in the
tanker's livid flesh, though a better judge than
Kruse might have noted that Pritchard's eyes
were as hard as his voice was mild.

"They'll help us save ourselves when the time
comes," Kruse retorted.

"If you'd gotten powerguns from French civilians instead of the mercs directly, you might
have been all right," the captain said. He was
coldly aware that the lie he was telling was more
likely to be believed in this situation than it
would have been in any setting he might deliberately have contrived. There had to be an incident, the French civilians *had* to think they
were safe in using their illegal weapons. . . .
"The Portelans, say, couldn't admit to having
guns to lose. But anything you take from mercs
—us or Barthe, it doesn't matter—we'll take
back the hard way. You don't know what you're
buying into."

Kruse's face did not change, but his fist drew
back for another blow. The mayor caught the
younger man's arm and snapped, "Franz, we're
here to show him that it's not a few of us, it's
every family in the village behind . . . our holding him." Van Oosten nodded around the room.
"More of us than your colonel could dream of
trying to punish," he added naively to Pritchard.
Then he flashed back at Kruse, "If you act like
a fool, he'll want revenge anyway."

"You may never believe this," Pritchard interjected wearily, "but I just want to do my job. If you let me go now, it—may be easier in the long run."

"Fool," Kruse spat and turned his back on the tanker.

A trap door opened in the ceiling, spilling more light into the cellar. "Pauli!" a woman shouted down the opening, "Hals is on the radio. There's tanks coming down the road, just like before!"

"The Lord's wounds!" van Oosten gasped. "We must—"

"They can't know!" Kruse insisted. "But we've got to get everybody out of here and back to their own houses. Everybody but me and him —" a nod at Pritchard—"and this." The musket lowered so that its round black eye pointed straight into the bound man's face.

"No, by the side door!" van Oosten called to the press of conspirators clumping up toward the street. "Don't run right out in front of them." Cursing and jostling, the villagers climbed the ladder to the ground floor, there presumably to exit on an alley.

Able only to twist his head and legs, Pritchard watched Kruse and the trembling muzzle of his weapon. The village must have watchmen with radios at either approach through the forests. If Hals was atop the heap of mine tailings—where Pritchard would have placed his outpost if he were in charge, certainly—then he'd gotten a nasty surprise when the main gun splashed the rocks with Hell. The captain grinned at the thought. Kruse misunderstood and snarled, "If they *are* coming for you, you're dead, you treacherous bastard!" To the backs of his departing fellows, the young Dutchman called, "Turn out the light here, but leave the trap door open. That won't show on the street, but it'll give me enough light to shoot by."

The tanks weren't coming for him, Pritchard knew, because they couldn't have any idea where he was. Perhaps his disappearance had stirred up some patrolling, for want of more directed action; perhaps a platoon was just changing ground because of its commander's whim. Pritchard had encouraged random motion. Tanks that freeze in one place are sitting targets, albeit hard ones. But whatever the reason tanks were approaching Haacin, if they whined by in the street outside they would be well within range of his implanted transmitter.

The big blowers were audible now, nearing with an arrogant lack of haste as if bears headed for a beehive. They were moving at about 30 kph, more slowly than Pritchard would have expected even for a contact patrol. From the sound there were four or more of them, smooth and gray and deadly.

"Kruse, I'm serious," the Slammer captain said. Light from the trap door back-lit the civilian into a hulking beast with a musket. "If you—"

"Shut up!" Kruse snarled, prodding his prisoner's bruised forehead with the gun muzzle. "One more word, any word, and—"

Kruse's right hand was so tense and white

that the musket might fire even without his deliberate intent.

The first of the tanks slid by outside. Its cushion of air was so dense that the ground trembled even though none of the blower's 170 tonnes was in direct contact with it. Squeezed between the pavement and the steel curtain of the plenum chamber, the air spurted sideways and rattled the cellar windows. The rattling was inaudible against the howling of the fans themselves, but the trembling shutters chopped facets in the play of the tank's running lights. Kruse's face and the far wall flickered in blotched abstraction.

The tank moved on without pausing. Pritchard had not tried to summon it.

"That power," Kruse was mumbling to himself, "that should be for us to use to sweep the beasts—" The rest of his words were lost in the growing wail of the second tank in the column.

Pritchard tensed within. Even if a passing tank picked up his implant's transmission, its crew would probably ignore the message. Unless Pritchard identified himself, the tankers would assume it was babbling thrown by the ionosphere. And if he did identify himself, Kruse—

Kruse thrust his musket against Pritchard's skull again, banging the tanker's head back against the cellar wall. The Dutchman's voice was lost in the blower's howling, but his blue-lit lips clearly were repeating, "One word. . . ."

The tank moved on down the highway toward Portela.

". . . and maybe I'll shoot you anyway," Kruse was saying. "That's the way to serve traitors, isn't it? *Mercenary!*"

The third blower was approaching. Its note seemed slightly different, though that might be the aftereffect of the preceding vehicles' echoing din. Pritchard was cold all the way to his heart, because in a moment he was going to call for help. He knew that Kruse would shoot him, knew also that he would rather die now than live after hope had come so near but passed on, passed on. . . .

The third tank smashed through the wall of the house.

The Plow's skirts were not a bulldozer blade, but they were thick steel and backed with the mass of a 150 tonne command tank. The slag wall repowdered at the impact. Ceiling joists buckled into pretzel shape and ripped the cellar open to the floor above. Kruse flung his musket up and fired through the cascading rubble. The boom and red flash were lost in the chaos, but the blue-green fire stabbing back across the cellar laid the Dutchman on his back with his parka aflame. Pritchard rolled to the floor at the first shock. He thrust himself with corded legs and arms back under the feeble protection of the bunk. When the sound of falling objects had died away, the captain slitted his eyelids against the rock dust and risked a look upward.

The collision had torn a gap ten feet long in the house wall, crushing it from street level to the beams supporting the second story. The tank blocked the hole with its gray bulk. Fresh scars

brightened the patina of corrosion etched onto
its skirts by the atmospheres of a dozen planets.
Through the buckled flooring and the dust
whipped into arabesques by the idling fans,
Pritchard glimpsed a slight figure clinging left-
handed to the turret. Her right hand still threatened the wreckage with a submachinegun.
Carpeting burned on the floor above, ignited by
the burst that killed Kruse. Somewhere a woman
was screaming in Dutch.

"Margritte!" Pritchard shouted. "Margritte!
Down here!"

The helmeted woman swung up her face
shield and tried to pierce the cellar gloom with
her unaided eyes. The tank-battered opening
had sufficed for the exchange of shots, but the
tangle of structural members and splintered
flooring was too tight to pass a man—or even a
small woman. Sooty flames were beginning to
shroud the gap. Margritte jumped to the ground
and struggled for a moment before she was able
to heave open the door. The Plow's turret swung
to cover her, though neither the main gun nor
the tribarrel in the cupola could depress enough
to rake the cellar. Margritte ran down the steps
to Pritchard. Coughing in the rock dust, he
rolled out over the rubble to meet her. Much of
the smashed sidewall had collapsed onto the
street when the tank backed after the initial impact. Still, the crumpled beams of the ground
floor sagged further with the additional weight of
the slag on them. Head-sized pieces had
splanged on the cot above Pritchard.

Margritte switched the submachinegun to her

left hand and began using a clasp knife on her captain's bonds. The cord with which he was tied bit momentarily deeper at the blade's pressure.

Pritchard winced, then began flexing his freed hands. "You know, Margi," he said, "I don't think I've ever seen you with a gun before."

The commo tech's face hardened as if the polarized helmet shield had slipped down over it again. "You hadn't," she said. The ankle bindings parted and she stood, the dust graying her helmet and her foam-filled coveralls. "Captain, Kowie had to drive and we needed Rob in the cupola at the gun. That left me to—do anything else that had to be done. I did what had to be done."

Pritchard tried to stand, using the technician as a post on which to draw himself upright. Margritte looked frail, but with her legs braced she stood like a rock. Her arm around Pritchard's back was as firm as a man's.

"You didn't ask Capt. Riis for help, I guess," Pritchard said, pain making his breath catch. The line tanks had two-man crews with no one to spare for outrider, of course.

"We didn't report you missing," Margritte said, "even to First Platoon. They just went along like before, thinking you were in The Plow giving orders." Together, captain and technician shuffled across the floor to the stairs. As they passed Kruse's body, Margritte muttered cryptically, "That's four."

Pritchard assumed the tremors beginning to shake the woman's body were from physical

strain. He took as much weight off her as he
could and found his numbed feet were beginning
to function reasonably well. He would never
have been able to board The Plow without Sgt.
Jenne's grip on his arm, however.

The battered officer settled in the turret with
a groan of comfort. The seat cradled his body
with gentle firmness, and the warm air blown
across him was just the near side of heaven.

"Captain," Jenne said, "what d'we do about
the slopes who grabbed you? Shall we call in an
interrogation team and—"

"We don't do anything," Pritchard interrupted. "We just pretend none of this happened
and head back to. . . ." He paused. His flesh
wavered both hot and cold as Margritte sprayed
his ankles with some of the apparatus from the
medical kit. "Say, how did you find me, anyway?"

"We shut off coverage when you—went into
your room," Jenne said, seeing that the commo
tech herself did not intend to speak. He meant,
Pritchard knew, they had shut off the sound
when their captain had said, "Sal." None of the
three of them were looking either of the other
two in the eyes. "After a bit, though, Margi noticed the carrier line from your implant had
dropped off her oscilloscope. I checked your
room, didn't find you. Didn't see much point
talking it over with the remfs on duty, either.

"So we got satellite recce and found two
trucks'd left the area since we got back. One was
Riis', and the other was a civvie junker before
that. It'd been parked in the woods out of sight,

half a kay up the road from the buildings. Both
trucks unloaded in Haacin. We couldn't tell
which load was you, but Margi said if we got
close, she'd home on your carrier even though
you weren't calling us on the implant. Some girl
we got here, hey?''

Pritchard bent forward and squeezed the commo tech's shoulder. She did not look up, but she
smiled. "Yeah, always knew she was something," he agreed, "but I don't think I realized
quite what a person she was until just now."

Margritte lifted her smile. "Rob ordered First
Platoon to fall in with us," she said. "He set up
the whole rescue." Her fine-fingered hands
caressed Pritchard's calves.

But there was other business in Haacin, now.
Riis had been quicker to act than Pritchard had
hoped. He asked, "You say one of the infantry's
trucks took a load here a little bit ago?"

"Yeah, you want the off-print?" Jenne agreed,
searching for the flimsy copy of the satellite picture. "What the Hell would they be doing, anyhow?"

"I got a suspicion," his captain said grimly,
"and I suppose it's one we've got to check out."

"Michael First-Three to Michael One," the
radio broke in. "Vehicles approaching from the
east on the hardball."

"Michael One to Michael First," Pritchard
said, letting the search for contraband arms wait
for this new development. "Reverse and form a
line abreast beyond the village. Twenty meter
intervals. The Plow'll take the road." More
weapons from Riis? More of Barthe's troops

when half his sector command was already in
Portela? Pritchard touched switches beneath the
vision blocks as Kowie slid the tank into position. He split the screen between satellite coverage and a ground-level view at top magnification. Six vehicles, combat cars, coming fast.
Pritchard swore. Friendly, because only the
Slammers had armored vehicles on Kobold, not
that cars were a threat to tanks anyway. But no
combat cars were assigned to this sector; and the
unexpected is always bad news to a company
commander juggling too many variables already.

"Platoon nearing Tango Sigma four-two,
three-two, please identify to Michael One,"
Pritchard requested, giving Haacin's map coordinates.

Margritte turned up the volume of the main
radio while she continued to bandage the
captain's rope cuts. The set crackled, "Michael
One, this is Alpha One and Alpha First. Stand
by."

"God's bleeding cunt!" Rob Jenne swore under his breath. Pritchard was nodding in equal
agitation. Alpha was the Regiment's special
duty company. Its four combat car platoons
were Col. Hammer's bodyguards and police.
The troopers of A Company were nicknamed the
White Mice, and they were viewed askance even
by the Slammers of other companies—men who
prided themselves on being harder than any other combat force in the galaxy. The White Mice
in turn feared their commander, Maj. Joachim
Steuben; and if that slightly-built killer feared

anyone, it was the man who was probably trav-
elling with him this night. Pritchard sighed and
asked the question. "Alpha One, this is Michael
One. Are you flying a pennant, sir?"

"Affirmative, Michael One."

Well, he'd figured Col. Hammer was along as
soon as he heard what the unit was. What the
Old Man was doing here was another question,
and one whose answer Pritchard did not look
forward to learning.

The combat cars glided to a halt under the
guns of their bigger brethren. The tremble of
their fans gave the appearance of heat ripples despite the snow. From his higher vantage point,
Pritchard watched the second car slide out of
line and fall alongside The Plow. The men at the
nose and right wing guns were both short,
garbed in nondescript battle gear. They differed
from the other troopers only in that their helmet
shields were raised and that the faces visible beneath were older than those of most Slammers:
Col. Alois Hammer and his hatchetman.

"No need for radio, Captain," Hammer called
in a husky voice. "What are you doing here?"

Pritchard's tongue quivered between the truth
and a lie. His crew had been covering for him,
and he wasn't about to leave them holding the
bag. All the breaches of regulations they had
committed were for their captain's sake. "Sir, I
brought First Platoon back to Haacin to check
whether any of the powerguns they'd hijacked
from Barthe were still in civvie hands."
Pritchard could feel eyes behind the cracked
shutters of every east-facing window in the village.

"And have you completed your check?" the Colonel pressed, his voice mild but his eyes as hard as those of Maj. Steuben beside him; as hard as the iridium plates of the gun shields.

Pritchard swallowed. He owed nothing to Capt. Riis, but the young fool *was* his superior— and at least he hadn't wanted the Dutch to kill Pritchard. He wouldn't put Riis' ass in the bucket if there were neutral ways to explain the contraband. Besides, they were going to need Riis and his Dutch contacts for the rest of the plan. "Sir, when you approached I was about to search a building where I suspect some illegal weapons are stored."

"And instead you'll provide back-up for the Major here," said Hammer, the false humor gone from his face. His words rattled like shrapnel. "He'll retrieve the twenty-four powerguns which Capt. Riis saw fit to turn over to civilians tonight. If Joachim hadn't chanced, *chanced* onto that requisition . . ." Hammer's left glove shuddered with the strength of his grip on the forward tribarrel. Then the Colonel lowered his eyes and voice, adding, "The quartermaster who filled a requisition for twenty-four pistols from Central Supply is in the infantry again tonight. And Capt. Riis is no longer with the Regiment."

Steuben tittered, loose despite the tension of everyone around him. The cold was bitter, but Joachim's right hand was bare. With it he traced the baroque intaglios of his holstered pistol. "Mr. Riis is lucky to be alive," the slight Newlander said pleasantly. "Luckier than some would have wished. But Colonel, I think we'd best go pick up the merchandise before anybody nerves themself to use it on us."

Hammer nodded, calm again. "Interfile your blowers with ours, Captain," he ordered. "Your panzers watch street level while the cars take care of upper floors and roofs."

Pritchard saluted and slid down into the tank, relaying the order to the rest of his platoon. Kowie blipped The Plow's throttles, swinging the turreted mass in its own length and sending it back into the village behind the lead combat car. The tank felt light as a dancer, despite the constricting sidestreet Kowie followed the car into. Pritchard scanned the full circuit of the vision blocks. Nothing save the wind and armored vehicles moved in Haacin. When Steuben had learned a line company was requisitioning two dozen extra sidearms, the Major had made the same deductions as Pritchard had and had inspected the same satellite tape of a truck unloading. Either Riis was insane or he really thought Col. Hammer was willing to throw away his life's work to arm a village—inadequately. Lord and Martyrs! Riis would have *had* to be insane to believe that!

Their objective was a nondescript two-story building separated from its neighbors by narrow alleys. Hammer directed the four rearmost blowers down a parallel street to block the rear. The searchlights of the vehicles chilled the flat concrete and glared back from the windows of the building. A battered surface truck was parked in the street outside. It was empty. Nothing stirred in the house.

Hammer and Steuben dismounted without haste. The major's helmet was slaved to a loudspeaker in the car. The speaker boomed, "Everyone out of the building. You have thirty seconds. Anyone found inside after that'll be shot. Thirty seconds!"

Though the residents had not shown themselves earlier, the way they boiled out of the doors proved they had expected the summons. All told there were eleven of them. From the front door came a well-dressed man and woman with their three children: a sexless infant carried by its mother in a zippered cocoon; a girl of eight with her hood down and her hair coiled in braids about her forehead; and a twelve-year-old boy who looked nearly as husky as his father. Outside staircases disgorged an aged couple on the one hand and four tough-looking men on the other.

Pritchard looked at his blower chief. The sergeant's right hand was near the gun switch and he mumbled an old ballad under his breath. Chest tightening, Pritchard climbed out of his hatch. He jumped to the ground and paced quietly over to Hammer and his aide.

"There's twenty-four pistols in this building," Joachim's amplified voice roared, "or at least you people know where they are. I want somebody to save trouble and tell me."

The civilians tensed. The mother half-turned to swing her body between her baby and the officers.

Joachim's pistol was in his hand, though Pritchard had not seen him draw it. "Nobody to speak?" Joachim queried. He shot the eight-year-old in the right knee. The spray of blood was momentary as the flesh exploded. The girl's mouth pursed as her buckling leg dropped her face-down in the street. The pain would come later. Her parents screamed, the father falling to his knees to snatch up the child as the mother pressed her forehead against the door jamb in blind panic.

Pritchard shouted, "You son of a bitch!" and clawed for his own sidearm. Steuben turned with the precision of a turret lathe. His pistol's muzzle was a white-hot ring from its previous discharge. Pritchard knew only that and the fact that his own weapon was not clear of its holster. Then he realized that Col. Hammer was shouting, "*No!*" and that his open hand had rocked Joachim's head back.

Joachim's face went pale except for the hand-print burning on his cheek. His eyes were empty. After a moment, he holstered his weapon and turned back to the civilians. "Now, who'll tell us where the guns are?" he asked in a voice like breaking glassware.

The tear-blind woman, still holding her infant, gurgled, "Here! In the basement!" as she threw open the door. Two troopers followed her within at a nod from Hammer. The father was trying to close the girl's wounded leg with his hands, but his palms were not broad enough.

Pritchard vomited on the snowy street.

Margritte was out of the tank with a medikit in her hand. She flicked the civilian's hands aside and began freezing the wound with a

spray. The front door banged open again. The
two White Mice were back with their submachineguns slung under their arms and a
heavy steel weapons-chest between them. Hammer nodded and walked to them.

"You could have brought in an interrogation
team!" Pritchard shouted at the backs of his superiors. "You don't shoot children!"

"Machine interrogation takes time, Captain,"
Steuben said mildly. He did not turn to acknowl-
edge the tanker. "This was just as effective."

"That's a little girl!" Pritchard insisted with
his hands clenched. The child was beginning to
cry, though the local anesthetic in the skin-sealer
had probably blocked the physical pain. The
psychic shock of a body that would soon end at
the right knee would be worse, though. The
child was old enough to know that no local doc-
tor could save the limb. "This isn't something
that human beings *do*!"

"Captain," Steuben said, "they're lucky I
haven't shot all of them."

Hammer closed the arms chest. "We've got
what we came for," he said. "Let's go."

"Stealing guns from my Colonel," the Newlander continued as if Hammer had not spoken.
The handprint had faded to a dull blotch. "I really ought to—"

"Joachim, shut it off!" Hammer shouted.
"We're going to talk about what happened tonight, you and I. I'd rather do it when we were
alone—but I'll tell you now if I have to. Or in
front of a court martial."

Steuben squeezed his forehead with the fingers of his left hand. He said nothing.

"Let's go," the Colonel repeated.

Pritchard caught Hammer's arm. "Take the kid back to Central's medics," he demanded.

Hammer blinked. "I should have thought of that," he said simply. "Some times I lose track of . . . things that aren't going to shoot at me. But we don't need this sort of reputation."

"I don't care cop for public relations," Pritchard snapped. "Just save that little girl's leg."

Steuben reached for the child, now lying limp. Margritte had used a shot of general anesthetic. The girl's father went wild-eyed and swung at Joachim from his crouch. Margritte jabbed with the injector from behind the civilian. He gasped as the drug took hold, then sagged as if his bones had dissolved. Steuben picked up the girl.

Hammer vaulted aboard the combat car and took the child from his subordinate's arms. Cutting himself into the loudspeaker system, the stocky colonel thundered to the street, "Listen you people. If you take guns from mercs—either Barthe's men or my own—we'll grind you to dust. Take 'em from civilians if you think you can. You may have a chance, then. If you rob mercs, you just get a chance to die."

Hammer nodded to the civilians, nodded again to the brooding buildings to either side. He gave an unheard command to his driver. The combat cars began to rev their fans.

Pritchard gave Margritte a hand up and followed her. "Michael One to Michael First," he said. "Head back with Alpha First."

*   *   *

Pritchard rode inside the turret after they left Haacin, glad for once of the armor and the cabin lights. In the writhing tree-limbs he had seen the Dutch mother's face as the shot maimed her daughter.

Margritte passed only one call to her commander. It came shortly after the combat cars had separated to return to their base camp near Midi, the planetary capital. The Colonel's voice was as smooth as it ever got. It held no hint of the rage which had blazed out in Haacin. "Capt. Pritchard," Hammer said, "I've transferred command of Sigma Company to the leader of its First Platoon. The sector, of course, is in your hands now. I expect you to carry out your duties with the ability you've already shown."

"Michael One to Regiment," Pritchard replied curtly. "Acknowledged."

Kowie drew up in front of the command post without the furious caracole which had marked their most recent approach. Pritchard slid his hatch open. His crewmen did not move. "I've got to worry about being sector chief for a while," he said, "but you three can rack out in the barracks now. You've put in a full tour in my book."

"Think I'll sleep here," Rob said. He touched a stud, rotating his seat into a couch alongside the receiver and loading tube of the main gun.

Pritchard frowned. "Margritte?" he asked.

She shrugged. "No, I'll stay by my set for a while." Her eyes were blue and calm.

On the intercom, Kowie chimed in with,

"Yeah, you worry about the sector, we'll worry about ourselves. Say, don't you think a tank platoon'd be better for base security than these pongoes?"

"Shut up, Kowie," Jenne snapped. The blond Burlager glanced at his captain. "Everything'll be fine, so long as we're here," he said from one elbow. He patted the breech of the 200 mm gun.

Pritchard shrugged and climbed out into the cold night. He heard the hatch grind shut behind him.

Until Pritchard walked in the door of the building, it had not occurred to him that Riis' replacement was Sally Schilling. The words "First Platoon leader" had not been a name to the tanker, not in the midst of the furor of his mind. The little blonde glanced up at Pritchard from the map display she was studying. She spat cracklingly on the electric stove and faced around again. Her aide, the big corporal, blinked in some embarrassment. None of the headquarters staff spoke.

"I need the display console from my room," Pritchard said to the corporal.

The infantryman nodded and got up. Before he had taken three steps, Lt. Schilling's voice cracked like pressure-heaved ice, "Cpl. Webbert!"

"Sir?" The big man's face went tight as he found himself a pawn in a game whose stakes went beyond his interest.

"Go get the display console for our new commander. It's in his room."

Licking his lips with relief, the corporal

obeyed. He carried the heavy four-legged console back without effort.

Sally was making it easier for him, Pritchard thought. But how he wished that Riis hadn't made so complete a fool of himself that he had to be removed. Using Riis to set up a double massacre would have been a lot easier to justify when Danny awoke in the middle of the night and found himself remembering. . .

Pritchard positioned the console so that he sat with his back to the heater. It separated him from Schilling. The top of the instrument was a slanted, 40 cm screen which glowed when Pritchard switched it on. "Sector Two display," he directed. In response to his words the screen sharpened into a relief map. "Population centers," he said. They flashed on as well, several dozen of them ranging from a few hundred souls to the several thousand of Haacin and Dimo. Portela, the largest Francophone settlement west of the Aillet, was about twenty kilometers west of Haacin.

And there were now French mercenaries on both sides of that division line. Sally had turned from her own console and stood up to see what Pritchard was doing. The tanker said, "All mercenary positions, confirmed and calculated."

The board spangled itself with red and green symbols, each of them marked in small letters with a unit designation. The reconnaissance satellites gave unit strengths very accurately, and computer analysis of radio traffic could generally name the forces. In the eastern half of the sector, Lt. Col. Benoit had spread out one battalion in platoon-strength billets. The guardposts were close enough to most points to put down trouble immediately. A full company near Dimo guarded the headquarters and two batteries of rocket howitzers.

The remaining battalion in the sector, Benoit's own, was concentrated in positions blasted into the rocky highlands ten kays west of Portela. It was not a deployment that would allow the mercs to effectively police the west half of the sector, but it was a very good defensive arrangement. The forest that covered the center of the sector was ideal for hit-and-run sniping by small units of infantry. The tree boles were too densely woven for tanks to plow through them. Because the forest was so flammable at this season, however, it would be equally dangerous to ambushers. Benoit was wise to concentrate in the barren high-ground.

Besides the highlands, the fields cleared around every settlement were the only safe locations for a modern firefight. The fields, and the broad swathes cleared for roads through the forest. . . .

"Incoming traffic for Sector Chief," announced a radioman. "It's from the skepsel colonel, sir." He threw his words into the air, afraid to direct them at either of the officers in the orderly room.

"Voice only, or is there visual?" Pritchard asked. Schilling held her silence.

"Visual component, sir."

"Patch him through to my console," the tanker decided. "And son—watch your language. Otherwise, you say 'beast' when you shouldn't.''

The map blurred from the display screen and was replaced by the hawk features of Lt. Col. Benoit. A pick-up on the screen's surface threw Pritchard's own image onto Benoit's similar console.

The Frenchman blinked. "Capt. Pritchard? I'm very pleased to see you, but my words must be with Capt. Riis directly. Could you wake him?''

"There've been some changes,'' the tanker said. In the back of his mind, he wondered what had happened to Riis. Pulled back under arrest, probably. "I'm in charge of Sector Two, now. Co-charge with you, that is.''

Benoit's face steadied as he absorbed the information without betraying an opinion about it. Then he beamed like a feasting wolf and said, "Congratulations, Captain. Some day you and I will have to discuss the . . . events of the past few days. But what I was calling about is far less pleasant, I'm afraid.''

Benoit's image wavered on the screen as he paused. Pritchard touched his tongue to the corner of his mouth. "Go ahead, Colonel,'' he said. "I've gotten enough bad news today that a little more won't signify.''

Benoit quirked his brow in what might or might not have been humor. "When we were proceeding to Portela,'' he said, "some of my troops mistook the situation and set up passive tank interdiction points. Mines, all over the sector. They're booby-trapped, of course. The only safe way to remove them is for the troops responsible to do it. They will of course be punished later."

Pritchard chuckled. "How long do you estimate it'll take to clear the roads, Colonel?" he asked.

The Frenchman spread his hands, palms up. "Weeks, perhaps. It's much harder to clear mines safely than to lay them, of course."

"But there wouldn't be anything between *here* and Haacin, would there?" the tanker prodded. It was all happening just as Hammer's informant had said Barthe planned it. First, hem the tanks in with nets of forest and minefields; then, break the most important Dutch stronghold while your mercs were still around to back you up. . . . "The spur road to our HQ here wasn't on your route; and besides, we just drove tanks over it a few minutes ago."

Behind Pritchard, Sally Schilling was cursing in a sharp, carrying voice. Benoit could probably hear her, but the colonel kept his voice as smooth as milk as he said, "Actually, I'm afraid there *is* a field—gas, shaped charges, and glass-shard antipersonnel mines—somewhere on that road, yes. Fortunately, the field was signal activated. It wasn't primed until after you had passed through. I assure you, Capt. Pritchard, that all the roads west of the Aillet may be too dangerous to traverse until I have cleared them. I warn you both as a friend and so that we will not be charged with damage to any of your vehicles— and men. You have been fully warned of the danger; anything that happens now is your responsibility."

Pritchard leaned back in the console's integral seat, chuckling again. "You know, Colonel," the tank captain said, "I'm not sure that the Bonding Authority wouldn't find those mines were a hostile act justifying our retaliation." Benoit stiffened, more an internal hardness than anything that showed in his muscles. Pritchard continued to speak through a smile. "We won't, of course. Mistakes happen. But one thing, Col. Benoit—"

The Frenchman nodded, waiting for the edge to bite. He knew as well as Pritchard did that, at best, if there were an Authority investigation, Barthe would have to throw a scapegoat out. A high-ranking scapegoat.

"Mistakes happen," Pritchard repeated, "but they can't be allowed to happen twice. You've got my permission to send out a ten-man team by daylight—only by daylight—to clear the road from Portela to Bever. That'll give you a route back to your side of the sector. If any other troops leave their present position, for any reason, I'll treat it as an attack."

"Captain, this demarcation within the sector was not a part of the contract—"

"It was at the demand of Col. Barthe," Pritchard snapped, "and agreed to by the demonstrable practice of both regiments over the past three months." Hammer had briefed Pritchard very carefully on the words to use here, to be recorded for the benefit of the Bonding Authority. "You've heard the terms, Colonel. You can either take them or we'll put the whole thing—the minefields and some other matters that've come up recently—before the Authority right now. Your choice."

Benoit stared at Pritchard, apparently calm but tugging at his upper lip with thumb and forefinger. "I think you are unwise, Captain, in taking full responsibility for an area in which your tanks cannot move; but that is your affair, of course. I will obey your mandate. We should have the Portela-Haacin segment cleared by evening; tomorrow we'll proceed to Bever. Good day."

The screen segued back to the map display. Pritchard stood up. A spare helmet rested beside one of the radiomen. The tank captain donned it —he had forgotten to requisition a replacement from stores—and said, "Michael One to all Michael units." He paused for the acknowledgment lights from his four platoons and the command vehicle. Then, "Hold your present positions. Don't attempt to move by road, any road, until further notice. The roads have been mined. There are probably safe areas, and we'll get you a map of them as soon as Command Central works it up. For the time being, just stay where you are. Michael One, out."

"Are you really going to take that?" Lt. Schilling demanded in a low, harsh voice.

"Pass the same orders to your troops, Sally," Pritchard said. "I know they can move through the woods where my tanks can't, but I don't want any friendlies in the forest right now either." To the intelligence sergeant on watch, Pritchard added, "Samuels, get Central to run a plot of all activity by any of Benoit's men. That won't tell us where they've laid mines, but it'll let us know where they can't have."

"What happens if the bleeding skepsels ignore you?" Sally blazed. "You've bloody taught them to ignore you, haven't you? Knuckling under every time somebody whispers 'contract'? You can't move a tank to stop them if they do leave their base, and *I've* got 198 effectives. A battalion'd laugh at me, *laugh!*"

Schilling's arms were akimbo, her face as pale with rage as the snow outside. Speaking with deliberate calm, Pritchard said, "I'll call in artillery if I need to. Benoit only brought two calliopes with him, and they can't stop all the shells from three firebases at the same time. The road between his position and Portela's just a snake-track cut between rocks. A couple firecracker rounds going off above infantry strung out there—Via, it'll be a butcher shop."

Schilling's eyes brightened. "Then for tonight, the sector's just like it was before we came," she thought out loud. "Well, I suppose you know best," she added in false agreement, with false nonchalance. "I'm going back to the barracks. I'll brief First Platoon in person and radio the others from there. Come along, Webbert."

The corporal slammed the door behind himself and his lieutenant. The gust of air that licked about the walls was cold, but Pritchard was already shivering at what he had just done to a woman he loved.

It was daylight by now, and the frosted windows turned to flame in the ruddy sun. Speaking to no one but his console's memory, Pritchard began to plot tracks from each tank platoon. He used a topographic display, ignoring the existence of the impenetrable forest which covered the ground.

Margritte's resonant voice twanged in the implant, "Captain, would you come to the blower for half a sec?"

"On the way," Pritchard said, shrugging into his coat. The orderly room staff glanced up at him.

Margritte poked her head out of the side hatch. Pritchard climbed onto the deck to avoid some of the generator whine. The skirts sang even when the fans were cut off completely. Rob Jenne, curious but at ease, was visible at his battle station beyond the commo tech. "Sir," Margritte said, "we've been picking up signals from —there." The blue-eyed woman thumbed briefly at the infantry barracks without letting her pupils follow the gesture.

Pritchard nodded. "Lt. Schilling's passing on my orders to her company."

"Danny, the transmission's in code, and it's not a code of ours." Margritte hesitated, then touched the back of the officer's gloved left hand. "There's answering signals, too. I can't triangulate without moving the blower, of course, but the source is in line with the tailings pile at Haacin."

It was what he had planned, after all. Someone the villagers could trust had to get word of the situation to them. Otherwise they wouldn't draw the Portelans and their mercenary backers into a fatal mistake. Hard luck for the villagers who were acting as bait, but very good luck for every other Dutchman on Kobold. . . . Pritchard

had no reason to feel anything but relief that it
had happened. He tried to relax the muscles
which were crushing all the breath out of his
lungs. Margritte's fingers closed over his hand
and squeezed it.

"Ignore the signals," the captain said at last.
"We've known all along they were talking to the
civilians, haven't we?" Neither of his crewmen
spoke. Pritchard's eyes closed tightly. He said,
"We've known for months, Hammer and I, every
damned thing that Barthe's been plotting with
the skepsels. They want a chance to break
Haacin now, while they're around to cover for
the Portelans. We'll give them their chance and
ram it up their ass crosswise. The Old Man
hasn't spread the word for fear the story'd get
out, the same way Barthe's plans did. We're all
mercenaries, after all. But I want you three to
know. And I'll be glad when the only thing I
have to worry about is the direction the shots are
coming from."

Abruptly, the captain dropped back to the
ground. "Get some sleep," he called. "I'll be
needing you sharp tonight."

Back at his console, Pritchard resumed plotting courses and distances. After he figured each
line, he called in a series of map coordinates to
Command Central. He knew his radio traffic
was being monitored and probably unscrambled
by Barthe's intelligence staff; knew also that
even if he had read the coordinates out in clear,
the French would have assumed it was a code.
The locations made no sense unless one knew

they were ground zero for incendiary shells.

As Pritchard worked, he kept close watch on the French battalions. Benoit's own troops held their position, as Pritchard had ordered. They used the time to dig in. At first they had blasted slit trenches in the rock. Now they dug covered bunkers with the help of mining machinery trucked from Portela by civilians. Five of the six anti-tank guns were sited atop the eastern ridge of the position. They could rake the highway as it snaked and switched back among the foothills west of Portela.

Pritchard chuckled grimly again when Sgt. Samuels handed him high-magnification off-prints from the satellites. Benoit's two squat, bulky calliopes were sited in defilade behind the humps of the eastern ridge line. There the eight-barrelled powerguns were safe from the smashing fire of M Company's tanks, but their ability to sweep artillery shells from the sky was degraded by the closer horizon. The Slammers did not bother with calliopes themselves. Their central fire director did a far better job by working through the hundreds of vehicle-mounted weapons. How much better, Benoit might learn very shortly.

The mine-sweeping team cleared the Portela-Haacin road, as directed. The men returned to Benoit's encampment an hour before dusk. The French did not come within five kilometers of the Dutch village.

Pritchard watched the retiring mine sweepers, then snapped off the console. He stood. "I'm going out to my blower," he said.

His crew had been watching for him. A hatch shot open, spouting condensate, as soon as Pritchard came out the door. The smooth bulk of the tank blew like a restive whale. On the horizon, the sun was so low that the treetops stood out in silhouette like a line of bayonets.

Wearily, the captain dropped through the hatch into his seat. Jenne and Margritte murmured greeting and waited, noticeably tense. "I'm going to get a couple hours' sleep," Pritchard said. He swung his seat out and up, so that he lay horizontal in the turret. His legs hid Margritte's oval face from him. "Punch up coverage of the road west of Haacin, would you?" he asked. "I'm going to take a tab of Glirine. Slap me with the antidote when something moves there."

"If something moves," Jenne amended.

"When." Pritchard sucked down the pill. "The squareheads think they've got one last chance to smack Portela and hijack the powerguns again. Thing is, the Portelans'll have already distributed the guns and be waiting for the Dutch to come through. It'll be a damn short fight, that one. . . ." The drug took hold and Pritchard's consciousness began to flow away like a sugar cube in water. "Damn short. . . ."

At first Pritchard felt only the sting on the inside of his wrist. Then the narcotic haze ripped away and he was fully conscious again.

"There a line of trucks, looks like twenty, moving west out of Haacin, sir. They're blacked out, but the satellite has 'em on infra-red."

"Red alert," Pritchard ordered. He locked his seat upright into its combat position. Margritte's soft voice sounded the general alarm. Pritchard slipped on his radio helmet. "Michael One to all Michael units. Check off." Five green lights flashed their silent acknowledgements across the top of the captain's face-shield display. "Michael One to Sigma One," Pritchard continued.

"Go ahead, Michael One." Sally's voice held a note of triumph.

"Sigma One, pull all your troops into large, clear areas—the fields around the towns are fine, but stay the hell away from Portela and Haacin. Get ready to slow down anybody coming this way from across the Aillet. Over."

"Affirmative, Danny, affirmative!" Sally replied. Couldn't she use the satellite reconnaissance herself and see the five blurred dots halfway between the villages? They were clearly the trucks which had brought the Portelans into their ambush positions. What would she say when she realized how she had set up the villagers she was trying to protect? Lambs to the slaughter. . . .

The vision block showed the Dutch trucks more clearly than the camouflaged Portelans. The crushed stone of the roadway was dark on the screen, cooler than the surrounding trees and the vehicles upon it. Pritchard patted the breech of the main gun and looked across it to his blower chief. "We got a basic load for this aboard?" he asked.

"Do bears cop in the woods?" Jenne grinned.

"We gonna get a chance to bust caps tonight, Captain?"

Pritchard nodded. "For three months we've been here, doing nothing but selling rope to the French. Tonight they've bought enough that we can hang'em with it." He looked at the vision block again. "You alive, Kowie?" he asked on intercom.

"Ready to slide any time you give me a course," said the driver from his closed cockpit.

The vision block sizzled with bright streaks that seemed to hang on the screen though they had passed in microseconds. The leading blobs expanded and brightened as trucks blew up.

"Michael One to Fire Central," Pritchard said.

"Go ahead, Michael One," replied the machine voice.

"Prepare Fire Order Alpha."

"Roger, Michael One."

"Margritte, get me Benoit."

"Go ahead, Captain."

"Slammers to Benoit. Pritchard to Benoit. Come in please, Colonel."

"Capt. Pritchard, Michel Benoit here." The colonel's voice was smooth but too hurried to disguise the concern underlying it. "I assure you that none of my men are involved in the present fighting. I have a company ready to go out and control the disturbance immediately, however."

The tanker ignored him. The shooting had already stopped for lack of targets. "Colonel, I've got some artillery aimed to drop various places in the forest. It's coming nowhere near your troops or any other human beings. If you interfere with this necessary shelling, the Slammer'll treat it as an act of war. I speak with my colonel's authority."

"Captain, I don't—"

Pritchard switched manually. "Michael One to Fire Central. Execute Fire Order Alpha."

"On the way, Michael One."

"Michael One to Michael First, Second, Fourth. Command Central has fed movement orders into your map displays. Incendiary clusters are going to burst over marked locations to ignite the forest. Use your own main guns to set the trees burning in front of your immediate positions. One round ought to do it. Button up and you can move through the fire—the trees just fall to pieces when they've burned."

The turret whined as it slid under Rob's control. "Michael Third, I'm attaching you to the infantry. More Frenchmen're apt to be coming this way from the east. It's up to you to see they don't slam a door on us."

The main gun fired, its discharge so sudden that the air rang like a solid thing. Seepage from the ejection system filled the hull with the reek of superheated polyurethane. The side vision blocks flashed cyan, then began to flood with the mounting white hell-light of the blazing trees. In the central block, still set on remote, all the Dutch trucks were burning as were patches of forest which the ambush had ignited. The Portelans had left the concealment of the trees and swept across the road, mopping up the Dutch.

"Kowie, let's move," Jenne was saying on intercom, syncopated by the mild echo of his voice in the turret. Margritte's face was calm, her lips moving subtly as she handled some traffic that she did not pass on to her captain. The tank slid forward like oil on a lake. From the far distance came the thumps of incendiary rounds scattering their hundreds of separate fireballs high over the trees.

Pritchard slapped the central vision block back on direct; the tank's interior shone white with transmitted fire. The Plow's bow slope sheared into a thicket of blazing trees. The wood tangled and sagged, then gave in a splash of fiery splinters whipped aloft by the blower's fans. The tank was in Hell on all sides, Kowie steering by instinct and his inertial compass. Even with his screens filtered all the way down, the driver would not be able to use his eyes effectively until more of the labyrinth had burned away.

Benoit's calliopes had not tried to stop the shelling. Well, there were other ways to get the French mercs to take the first step over the line. For instance—

"Punch up Benoit again," Pritchard ordered. Even through the dense iridium plating, the roar of the fire was a subaural presence in the tank.

"Go ahead," Margritte said, flipping a switch on her console. She had somehow been holding the French officer in conversation all the time Pritchard was on other frequencies.

"Colonel," Pritchard said, "we've got clear running through this fire. We're going to chase down everybody who used a powergun tonight;

then we'll shoot them. We'll shoot everybody in
their families, everybody with them in this ambush, and we'll blow up every house that anybody involved lived in. That's likely to be every
house in Portela, isn't it?"

More than the heat and ions of the blazing
forest distorted Benoit's face. He shouted, "Are
you mad? You can't think of such a thing,
Pritchard!"

The tanker's lips parted like a wolf's. He could
think of mass murder, and there were plenty of
men in the Slammers who would really be willing to carry out the threat. But Pritchard
wouldn't have to, because Benoit was like Riis
and Schilling: too much of a nationalist to remember his first duty as a merc. . . . "Col.
Benoit, the contract demands we keep the peace
and stay impartial. The record shows how we
treated people in Haacin for *having* powerguns.
For what the Portelans did tonight—don't
worry, we'll be impartial. And they'll never
break the peace again."

"Captain, I will not allow you to massacre
French civilians," Benoit stated flatly.

"Move a man out of your present positions
and I'll shoot him dead," Pritchard said. "It's
your choice, Colonel. Over and out."

The Plow bucked and rolled as it pulverized
fire-shattered trunks, but the vehicle was meeting nothing solid enough to slam it to a halt.
Pritchard used a side block on remote to examine Benoit's encampment. The satellite's
enhanced infra-red showed a stream of sparks
flowing from the defensive positions toward the

Portela road: infantry on skimmers. The pair of
larger, more diffuse blobs were probably anti-
tank guns. Benoit wasn't moving his whole battalion, only a reinforced company in a show of
force to make Pritchard back off.

The fool. Nobody was going to back off now.

"Michael One to all Michael and Sigma
units," Pritchard said in a voice as clear as the
white flames around his tank. "We're now in a
state of war with Barthe's Company and its civilian auxiliaries. Michael First, Second and
Fourth, we'll rendezvous at the ambush site as
plotted on your displays. Anybody between
there and Portela is fair game. If we take any fire
from Portela, we go down the main drag in line
and blow the cop out of it. If any of Barthe's
people are in the way, we keep on sliding west.
Sigma One, mount a fluid defense, don't push,
and wait for help. It's coming. If this works, it's
Barthe against Hammer—and that's wheat
against the scythe. Acknowledged?"

As Pritchard's call board lit green, a raspy
new voice broke into the sector frequency. "Wish
I was with you, panzers. We'll cover your butts
and the other sectors—if anybody's dumb
enough to move. Good hunting!"

"I wish you *were* here and not me, Colonel,"
Pritchard whispered, but that was to himself . . .
and perhaps it was not true even in his heart.
Danny's guts were very cold, and his face was a
cold as death.

To Pritchard's left, a lighted display segre-
gated the area of operations. It was a computer
analog, not direct satellite coverage. Doubtful

images were brightened and labeled—green for the Slammers, red for Barthe; blue for civilians unless they were fighting on one side or the other. The green dot of The Plow converged on the ambush site at the same time as the columns of First and Fourth Platoons. Second was a minute or two farther off. Pritchard's breath caught. A sheaf of narrow red lines was streaking across the display toward his tanks. Barthe had ordered his Company's artillery to support Benoit's threatened battalion.

The salvo frayed and vanished more suddenly than it had appeared. Other Slammers' vehicles had ripped the threat from the sky. Green lines darted from Hammer's own three firebases, off-screen at the analog's present scale. The fighting was no longer limited to Sector Two. If Pritchard and Hammer had played their hand right, though, it would stay limited to only the Slammers and Compagnie de Barthe. The other Francophone regiments would fear to join an unexpected battle which certainly resulted from someone's contract violation. If the breach were Hammer's, the Dutch would not be allowed to profit by the fighting. If the breach were Barthe's, anybody who joined him was apt to be punished as sternly by the Bonding Authority.

So violent was the forest's combustion that the flames were already dying down into sparks and black ashes. The command tank growled out into the broad avenue of the road west of Haacin. Dutch trucks were still burning—fabric, lubricants, and the very paint of their frames had been ignited by the powerguns. Many of the bodies sprawled beside the vehicles were smouldering also. Some corpses still clutched their useless muskets. The dead were victims of six centuries of progress which had come to Kobold pre-packaged, just in time to kill them. Barthe had given the Portelans only shoulder weapons, but even that meant the world here. The powerguns were repeaters with awesome destruction in every bolt. Without answering fire to rattle them, even untrained gunmen could be effective with weapons which shot line-straight and had no recoil. Certainly the Portelans had been effective.

Throwing ash and fire like sharks in the surf, the four behemoths of First Platoon slewed onto the road from the south. Almost simultaneously, Fourth joined through the dying hellstorm to the other side. The right of way was fifty meters wide and there was no reason to keep to the center of it. The forest, ablaze or glowing embers, held no ambushes any more.

The Plow lurched as Kowie guided it through the bodies. Some of them were still moving. Pritchard wondered if any of the Dutch had lived through the night, but that was with the back of his mind. The Slammers were at war, and nothing else really mattered. "Triple line ahead," he ordered. "First to the left, Fourth to the right; The Plow'll take the center alone till Second joins. Second, wick up when you hit the hardball and fall in behind us. If it moves, shoot it."

At 100 kph, the leading tanks caught the Portelans three kilometers east of their village. The settlers were in the trucks that had been

hidden in the forest fringe until the fires had
been started. The ambushers may not have
known they were being pursued until the rearmost truck exploded. Rob Jenne had shredded it
with his tribarrel at five kilometers' distance.
The cyan flicker and its answering orange blast
signaled the flanking tanks to fire. They had just
enough parallax to be able to rake the four remaining trucks without being blocked by the one
which had blown up. A few snapping discharges
proved that some Portelans survived to use their
new powerguns on tougher meat than before.
Hits streaked ashes on the tanks' armor. No one
inside noticed.

From Portela's eastern windows, children
watched their parents burn.

A hose of cyan light played from a distant roof
top. It touched the command tank as Kowie
slewed to avoid a Portelan truck. The burst was
perfectly aimed, an automatic weapon served by
professionals. Professionals should have known
how useless it would be against heavy armor. A
vision block dulled as a few receptors fused.
Jenne cursed and trod the foot-switch of the
main gun. A building leaped into dazzling prom-
inence in the microsecond flash. Then it and
most of the block behind collapsed into internal
fires, burying the machinegun and everything
else in the neighborhood. A moment later, a
salvo of Hammer's high explosive got through
the calliopes' inadequate screen. The village
began to spew skyward in white flashes.

The Portelans had wanted to play soldier,
Pritchard thought. He had dammed up all pity

for the villagers of Haacin; he would not spend it
now on these folk.

"Line ahead—First, Fourth, and Second,"
Pritchard ordered. The triple column slowed
and reformed with The Plow the second vehicle
in the new line. The shelling lifted from Portela
as the tanks plunged into the village. Green trails
on the analog terminated over the road crowded
with Benoit's men and over the main French
position, despite anything the calliopes could do.
The sky over Benoit's bunkers rippled and flared
as firecracker rounds sleeted down their
thousands of individual bomblets. The defensive
fire cut off entirely. Pritchard could imagine the
carnage among the unprotected calliope crews
when the shrapnel whirred through them.

The tanks were firing into the houses on either
side, using tribarrels and occasional wallops
from their main guns. The blue-green flashes
were so intense they colored even the flames they
lit among the wreckage. At 50 kph the thirteen
tanks swept through the center of town, hin-
dered only by the rubble of houses spilled across
the street. Barthe's men were skittering white
shadows who burst when powerguns hit them
point blank.

The copper mine was just west of the village
and three hundred meters north of the highway.
As the lead tank bellowed out around the last
houses, a dozen infantrymen rose from where
they had sheltered in the pit head and loosed a
salvo of buzzbombs. The tank's automatic defense system was live. White fire rippled from
just above the skirts as the charges there flailed

pellets outward to intersect the rockets. Most of the buzzbombs exploded ten meters distant against the steel hail. One missile soared harmlessly over its target, its motor a tiny flare against the flickering sky. Only one of the shaped charges burst alongside the turret, forming a bell of light momentarily bigger than the tank. Even that was only a near miss. It gouged the iridium armor like a misthrust rapier which tears skin but does not pierce the skull.

Main guns and tribarrels answered the rockets instantly. Men dropped, some dead, some reloading. "Second Platoon, go put some HE down the shaft and rejoin," Pritchard ordered. The lead tank now had expended half its defensive charges. "Michael First-Three, fall in behind First-One. Michael One leads," he went on.

Kowie grunted acknowledgement. The Plow revved up to full honk. Benoit's men were on the road, those who had not reached Portela when the shooting started or who had fled when the artillery churned the houses to froth. The infantry skimmers were trapped between sheer rocks and sheer drop-offs, between their own slow speed and the onrushing frontal slope of The Plow. There were trees where the rocks had given them purchase. Scattered incendiaries had made them blazing cressets lighting a charnel procession.

Jenne's tribarrel scythed through body armor and dismembered men in short bursts. One of the anti-tank guns—was the other buried in Portela?—lay skewed against a rock wall, its driver killed by a shell fragment. Rob put a

round from the main gun into it. So did each of
the next two tanks. At the third shot, the ammunition ignited in a blinding secondary explosion.

The anti-tank guns still emplaced on the ridge
line had not fired, though they swept several
stretches of the road. Perhaps the crews had
been rattled by the shelling, perhaps Benoit had
held his fire for fear of hitting his own men. A
narrow defile notched the final ridge. The Plow
heaved itself up the rise, and at the top three
bolts slapped it from different angles.

Because the bow was lifted, two of the shots
vaporized portions of the skirt and the front fans.
The tank nosed down and sprayed sparks with
half its length. The third bolt grazed the left top
of the turret, making the iridium ring as it expanded. The interior of the armor streaked white
though it was not pierced. The temperature inside the tank rose 30°. Even as The Plow
skidded, Sgt. Jenne was laying his main gun on
the hot spot that was the barrel of the leftmost
anti-tank weapon. The Plow's shot did what
heavy top cover had prevented Hammer's rocket
howitzers from accomplishing with shrapnel.
The anti-tank gun blew up in a distance-muffled
flash. One of its crewmen was silhouetted high in
the air by the vaporizing metal of his gun.

Then the two remaining weapons ripped the
night and the command blower with their
charges.

The bolt that touched the right side of the
turret spewed droplets of iridium across the interior of the hull. Air pistoned Pritchard's
eardrums. Rob Jenne lurched in his harness,

right arm burned away by the shot. His left hand blackened where it touched bare metal that sparked and sang as circuits shorted. Margritte's radios were exploding one by one under the overloads. The vision blocks worked and the turret hummed placidly as Pritchard rotated it to the right with his duplicate controls.

"Cut the power! Rob's burning!" Margritte was shrieking. She had torn off her helmet. Her thick hair stood out like tendrils of bread mold in the gathering charge. Then Pritchard had the main gun bearing and it lit the ridge line with another secondary explosion.

"Danny, our ammunition! It'll—"

Benoit's remaining gun blew the tribarrel and the cupola away deafeningly. The automatic's loading tube began to gang-fire down into the bowels of the tank. It reached a bright tendril up into the sky. But the turret still rolled.

Electricity crackled around Pritchard's boot and the foot trip as he fired again. The bolt stabbed the night. There was no answering blast. Pritchard held down the switch, his nostrils thick with ozone and superheated plastic and the sizzling flesh of his friend. There was still no explosion from the target bunker. The rock turned white between the cyan flashes. It cracked and flowed away like sun-melted snow, and the anti-tank gun never fired again.

The loading tube emptied. Pritchard slapped the main switch and cut off the current. The interior light and the dancing arcs died, leaving only the dying glow of the bolt-heated iridium. Tank after tank edged by the silent command vehicle and roared on toward the ridge. Benoit's demoralized men were already beginning to throw down their weapons and surrender.

Pritchard manually unlatched Jenne's harness and swung it horizontal. The blower chief was breathing but unconscious. Pritchard switched on a battery-powered handlight. He held it steady as Margritte began to spray sealant on the burns. Occasionally she paused to separate clothing from flesh with a stylus.

"It had to be done," Pritchard whispered. By sacrificing Haacin, he had mousetrapped Benoit into starting a war the infantry could not win. Hammer was now crushing Barthe's Company, one on one, in an iridium vise. Friesland's Council of State would not have let Hammer act had they known his intentions, but in the face of a stunning victory they simply could not avoid dictating terms to the French.

"It had to be done. But I look at *what* I did—" Pritchard swung his right hand in a gesture that would have included both the fuming wreck of Portela and the raiders from Haacin, dead on the road beyond. He struck the breech of the main gun instead. Clenching his fist, he slammed it again into the metal in self-punishment. Margritte cried out and blocked his arm with her own.

"Margi," Pritchard repeated in anguish, "it isn't something that human beings *do* to each other."

But soldiers do.

And hangmen.

INTERLUDE: TABLE OF ORGANIZATION AND EQUIPMENT, HAMMER'S REGIMENT

Sec I: Headquarters Battalion

Except for Artillery and Replacement, all the support elements were grouped for administrative convenience in HQ Battalion. In practice, a large percentage of the strength of these units was parcelled out to line companies according to need.

a) Headquarters Company—Col Hammer and his personal staff, including battalion officers; satellite launch and maintenance personnel; finance; and a security element. Total: 153 effectives.

b) Maintenance—Capable of handling anything short of full hull rebuilds and internal work on fusion units. Company included 3 tank and 6 combat car transporters, stretched-chassis vehicles with fans at either end; ACVs cannot, of course, be towed. Total: 212 effectives.

c) Communications—Included not only the staff of Command Central, but the staffs of local headquarters with area responsibilities. Total: 143 effectives.

d) Medical—Twenty-four first line medics with medicomps linked to Central, and a field hospital with full life-support capability. Total: 60 effectives.

e) Supply—Included Mess and Quartermaster functions. Total: 143 effectives.

f) Intelligence—Order of Battle was performed mostly by computer. Imagery Interpretation, study of satellite recce, was in large measure still a human function. There were three mechanical interrogation (i.e., mind probe) teams. Total: 84 effectives.

g) Transport—312 men (heavily supplemented from Replacement Battalion) and 288 air cushion trucks for local unit supply from spaceport or planetary logistics centers. True aircraft, flying above the nape of the earth, would have been suicidally vulnerable to powerguns.

h) Combat Engineers—Carried out bridging, clearing, mine-sweeping, and very frequently fighting tasks. Formed in three 16-man platoons, each mounted on a pair of tank-chassis Engineer Vehicles. Total: 50 effectives.

i) Recreation—Field brothels. The strength and composition of this unit varied from world to world. Generally, teams of 3–6 were put under the direct control of company supply personnel.

Sec. II: Combat Cars

Eight combat car companies, each of a command section (one car) and four line platoons. Each platoon contained a command car and five combat cars, or six combat cars. Company total: 100 effectives.

Sec III: Tanks

Four tank companies, each of a command tank and four line platoons. Each line platoon contained four tanks. Company total: 36 effectives.

Sec IV: Infantry

Four companies, each of four platoons. Each platoon contained four 10-man line squads; two 2-man tribarrel teams (jeep-mounted); one 2-man 100 mm mortar team (jeep-mounted); and a command element. All but Heavy Weapons were on one-man skimmers. Buzz-bombs could be issued for special purposes; but in general, support from the armored vehicles allowed the Slammers' infantry to travel lighter than most pongoes. Company total: 202 effectives.

Sec V: Artillery

Three batteries of self-propelled 200 mm rocket howitzers. Each battery contained six tubes; one command car; and two munitions haulers. Battery total: 37 effectives.

Sec VI: Replacement

The training and reserve component of the Slammers, normally totalling 1500 men (including cadre) with about ten tanks, twenty-five combat cars, and a hundred trucks. Because

Hammer had no permanent base world, training had to be performed wherever the Regiment was located. Because men were more vulnerable than the armored vehicles they rode, and the vehicles were too valuable to run under-crewed or held out of service while replacements were trained, a pool of trained men had to be on hand to fill gaps immediately. Until they were needed in combat slots, they acted as extra drivers, loading crews, camp police, and firebase security.

Note: As personal weapons line infantry were issued 2 cm shoulder powerguns and grenades. Vehicle and Heavy Weapons crewmen carried 1 cm pistols (unless they had picked up shoulder arms on their own). Officers carried pistols or 1 cm submachineguns as they desired.

STANDING DOWN

"LOOK, I'M NOT about to wear a goon suit like that, even to my wedding," Col. Hammer said, loudly enough to be heard through the chatter. There were a dozen officers making last-minute uniform adjustments in the crowded office and several civilians besides. "Joachim, where's Maj. Pritchard? I want him in the car with us, and it's curst near jump-off now."

Joachim Steuben was settled nonchalantly on the corner of a desk, unconcerned about the state of his dress because he knew it was perfect—as always. He shrugged. "Pritchard hasn't called in," the Newlander said. His fine features brightened in a smile. "But go ahead, Alois, put the armor on."

"Yes indeed, sir," said the young civilian. He was holding the set of back-and-breast armor carefully by the edges so as not to smear its bright chrome. Rococo whorls and figures decorated the plastron, but despite its ornateness, the metal/ceramic sandwich beneath the brightwork was quite functional. "Really, the image you'll project to the spectators will be ideal, quite ideal. And there couldn't be a better time for it, either."

Lt. Col. Miezierk frowned, wrinkling his forehead to the middle of his bald skull. He said, "Yes, Colonel. After all, Mr van Meter's firm studied the matter very carefully and I think—" Joachim snickered; Miezierk's scalp reddened but he went on—"that you ought to follow his advice here."

"Lord!" Hammer said, but he thrust his hands through the armholes and let Miezierk lock the clamshell back.

Someone tapped on the door. A lieutenant was leaning over the front desk, combing his hair in the screen of the display console. He cursed and straightened so that the door could open to admit Capt. Fallman. The Intelligence captain was duty officer for the afternoon, harried by the inevitable series of last-minute emergencies. "Colonel," he said, "there's a Mr. Wang here to see you."

"Lord curse it, Fallman, he can wait till tomorrow!" Hammer blazed. "He can wait till Hell freezes over. Miezierk, get this bloody can off me, it's driving the stylus in my pocket clear through my rib cage."

"Sir, we can take the stylus—" Miezierk began.

"Sir, he's from the Bonding Authority," Fallman was saying. "It's about President Theismann's—death."

Hammer swore, brushing the startled Miezierk's hands away. The room grew very silent. "Joachim, what's in the office next door?" Hammer asked.

"Dust, three walls, and some stains from the

Iron Guards who decided to make a stand there," the Newlander replied.

"Bring him next door, Captain, I'll talk to him there," Hammer said. He met his bodyguard's eyes. "Come along too, Joachim."

At the door the Colonel paused, looking back at his still-faced officers. "Don't worry," he said. "Everything's going to work out fine."

The closing door cut off the babble of nervous speculation from within.

A moment after Hammer and his aide had entered the side office, Capt. Fallman ushered in a heavy Oriental. Joachim bowed to the civilian and closed the door, leaving the duty officer alone in the hallway

An automatic weapon had punched through the outer wall of the office, starting fires which the grenade thrown in a moment later had snuffed. There was still a scorched-plastic afterstench mingling with that of month-dead meat. Joachim had been serious about the Iron Guards.

"I'm Hammer," the Colonel said, smiling but not offering the Authority representative his hand for fear it might be refused.

"Wang An-wei," said the Oriental, nodding curtly. He held a flat briefcase. It seemed to be more an article of dress than a tool he intended to use this morning. "I was sent here as Site Officer when Councillor Theismann—"

"President Theismann, he preferred," interjected Hammer. He seated himself in feigned relaxation on a blast-warped chair.

Wang's answering smile was brief and as sharp as the lightning. "He was never awarded the title by a quorum of the Council," the Terran said. "As you no doubt are aware, Site Officers are expected to be precise. If I may continue?"

Hammer nodded. Steuben snickered. His left thumb was hooked in the belt which tucked his tailored blouse in at the waist, but his right hand dangled loose at his side.

"When Councillor Theismann hired you to make him dictator," Wang continued coolly. "Naturally I have been investigating the death of your late employer. There have been—and I'm sure you're aware of this—accusations that you murdered Councillor Theismann yourself in order to replace him as head of the successful coup."

The Site Officer looked at the men in turn. The two Slammers looked back.

"I started with the autopsy data. In addition, I have interrogated the Councillor's guards, both his personal contingent and the platoon of— White Mice—on security detail here at Government House." Wang stared at Hammer. "I assume you were informed of this?"

Hammer nodded curtly. "I signed off before they'd let you mind-probe my men."

"I used mechanical interrogation on all troops below officer rank involved," Wang agreed, "as your bond agreement specifies the Site Officer may require." When Hammer made no reply, he continued, "The evidence is uncontroverted that Councillor Theismann, accompanied by you,

Colonel—" Hammer nodded again—"stepped out onto his balcony and was struck in the forehead by a pistol bolt."

Wang paused again. The room was very tense. "The pistol must have been fired from at least a kilometer away. Because of the distance and the fact that fighting was going on at several points within the city, I have reported to my superiors that it was a stray shot, and that the Councillor's death was accidental."

Joachim's fingers ceased toying with the butt of the powergun holstered high on his right hip. "We were clearing some of van Vorn's people out of the Hotel Zant," he said. "Pistol and submachinegun work. There might have been a stray shot from that. It'd be very difficult to brain a man that far away with a pistol, wouldn't it?"

"Impossible, of course," Wang said. His gaze flicked to Steuben's ornate pistol, flicked up to the bodyguard's eyes. For the first time the Oriental looked startled. He looked away from Steuben very quickly and said, "Since the investigation has cleared you, and your employment has ended for the time, I'll be returning to Earth now. I wish you good fortune, and I hope we may do business again in the near future."

Hammer laughed, clapping the civilian on the shoulder with his left hand while their right hands shook. "That's all over, Mr. Wang. The Slammers're out of the merc business for good, now. But I appreciate your wishes."

Wang turned to the door, smiling by reflex. He looked at Joachim's face again: the Cupid grin and unlined cheeks; the hair which, though naturally graying, still fell across the Newlander's forehead in an attractive page-boy; and the eyes. Wang was shivering as he stepped into the hall.

Danny Pritchard stood outside the door, watching the Site Officer leave. He was dressed in civilian clothing.

Spaceport buses did not serve the cargo ships for the man or two they might bring, so Rob Jenne hiked toward the barrier on foot. At first he noticed only that the short man marching toward the terminal from the other recently-landed freighter was also missing an arm. Then the other's crisp stride rang a bell in Jenne's mind. He shouted, "Top! Sgt. Horthy! What the hell're *you* doing here?"

Horthy turned with the wary quickness of a man uncertain as to any caller's interest. At Jenne's grin he broke into a smile himself. The two men dropped their bags and shook hands awkwardly, Jenne's left in Horthy's right. "Same thing you're doing, trooper," Horthy said. The Magyar's goatee was white against his swarthy skin, but his grip was as firm as it had been when Rob Jenne was Horthy's right wing gunner. "Comin' here to help the Colonel put some backbone in this place. You don't know how glad I was when the call came, snake."

"Don't I though?" Jenne murmured. Side by side, talking simultaneously, the two veterans walked toward the spaceport barrier. There was already a line waiting at the customs kiosk. Jenne knew very well what his old sergeant meant. Seven years of retirement had been hard on the younger man, too. He hadn't lacked money—his pension put him well above the norm for the Burlage quarrymen to whom he had returned—but he was useless. To himself, to Burlage, to the entire human galaxy. Jenne had shouted for joy when Col. Hammer summoned all pensioned Slammers who wanted to come. The Old Man needed supervisors and administrators, now. It didn't matter any more that gaseous iridium had burned off Jenne's right arm, right eye, and his gonads; it was enough that Hammer knew where his loyalties lay.

A gray bus with wire-mesh windows and SECURITY stencilled on its side pulled up to the barrier. The faces and clothing of the prisoners within were as drab as the air cushion vehicle's exterior. A guard wearing the blue of the civil police stepped out and walked to the barrier. His submachinegun was slung carelessly under his right arm.

Horthy nudged his companion. "It's a load a' politicals for the Borgo Mines," he muttered. "Bet they're bein' hauled out on the ship that brought me in. *And* I'll bet that bus'll be heading back to wherever the Colonel is, just as quick as it unloads. Let's see if that cop'll offer us a ride, snake."

As he spoke, the Magyar veteran stepped to the waist-high barrier. The customs official bustled over from his kiosk and shouted in Horthy's face. Horthy ignored him. The official unsnapped the flap of his pistol holster. Other travellers waiting for entry scattered, more afraid of losing their lives than their places in line. Jenne, his good eye flashing across the tension, knowing as well as any man alive that his muscles were nothing to the blast of a powergun, cursed and closed the Magyar's rear.

A second bus, civilian in stripes of white and bright orange, pulled up behind the prison vehicle. The policeman turned and waved angrily. The bus hissed and settled to the pavement despite him. The policeman fumbled with his submachinegun.

A shot from the bus cut him down.

A man with a pistol swung to the loading step of the striped vehicle. He roared, "Just hold it, everybody. We got a load of hostages here. Either we get out of here with our friends or nobody gets out!"

The customs official had paused, staring with his mouth open and his fingers brushing the butt of the gun whose existance he had forgotten. Horthy, behind him, drew the pistol and fired. The rebel doubled over, his jacket afire over his sternum. Someone aboard the civilian bus screamed. Another gun fired. Horthy was prone, his pistol punching out windows in answer to the burst that had sawed the customs official in half.

Rob rolled over the barrier, coming up with the guard's automatic weapon.

The striped bus was moving, dragging the fallen gunman's torso on the concrete. The ex-tanker's mind raced in the old channels. The fans of the bus were not armored like those of a military vehicle. Rob aimed low. A powergun bolt sprayed lime dust over his head and shoul-

ders. His own burst ripped across the plenum
chamber. The driving fans disintegrated, flaying
the air with steel like a bursting shell. The bus
rolled over on its left side. Metal and humans
screamed together. A gray-suited prisoner
jumped from the door of the government bus.
Horthy shot her in the face.

The ruptured fuel cell of the overturned vehicle ignited. The explosion slapped the area with
a pillow of warm air. The screaming took a
minute to die. Then there was just the rush of
wind feeding the fire, and the nearing wail of
sirens.

Jenne's cheek and shoulder-stub were oozing
where the concrete had ground against them.
The tall man rose to his knees, keeping his eye
and the submachinegun trailed on the gray bus.
No one else was trying to get out of it. The police
could sort through whatever had happened inside in their own good time.

Horthy stood, heat rippling from the barrel of
the weapon he had appropriated. He glanced at
the mangled customs official as if he would rather have spit on the body. "Oh, yes," the veteran
said. "They need us here, trooper. They need
people to teach 'em the facts of life."

"Pritchard, where the Hell have you been?"
Hammer demanded, pretending that he did not
understand the implications of his subordinate's
business suit.

"I need to talk to you, Colonel," the brown-
haired major said.

Hammer stood aside. "Then come on in.

Joachim, we'll join the group next door in a moment. Wait for us there, if you will."

Pritchard took a step forward. He hesitated when he realized that Joachim was not moving. The Newlander had been as relaxed as a sunning adder during the interview with Wang Anwei. Now he was white and tense. "Colonel, he's a traitor to you," Joachim said. "He's going to walk out." His voice was quiet but not soft.

"Joachim, I told you—"

"You don't talk to traitors, Colonel. What you do to traitors—" The Newlander's hand was dipping to his gunbutt. Hammer grappled with him. He was not as fast as his aide, but he knew Joachim's mind even better than the gunman did himself. The extra fraction of a second saved Pritchard's life.

The two men stood, locked like wrestlers or lovers. Pritchard did not move, knowing that emphasizing his presence would be the worst possible course under the circumstances. Hammer said, "Joachim are you willing to shoot me?"

The bodyguard winced, a tic that momentarily disfigured his face. "Alois! You know I wouldn't. . . ."

"Then do as I say. Or you'll have to shoot me. To keep me from shooting you."

Hammer stepped away from his aide. Joachim lurched through the doorway, bumping Pritchard as he passed because his eyes had filled with tears.

Pritchard swung the door shut behind him. "I told you last week I was going to resign from the Slammers, sir."

Hammer nodded. "And I told you you weren't."

Pritchard looked around at the dust and rubble of the room, the bloodstains. "I've decided there's been enough killing, Colonel. For me. We're going somewhere else."

"Danny, the killing's over!"

The taller man gave a short snap of his head. He said, "No, it'll never be over—not any place you are." He spread his hands, then clenched them. He was staring at his knuckles because he would not look at his commander. "Right now we're chasing van Vorn's guards like rabbits, shooting 'em down or sticking 'em behind wire where they're not a curse a' good to you or themselves or this planet."

He faced Hammer, the outrage bubbling out at a human being, not the Colonel he had served for all his adult life. "And the ones we kill—doesn't every one a' them have a wife or a brother or a nephew? And they'll put a knife in a Slammer some night and be shot the same way because of it!"

"All right," said Hammer calmly. "What else?"

"How about the Social Unity Party, then?" Pritchard blazed. "Maybe the one chance to get this place a work force that *works* instead of the robots the Great Houses've been trying to make them. And does anybody listen? Hell, no! The Council tinkers with the franchise to make sure they don't get a majority of the Estates-General; van Vorn outlaws the party and makes their leaders terrorists instead of politicians. And you, *you* ship them off-planet to rot in state-owned mines on Kobold!"

"All right," Hammer repeated. He sat down again, his stillness as compelling as that of the shattered room around him. "What would you do?"

Pritchard's eyes narrowed. He stretched his left hand out to the wall, not leaning on it but touching its firmness, its chill. "What do you care?" he asked quietly. "I didn't say the Slammers couldn't keep you in power here the rest of your life. I just don't want to be a part of it, is all."

Without warning, Hammer stood and slammed his fist into the wall. He turned back to his aide. His bleeding knuckles had flecked the panel more brightly than the remains of the Iron Guards. "Is that what you think?" he demanded. "That I'm a bandit who's found himself a bolthole? That for the past thirty years I've fought wars because that's the best way to make bodies?"

"Sir, I. . . ." But Pritchard had nothing more to say or need to say it.

Hammer rubbed his knuckles. He grinned wryly at his subordinate, but the grin slipped away. "It's my own fault," he said. "I don't tell people much. That's how it's got to be when you're running a tank regiment, but . . . that's not where we are now.

"Danny, this is my *home*." Hammer began to reach out to the taller man but stopped. He said, "You've been out there. You've seen how every world claws at every other one, claws its own guts too. The whole system's about to slag down, and there's nothing to stop it if *we* don't."

"You don't create order by ramming it down

peoples' throats on a bayonet! It doesn't work that way."

"Then show me a way that *does* work!" Hammer cried, gripping his subordinate's right hand with his own. "Are things going to get better because you're sitting on your butt in some farmhouse, living off the money *you* made killing? Danny, I *need* you. My *son* will need you."

Pritchard touched his tongue to his lips. "What is it you're asking me to do?" he said.

"Do you have a way to handle the Unionists?" Hammer shot back at him. "And the Iron Guards?"

"Maybe," Pritchard said with a frown. "Amnesty won't be enough—they won't believe it's real, for one thing. But a promise of authority . . . administrative posts in education, labor, maybe even security—that'd bring out a few of the Unionists because they couldn't afford *not* to take the chance. Most of the rest of them might follow when they saw you really were paying off."

The brown-haired man's enthusiasm was building without the hostility that had marked it before. "The Guards, that'll be harder because they're rigid, most of them. But if you *can* find some way to convince them there's nothing to gain by staying out, and—Hell, there'll be counter-protests, but work the ones who turn over their guns into the civil police. Not in big dollops, but scattered all over the planet. They'll feel more secure that way, and you can keep an eye on them easier anyhow."

Hammer nodded. "All right, bring me a pre-

liminary assessment of both proposals by, say,
0800 Tuesday. No, make that noon, you're going
to waste the rest of today watching a wedding
from the front row. You'll have the backing
you'll need, but these are *your* projects—I've got
too much blood on my hands to run them." His
eyes held Pritchard's. "Or don't you have the
guts to try?"

The taller man hesitated, then squeezed
Hammer's hand in return. "I rode your lead
tank," he said. "I ran your lead company. If you
need me now, you've got me." His face clouded.
"Only, Colonel—"

Hammer tightened. "Spit it out."

"I'm not ashamed of anything. But I swore to
Margritte I'd never wear another uniform or
carry another gun. And I won't."

Hammer cleared his throat. "Right now I
don't need a major as much as I do a con-
science," he said. He cleared his throat again.
"Now let's go. We've got a wedding to get to."

Cosimo Barracks was a fortress in the midst of
estates which had belonged for three hundred
years to the family of the late President van
Vorn. The Slammers had bypassed Cosimo in
the blitzkrieg which replaced van Vorn with
Theismann, their employer. But now, a month
after van Vorn had poisoned himself in Government House and three weeks after someone else
had burst Theismann's skull with a powergun,
the fortress still refused to surrender. Sally
Schilling, leading a 'battalion' made up of S
Company and six hundred local recruits, was on

hand to do something about the situation.

A burst of automatic fire combed the rim of the dugout, splashing Capt. Schilling with molten granite. "Via!" she snapped to the frightened recruit, "Keep your coppy head down and don't draw fire."

The sergeant who shared the dugout with Schilling and the recruit shook his own head in disgust. In her mind, Schilling seconded the opinion. To police a planet, Hammer needed more men than the five thousand he had brought with him. He wanted to give the new troops at least a taste of combat in the mopping-up operations. Schilling could understand that desire, but it was a pain in the ass trying to do her own job and act as baby-sitter besides.

She looked again through the eyepiece of her periscope. The machinegun had ceased firing, though cyan flickers across the perimeter showed someone else was catching it. The Iron Guards were political bullies rather than combat soldiers, but their fortress here was as tough as anything the Slammers had faced in their history. The fiber-optics periscope showed Cosimo Barracks only as a rolling knob. The grass covering the rock was streaked yellow in fans pointing back to hidden gunports. The ports themselves were easy enough targets, but the weapons within were on disappearing carriages and popped up only long enough to fire. The rest of the fortress, with an estimated five hundred Iron Guards plus enough food, water and ammunition to last a century, was deep underground.

Schilling glanced down at her console. On it Cosimo Barracks showed as a red knot of tunnels drawn from plans found in Government House. "Sigma Battalion," she said, "check off." Points of green light winked on the screen, an emerald necklace ringing the fortress. Each point was a squad guarding nearly 100 meters of front. That was adequate; the infantry was on hand primarily to prevent a breakout.

"Fire Central," Schilling said, "prepare Fire Order Tango-Niner."

"Ready," squawked the helmet.

"Ma'am," said the recruit, "w-why don't the tanks attack instead of us?"

"Shut it off, boy!" the sergeant snapped.

"No, Webbert, we're supposed to be teaching them," Schilling said. She gestured toward the knob. The recruit automatically raised his head. Webbert shoved him back down before another burst could decapitate him. The captain sighed. "Mines're as thick up there as flies on a fresh turd," she said, "and they've got more guns in that hill than the light stuff they've been using on us. Besides, we aren't going to attack."

The recruit nodded with his mouth and eyes both wide open. He began to rub the stock of his unfamiliar powergun.

"Fire Central, execute Tango-Niner," Schilling ordered.

"On the way."

Nothing happened. After a long half minute, the recruit burst out, "What went wrong? Dear Lord, will they make us charge—"

"Boy!" the sergeant shouted, his own knuckles tight on his weapon.

"Webbert!"

The sergeant cursed and turned away.

Schilling said, "The hogs're a long way away. It takes time, that's all. Everything takes time."

"Shot," said the helmet. Five seconds to impact. The sky overhead began to howl. The recruit was trembling, his own throat working as if to scream along with the shells.

The explosions were almost anticlimactic. They were only a rumbling through the bedrock, more noticed by one's feet than one's ears. Schilling, at the periscope, caught the spurts of earth as the first penetrator rounds struck. The detonations seconds later were lost in the shriek of further shells landing on the same points. Each tube's first shell ripped sod to the granite. The second salvo struck gravel; the third, sand. By the tenth salvo, the charges were bursting in the guts of Cosimo Barracks, thirty meters down. A magazine went off there, piercing earth and sky in a cyan blast that made the sun pale.

"Not an oyster born yet but a starfish can drill a hole through it," muttered Webbert. He had been a fisherman long years before when he saw one of Hammer's recruiting brochures.

"Sigma One, this is Sigma Eight-Six," said the helmet. "Our sensors indicate all three fortress elevators are rising."

With the words, circuits of meadow gaped. "Sigma Battalion," Schilling said as she rose and aimed over the lip of the dugout, "Time to earn our pay. And remember—no prisoners!"

Because of the way the ground pitched, it was hard for the captain to keep her submachinegun trained on the rising elevator car. But there were eight hundred guns firing simultaneously at the three elevator heads. The bolts converged like suns burning into the heart of the hillside.

"They were sending up their families!" the recruit suddenly screamed. "The children!"

Sally Schilling slid a fresh gas cylinder in place in the butt of her weapon, then reached for another magazine as well. "They had three months to turn in their guns," she said. "Half the ones down there were troops we beat at Maritschoon and paroled. So this was the second time, and *I'm* not going to have my ass blown away because I gave somebody three chances to do it. As for the families, well . . . there's a couple thousand more of van Vorn's folks mooching around in the Kronburg, and they won't know it was an accident: when word of this gets around, the ones that're still out are going to think again."

The fortress guns had fallen silent as the elevator cars rose. Now a few weapons opened up again, but in long, suicidal bursts which flailed the world until the Slammer's fire silenced them forever.

President van Vorn's Iron Guards had planned to use the garage beneath Government House for a last stand; which in a manner of speaking was what they did. The political soldiers had naively failed to consider gas. The Slammers introduced KD7 into the forced ventilation system, then spent three days neutralizing the toxin before they could safely enter the garage and remove the bloated corpses. Now the concrete walls, unmarred by shots or grenade fragments, echoed to the fans of two dozen combat cars readying for the parade.

"There's three layers a' gold foil," the bald maintenance chief was saying as he rapped the limousine's myrmillon bubble. "That'll diffuse most of a two see-emma bolt, but the folks, they'll still be able to *see* you, you see?"

"What I don't see is my wife," Hammer snapped to the stiff-faced noble acting as the Council's liaison with their new overlord. "She's agreed, I've agreed. If *you* think that the Great Houses can back out of this now—"

"Colonel," interrupted Pritchard, pointing at the closed car which was just entering the garage. The armored doors to the mews slammed shut behind the vehicle, cutting off the wash of sunlight which had paled the glow strips by comparison. The car hissed slowly between armored vehicles and support pillars, coming to a halt beside Hammer and his aides. Two men got out, dressed in the height of conservative fashion. The colors of Great Houses slashed their collar flares. A moment later, a pair of women stepped out between them.

One of them was sixty, as tall and heavy as either of the men. Her black garments were as harsh as the glare she turned on Hammer when he nodded to her.

The other woman was short enough to be petite. It was hard to tell, however, because she wore a dress of misty, layered fabric which gave the impression of spiderweb but hid even the outline of her body. The celagauze veil hanging from her cap-brim blurred her face similarly.

Before any of those around her could interfere, she had reached up and removed the cap.

"Anneke!" cried the woman in black. One of the escorting nobles shifted. Danny Pritchard motioned him back, using his left hand by reflex.

Anneke sailed the cap into the intake of a revving combat car. Shreds of white fabric softened the floor of the garage. "What, Aunt Ruth?" she asked. Her voice was clearly audible over the fans and the engines. "That's the idea, isn't it? Prove to the citizens that the Great Houses are still in charge because the Colonel is marrying one of us? But then they've got to see who I am, don't they?"

Hammer stepped forward. "Lady Brederode," he said, repeating his nod. The older woman looked away as if Hammer were a spot of offal on the pavement. "Lady Tromp."

Anneke Tromp extended her right hand. She had fine bones and skin as soft as the lining of a jewelry box. The fingernails looked metallic.

The Colonel knelt to kiss her hand, the gesture stiffened by his armor. "Well, Lady Tromp," he said, "are you ready?"

The woman smiled. Hammer became the commander again. He waved dismissingly toward his bride's aunt and escort. "I've made provisions for your seating at the church," he said, "but you'll not be needed for the procession. Lady Tromp will ride in my vehicle. We'll be accompanied by Majors—that is, by Maj. Steuben and Mr. Pritchard."

Anneke nodded graciously to the aides flanking Hammer. Unexpectedly, Joachim giggled.

His eyes were red. "Your family and I go back a long way, Lady," he said. "Did you know that I shot your father on Melpomene? Between the eyes, so that he could see it coming."

The Colonel's face changed, but he grinned as he turned. He threw an arm around his bodyguard's shoulders. "Joachim," he said, "let's talk in the car for a moment." Steuben looked away, blazing hatred at everyone else in the room, but he followed his commander into the sound-proofed compartment.

As the car door thudded shut, Anneke Tromp stepped idly to Pritchard's side. She was still smiling. Without looking at the limousine's bubble, she said, "That's a very jealous man, Mr. Pritchard. And jealous not only of me, I should think."

Danny shrugged. "Joachim's been with the Colonel a long time," he said. "He's not an . . . evil . . . man. Just loyal."

"A razor blade in a melon isn't evil, Mr. Pritchard," the woman said, gesturing as though they were discussing the markings of the nearest combat car. "It's just too dangerous to be permitted to exist."

Pritchard swallowed. Part of his duties involved checking the roster of veterans returning to the colors. He was remembering a big man with an engaging grin—as good a tank commander as had ever served under Pritchard, and the lightest touch he knew on the trigger of an automatic weapon. "We'll see," Danny said without looking at the woman.

"When I was a little girl," she murmured,

"my father ruled Friesland. I want to live to see my son rule."

The car door opened and both men got out. "Joachim has decided to ride up front with the driver instead of with us in back," Hammer said with a false smile. He held the door. "Shall we?"

Pritchard sat on a jump seat across from Hammer and Lady Tromp. The armored bubble was cloudy, like the sky on the morning of a snow storm. Hammer touched a plate on the console. "Six-two," he said. "Move 'em out."

Fans revved. The garage door lifted and began passing combat cars out into the mews. Hammer's driver slid the limousine into the line of cars waiting to exit. More armored vehicles edged in behind them. They accelerated up the ramp and into the Frisian sunlight. The whole west quarter of Government House had burned in the fighting, darkening the vitril panels there.

Pritchard leaned forward. "You don't really think that you can turn Friesland around, much less the galaxy?" he asked.

Hammer shrugged. "If I don't, they'll at least say that I died trying."

The limousine glided through the archway into Independence Boulevard. Tank companies were already closing either end of the block, eight tanks abreast. The panzers had been painted dazzlingly silver for the celebration. The combat cars aligned themselves in four ranks between the double caps of bigger vehicles, leaving the limousine to tremble alone in the midst of the waves of heavy armor. Hammer's breastplate was a sunblazed eye in the center of all.

On the front bench beside the driver, Joachim was trying nervously to scan the thousands of civilians. He knew that despite the armored bubble, the right man could kill Hammer as easily as he himself had murdered Councillor Theimsann. He wished he could kill every soul in the crowd.

Pritchard checked the time, then radioed a command. The procession began to slip forward toward the throngs lining the remaining three kilometers of the boulevard, all the way to the Church of the First Landfall.

"I've been a long time coming back to Friesland," said Hammer softly. He was not really speaking to his companions. "But now I'm back. And I'm going to put this place in order."

Anneke Tromp touched him. Her glittering fingernails lay like knife-blades across the back of his hand. "*We're* going to put it in order," she said.

"We'll see," said Danny Pritchard.

"Hammer!" shouted the crowd.

"Hammer!"

"Hammer!"

"Hammer!"